MANY STRANGE WOMEN

MANY STRANGE WOMEN

PARKER J. COLE

eLectio Publishing
Little Elm, TX
www.eLectioPublishing.com

To the Author and Finisher of my faith – thank you for everything.
To my family and my four best friends – Angie, Rachel, Torei, and Millie
who aren't the least bit surprised.
To my husband who loves me.

TABLE OF CONTENTS

ACKNOWLEDGMENTS

I think "acknowledge" is a clumsy word as it doesn't do justice to the efforts of some of the people who have walked with me through this journey of a writer. But, until there's another word, it will have to do.

This book would not have been written if it weren't for Allyson Carter. Ally opened her heart to a woman she barely knew and gave me advice, encouragement, and the fortitude to help me complete it. In the words of our Lord, 'I have called you friend'. Thank you from the bottom of my heart, Ally.

Roystonn Pruitt walked with me through this book, page by page, line by line. His invaluable insights are written in here as a testament to his friendship and his gift as a writer. Be blessed and thank you for everything.

Special acknowledgement goes to my agent, Vanessa Grossett. She believed in me and worked tirelessly to help me in my writing career. She offered advice, Godly counsel, and helped to create the brand that is becoming Parker J. Cole. Thank you so much for everything, Vanessa.

I also would like to thank Unoma Osiegbu-Nwankwor for her assistance with accurately depicting all things Yoruba. Any and all mistakes are mine.

"Let thy fountain be blessed: and rejoice with the wife of thy youth."

Proverbs 5:18 (KJV)

MR. AND MRS. SOLOMON GREENE

The thought of kissing her husband was repugnant. The idea had the attraction of eating an apple with a worm in it. The longer Celeste Greene thought about it, the more distasteful it became.

"I hope you don't actually intend for me to kiss this man, reverend," Celeste clipped out in a carefully controlled voice.

The minister was a short black man whose gray hair had receded until his head looked like a polished teak wood surface. Dark rimmed bifocals rested on his nose and gray bushy eyebrows lifted in surprise.

"Excuse me, Mrs. Grane?" His voice was deep and rumbled like gravel shifting at the bottom of a fish tank.

"I refuse to kiss this man."

The minister closed the Bible in his hand and pressed it against his Santa Claus belly. He cleared his throat.

"Mrs. Grane, I have married couples for a good many years. I can honestly say I've never heard a wife speak so about her husband. Although, the decision is yours, may one ask why you choose not to kiss your husband?"

"I don't know him."

Celeste could see the minister's confusion as he glanced over at the tall, silent man by her side. She looked at him, too, but only saw his profile. Her new husband reeked of unwashed body odor and alcohol. Although his clothes didn't display any hint of those noxious smells. In fact, his clothes were perfectly tailored to him. The dark blue suit with its sharp cut and the pastel colored green shirt under it gave her husband a handsome appearance.

Too bad the clothes could not do anything about his stench.

Celeste had no idea her husband had spoken until she realized his mouth moved. He still chose not to look at her but directed his statement to the minster.

"The name is Greene."

"Greene?"

"Yes, my wife's new name is Mrs. Solomon Greene. With an 'e'."

"Indeed? Well, I do apologize for the mistake."

Celeste folded her arms and turned fully toward her husband.

"Solomon, are you ready to sign the papers so we can get back to the hotel room?"

"Yes, Celeste. Let's get this over with."

A scant fifteen minutes later and Celeste felt the sun warm her face as she stepped out of the small church. Of course, the June sun blazed brightly in the sky on this, the most unexpected day of her life. The snow shrouded Rocky Mountains in the Denver skyline only added to the physical perfection of the day. Why couldn't it be rainy and gloomy? Why couldn't lightning and thunder shake the ground to mirror the feelings that swarmed inside of her? Why should the sky be the bluest she'd ever seen it and the sound of the birds that twittered from tree to tree create a song to accompany her discomfiture?

"I appreciate you married me, Celeste Greene," her husband said from somewhere behind her.

She turned, her arms still folded. "It's the least I could do."

Gratitude welled inside Solomon's heart as he once again realized his wife had none of the attributes he found sexy in a woman. He had hoped the woman he married would have the beauty of a gargoyle, but a plain face would do just as well.

He studied his new wife. The top of her head reached his shoulder. She held her body stiff, and her face remained devoid of expression. It emphasized her unattractiveness. If she never smiled at all, it would be wonderful.

She wore a peculiar outfit—a blue skirt that brushed the tops of her shoes, a blouse buttoned to her neck with long sleeves also buttoned at her wrist, and her hands were encased in plain white gloves. It had an old-fashioned look to it, like something from the pioneer days. It obscured her figure and Solomon breathed a sigh of relief. His belief in God had been restored.

God had sent an unattractive woman to be his wife. His eyes began to water, and he blinked furiously. He could hardly break down and cry a bucket of tears in joy right now.

"I've called my driver," he told her as a metallic glint caught his peripheral vision, and he whirled his head to see a sleek black Hummer limousine turn the corner and stop in front of them.

Celeste didn't respond. Her silence made him want to click his heels. A woman who didn't talk incessantly had to be a godsend. Perfect!

Moments later, he sat by her side as the vehicle moved. The scenery passed, and Solomon appreciated it as the light of the sun beamed on the ground. The leaves rustled as a gentle breeze wafted through them and the sight of birds as they flew by lifted his spirits. It was a lovely June day, and he'd found his wife.

"I anticipate, Mr. Greene, you will make use of the facilities once we attain our room at the hotel. Your odor is pungent enough to raise the dead." His new wife stated as she continued to focus her attention on the scenery.

"I know I smell like a pig, Celeste. I'll head dive into the shower once we get into the hotel."

"Thank you."

Solomon waited for her to say more, but Celeste simply fixed her gaze out the window and remained quiet. The limousine continued its trek on the road, and the shadows of trees and buildings flowed over their figures. A light vanilla fragrance titillated his nose. It came from his new wife. As the silence grew, he focused his thought on this sudden marriage. It had to be God's doing this woman would come to him when he needed her.

"Mr. Greene, you do understand you will not be allowed any connubial rights." Celeste spoke quietly as she sat on the bed in the chilled air conditioned room at the hotel.

"Connubial? What on earth does that mean?" Solomon stood in front of her, eyes staring with confusion.

"It means conjugal or marital rights. In plain English, you and I will not share a bed."

Celeste watched Solomon's chest heave a sigh of relief. "I'm glad. It's almost too good to be true. God has given me a wife, and she's not interested. I can't tell you how happy you've made me this day."

"As I have said, Mr. Greene, it's the least I could do."

"Do you think we can go over our itinerary in the morning? I've a killer headache." She watched as he rubbed the back of his neck. He closed his eyes and sighed.

"The ingurgitation of alcohol prefaces such symptoms," Celeste remarked quietly.

She saw the confusion on his face at her statement before he shrugged. "Yeah right," he answered and took off his shirt and threw himself on the separate king size bed across from her. He turned on his back and flung his arm over his head. Soft snores followed moments later.

Celeste stood and walked over to his bed and gazed down at him. With detachment, she noted her husband exuded sensuality. He was very tall with short spiked hair dark as coal, a wide forehead, thinly sliced eyebrows over green gold-flecked eyes, a beak-like nose and broad, full lips. He had a body like a Roman gladiator . . . bronze and chiseled with muscles. And he smelled awful.

"How unfortunate for you, husband, that I am not interested. Even if your odor wasn't deadly. " Celeste spoke to his silent frame.

His feet hung over the edge of the bed, and she noted he hadn't taken off his shoes.

A moment later, the shoes were on the floor.

She walked back to her side of the room, sat down on the king sized bed, picked up the phone and dialed a number.

"Hello Mama. It's Icy."

"Icy?" Her mother's voice screeched through the phone, and Celeste pulled it back from her ear. "Why in the world haven't you called me? It has been a week since you've last spoken to me, and you know how I feel when I don't hear from you. Do you have any idea what goes through a mother's mind when she doesn't hear from her children? Especially when they're in another state? How do you think that makes me feel?"

"Awful, Mama," Celeste answered without inflection.

"You got that right. It makes me feel absolutely awful."

"I have news to disclose to you Mama."

"What is it, Icy?"

"I married a man I met a week ago."

.

BROWN SUGAR CHAINS

Chains of brown sugar imprisoned him to the bed. Despite every effort, he could not free himself. Repeatedly, he lifted his wrists to break the crumbly manacles but the granules simply shifted, lengthened and then tightened themselves even more securely. The bed under him undulated and writhed violently back and forth like a body in pain. The milk colored silk sheet lifted above him to cascade gently across his body and wrap itself around him in a soft vise-like grip. It was a peculiar sort of torture to be held hostage by a bed, Solomon thought as he clenched his teeth and once again pulled futilely at his brown sugar chains.

A movement caught his attention, and he turned his head to see the woman. Exotic like an African flower, she had onyx skin that shimmered with a silver sheen. Short dark springy braids with iron pressed eyebrows rested above a pair of thickly lashed and kohl enhanced brown eyes. Her nose was snub and her mouth bow-shaped and full.

Fear slithered along his back as Solomon's mouth dropped open and his hands and feet began to wrestle ferociously against the chains that clasped him against the bed. His heart raced, and he felt his breath escape in short gasps. The woman started to walk to the bed, dressed sultrily in a coconut shaded negligée that molded to her form provocatively.

Her beauty terrified him.

He struggled against the grainy restraints. Solomon moaned as the woman drew closer, "Please, get away from me! Stay away!"

"Derrick Shaw," the woman spoke, her voice throaty and smooth.

"Go away! Go away!"

The woman stopped at the bed, and her brown eyes gazed at him. "No. I'll never go away."

She leaned over him, tilted her head to the side. "Never, Derrick Shaw."

Her left eye slid from its socket like a glob of melted ice cream and trailed down her cheek to fall onto his face. Solomon's lips open to scream when her right eye followed suit and landed on his tongue. He gasped as much as he could as he fought not to close his mouth over the eye.

The rest of her face became a morbid dark waterfall of fluid skin that splattered on the milk colored sheets and his face. "I'll never go away," the voice of the woman repeated all around him as she continued to disappear in a cascade of liquefied flesh that sheathed him. He closed his mouth . . . and opened his eyes.

The hum of the air conditioner brought him back to the present. His heart tap danced against his rib cage, and he exhaled noisily and lifted himself from the bed.

"Oh!" he bit out as the alcohol fairy with the two ton mallet began to strike against his brain.

"Mr. Greene?"

He jerked his head up and winced again at the action. Celeste stood over him, her face impassive, arms folded.

"My wife," he spoke slowly as he massaged his temple as he sat up.

"Indeed. Would you like for me to ring for coffee and a countermeasure for your cranial affliction?"

"Yes, please."

Ten minutes later, a knock on the door caused Solomon to groan, and an attendant entered with an ornate coffee service that included bagels, croissants, toast, eggs, and bacon with cream and sugar in high polished silver containers. On a small tray laid a pair of pills.

Solomon still sat on the bed and watched with one eye closed as Celeste went over to the tray.

"Shall I?" Celeste asked.

He nodded and then winced at the action. "Make it black."

She didn't answer him but poured the coffee. Solomon allowed his gaze to rove over her. She had changed from the last time he had seen her, but she had the same style of dress on. Her black skirt hung to her ankles, and the collar of her ivory blouse came to the back of her hair. If he didn't know better, he'd think he was looking at a school teacher circa 1865.

She turned around, her skirt slightly billowed out. He saw a brief glimpse of petticoats and a row of ruffles on her blouse.

Dear Lord, who in the world did I marry?

She came forward and with a half-smile he thanked her and took a sip of the hot coffee that scalded his tongue as well as the pills she held out to him from the small tray, her hands covered with black lacy gloves.

"What time is it?"

"One-thirty in the morning."

"I've been asleep for twelve hours?"

She walked away from him and sat in an armchair he didn't notice earlier. A large ball of yarn with two needles sticking out of it rested at her feet. She picked them up and began to knit.

"Why didn't you wake me?" he asked as he took more sips and watched her at her craft. Her gloved fingers zipped stitches off and on in a blur. Fascinated, he saw the piece of yarn she knitted growing before his eyes.

"You are a stranger. I have no inclination to discover whether or not violence is a component of your inebriated persona." She didn't glance up as she answered him.

Hitting women is not my problem, Solomon thought to himself. "I've never hit a woman in my life, Mrs. Greene. Sober or not."

"Very well."

The atmosphere was chilled by the air conditioner. Its hum and the faint click-clack of the needles kept away the silence that started to grow between them. Solomon studied his wife again as he ate the food on the tray. He could tell she had an abundance of hair although it was hidden in a bun. With her head bent over her work, the soft light from the lamp illuminated her cheeks. Her skin was smooth — it reminded him of nutmeg.

"You don't wear makeup," he stated as he finished the meal. Every woman he'd known since childhood dabbed their faces in foundation.

Celeste didn't answer or move as she continued to knit.

"Do you have any family?"

"Yes."

He waited for her to add more to her statement but when she continued to knit, he said slowly, "And?"

"Are you truly curious about my familial connections or simply seeking a way to fill the silence?"

Solomon felt his eyebrows arch. "Well I —"

"Mr. Greene, we were married thirteen hours ago. A man who joins in matrimony to a woman he scarcely knows should not expect much." Solomon's eyes were glued to her as he thought about what she'd said. It was true he didn't know his wife but he had hoped he could be friends with the woman he wedded on a whim. After all, he married her for protection.

"I understand we just met." He got up and stretched; the medicine had begun to vaporize the alcohol fairy in his head. The pain lessened to a dull throb. "But I would like to know more about my wife. After all, we are married."

"That is true, sir. However, this shall only last for a period of seven years. At that time, you will be free to dissolve this marriage. You wedded me for my lack of looks. I have my own reasons for why I agreed to marry you. You are merely a title - Husband. I am only a title - Wife. Have I made myself clear?"

He stared at her, his arms across his bare chest. Why wouldn't she look at him? "Will you look at me and put those needles down?"

She set them down and lifted her head. *Maple syrup eyes.*

"I want to get to know you. Is that too much to ask?"

"Yes."

His eyes widened in surprise. "Why is that too much to ask?"

"Mr. Greene, this marriage is a farce. We only joined in matrimony because we both have agendas that do not accommodate romantic notions. Why should we try to cultivate some sort of camaraderie when we have no intention to solidify this arrangement? Most assuredly, you comprehend a platonic formal relationship is all we can share."

Solomon stared at her. Her face was void of expression and voice without intonation. He sighed and rubbed the back of his neck. She sounded like an old-fashioned teacher. He sighed again and dropped his hand. Perhaps she was right.

"Well, Celeste—"

"Mrs. Greene."

His hand paused. "What?"

"Mrs. Greene. I prefer you address me by your surname."

He stared at her for a moment, not sure if he heard correctly. When he realized he had, he responded, "Woman you must be out your mind. Your name is Celeste, my wife."

She stared at him, her maple syrup eyes devoid of any emotion and then she broke contact and picked up her needles and started to knit once more.

"Celeste, I need to know about your family. You and I both know that as far as we're concerned our families will need to know about each other. Now tell me."

Silence pervaded for a few moments and then she spoke, her face averted from him. "I have one sister. Her name is Leah. She's shorter, plumper, and prettier than I am. She is an exquisite cook. Actually, Mr. Greene, you may be familiar with her. She appeared on television and became an Internet star two years ago because she terminated the reign of a serial rapist as she beat him within seconds of his life with her bare hands."

"The Kung Fu Sunday School Teacher?" Solomon couldn't believe it.

"Yes, although she doesn't know Kung Fu. Apparently, that peculiar designation was used as an attention grabber and not for accuracy." Her hands stilled and looked up at him. "May I continue?"

"Continue what?"

"I desire to make you *au courant* with my family."

He nodded as he ignored the fact he had no idea what the word meant. "Sure."

"My parents are Brenda and Samuel Martin. They have a very comfortable Internet business. My mother is a talker, and my father is a listener."

"When do I meet them?"

"We don't. I have made it quite clear."

Solomon recognized instantly that her appearance hid a bossy woman underneath the surface. Not his usual type of woman eager to be friendly and fun. And if he wasn't careful, his wife would walk over him.

"I'm not a kid, Celeste. I'm your husband. We'll go see your family in three days. We may not have a real marriage, but we will at least pretend we do in front of family. And what you need to know about me is that I have money, a lot of it."

He waited to see how she would respond, but she simply looked at him and said, "How fortunate for you."

So much for shock treatment!

"Hopefully, you needn't use all that money to take a shower now."

ICY AND BLAZE

"What! He married you because he thought you were ugly? Icy, are you serious?"

"Wholly," Celeste responded to her sister Leah as they sat in the kitchen, eating her sister's homemade crumpets. They were in Columbus, Ohio a few hours' drive from Mr. Greene's home in Michigan. Although they could have easily driven back to the house, Mr. Greene scheduled a flight from Columbus to Detroit where his driver would meet them.

"And you married him?" Leah's voice screeched like an antique record, and her eyes grew to the size of pincushions. Celeste had a fanciful notion they were set to fall out. She didn't answer but took another sip of her tea.

After a few moments, Celeste heard Leah sigh. "Icy, you gotta be kidding me."

"These are exquisite Blaze," Celeste remarked as she took a bite of her crumpet.

"I'm glad you like them. You're the only one who eats them." Leah leaned back in the chair and folded her arms. "Since we've gotten that useless comment out of the way, answer my question."

Celeste continued to chew as she studied her sister. Blaze had everything she didn't. She had accepted it some time ago. Very pretty, her sister possessed the subtle blend of baby innocence enhanced by adult maturity. One admirer compared her to a mythical Pillsbury Dough girl with stilettos.

No one had ever taken a second glance at Celeste. Instantly she stopped that train of thought and allowed a mental picture of ice to freeze over it.

"I have my reasons," Celeste finally remarked.

With a sense of detachment, she watched Leah pulled at her curls in a manner of frustration and howled a groan. "Icy, for Pete's sake, just tell me!"

"I don't intend to, dear sister."

Solomon had forgotten houses could be so small.

In the Martin's living room, the coziness of the place enveloped him. His family home loomed like a giant hidden in the forest. Huge with the living areas divided into suites. What the Martin's home lacked in size was made up in the warmth that exuded from it. Pale blue walls with white trim gave the living room a happy, carefree feel. To his left, an L-shaped creamy white sectional surrounded a glass table topped with a vase of fresh flowers and an unlit fireplace to his right. He saw a number of pictures interspersed with various knickknacks on the mantle. He sauntered over and studied it.

One picture showed a young woman with caramel baby skin, thick curly hair, and chocolate chip eyes. She had a bright smile, and it blazed from the photograph. *Juicy. I wonder what she would be like.*

Stop it Solomon! You have your wife. That was the deal, correct?

He pinched his nose and sighed. He took off his jacket, placed it in the crook of his arm, and jammed his hands into his pockets.

A picture of a young Celeste caught his eye. Not much to look at even as a child. She could have stepped off the set of the Big Valley. Two long braided ponytails nestled on either side of her head. Once again, she was dressed in pioneer clothes, her face devoid of expression.

Does she ever smile? He wondered.

"Are you my son-in-law?" A woman's voice said from behind him.

He turned and looked down and saw the modern version of a hobbit.

An older woman with toffee colored skin met his gaze. Her black hair streaked with gray was neatly styled in a French roll. Milk chocolate eyes crinkled and blazed with vibrancy as they assessed him. Her nose turned up at the tip. A beautiful smile made her thin lips attractive. She wasn't a slender woman but nicely shaped in a motherly way, dressed in a light blue dress and sandals.

"Are you my mother-in-law?" Solomon asked as he bent to give her a hug, inhaling a flowery scent.

"I certainly am. Though I must tell you, I was surprised to find out my dear Celeste had gotten married. I can't possibly understand why she would marry a complete stranger in a matter of days. I know sometimes that it can happen—one can find true love in a matter of minutes and know instantly he or she is the right one." For the next five minutes, Mrs. Martin babbled on. Before she finished, he'd hear about two different couples, eight children, and a bear. How all of it related to his and Celeste's marriage was anyone's guess.

"Why'd you marry my Celeste anyway?" The question came at the end of her soliloquy.

Solomon rocked back on his heels. He'd have to be very careful how he answered the question too. It would have to be as succinct as possible without giving too much away. He felt shame wash over him as he realized the fact if his mother-in-law knew why he married her daughter, she'd give him an earful. "She was the answer to my prayers."

I prayed to God for an ugly wife, and I got one.

"Are you a church man, son?"

"Not until lately, Mrs. Martin." *Not until three days ago, mother-in-law.*

"Well, I'm glad to hear that at least. My Celeste is not a real church-goer herself. I raised her like I did both my girls but one has to make up one's own mind. I remember when—"

"Is this my son-in-law, Brenda sweet?" A frog-like voice croaked.

Solomon lifted his head at the masculine tone. A tall older man dressed casually in a pair of black jeans and a polo shirt gazed at him. Celeste shared her father's complexion. He had shoulders like a linebacker and a small afro. His face could have been carved out of granite and just as expressionless except for his eyes. Underneath a pair of thick eyebrows, the coffee colored eyes glittered with bone-penetrating scrutiny.

"Hello Mr. Martin." Solomon reached out to shake the man's hand.

Mr. Martin didn't take his hand but left it suspended in the air.

Surprise swept through his body. He hardly expected hostility of any form. He had married their daughter, hadn't he? It didn't take long for anyone to know his wife was a bit of an oddball without her daily habit of dress-up.

"I will be upfront with you. The fact you're my daughter's husband means little. I don't know you, Solomon Greene. I am extremely skeptical of a man who marries a woman after a week and does not have the decency to meet her family. And you expect me to shake hands with you? You are mistaken. However, I will give you the benefit of the doubt. You must have some sort of feelings for my daughter, and as such, you will have to earn my respect. My daughter deserves a very special man, and I don't believe it is you. Only time will tell."

Solomon felt his eyebrows take residence in his hairline, and he withdrew his hand as it began to tingle from the lack of circulation. This man had to be out of his mind. He should be on his knees thankful he'd even had a husband for his daughter. No, that wasn't fair. He needed her; not the other way around. She didn't have to marry him, especially when he told her bluntly he was marrying since she wasn't his type by any stretch of the word.

"I'm sorry you feel that way, Mr. Martin," Solomon spoke after a brief silence. "I hope to show you I have only good intentions for your daughter, and I will provide for her as well." He had enough

20

money for her to have whatever she wished. And he did have pleasant feelings for her. Wasn't relief a pleasant feeling?

"We'll see." The man's voice dribbled with doubt.

"Sam," Mrs. Martin intervened, "why don't you call Leah and tell her to bring some of her afternoon treats. I'm sure you'd like to meet your sister-in-law. She's the Kung Fu Sunday School teacher."

She motioned to the couch with her hand. "Please sit down. Here's Leah now. Leah, this is your brother-in-law, Solomon. Celeste baby, come over and sit next to Solomon and Leah. Put the tray of goodies here. Would you like some lemonade, Solomon?"

Solomon lifted his eyes to see the girl from the picture. Older, her chocolate chip eyes locked with his. He gritted his teeth as her beauty hit him with a blast of fear even as a snake of desire slithered along his mind. Quickly, he darted his eyes to his wife. Her face smothered the small spark of flame and the fear receded. She was his personal life savior.

Green gold flares lit up in her husband's eyes as he saw her sister.

Celeste noted the reaction in a detached way. It always happened like this. Men saw Leah and responded. They didn't see the other side of her sister, and she refrained from enlightening them. Eventually those who dared to be enmeshed by her sister's trappings of beauty found out for themselves what she really was.

It was the spark of fright in his eyes that captured her attention. What could Mr. Greene be afraid of?

Cease and desist, Icy. Mr. Greene's fears are of no concern to you. He is merely your husband which means absolutely nothing.

"So Sol, oh brother-in-law, what made you marry my sister?"

21

Celeste glanced up at her sister as they all were seated on the sectional, she next to Leah and Mr. Greene between her parents. They sipped at the lemonade her sister brought out and ate a dish of strawberries and meringue topped with whipped cream. The question was innocently asked, but Celeste knew Leah. Her eyes narrowed, and Celeste could feel the tension radiate from her. Her sister barely had a rein on her temper.

"Like I told your mother, I married your sister because she's an answer to prayer," her husband replied.

Leah's fingers tightened on the glass. It was the only clue to what happened next. Even if Celeste had had the speed of a comic book superhero, only divine intervention could have prevented her sister from what she did. In a flash, she stood and began to pour the glass of lemonade over Mr. Greene's head. Her mother's crystal glass smashed to smithereens as she threw it blindly against a wall behind her.

Numb, Celeste watched the scene unfold before her.

Leah screeched, "Don't you ever try to make a mockery of God's name! And not at the expense of my sister!"

"Blaze! What in the world are you doing!?" Mrs. Martin yelled as she jumped up and clasped her hands to her face.

"Leah, what the devil is wrong with you? You don't treat a guest like that," her father remarked sternly as his eyebrows met to a V in the middle of his forehead.

"This man," she spat in a bitter tone that snapped like an elastic band, "is making a fool out of my sister and I'm not going to let him!" Leah screamed, as she gestured wildly toward Mr. Greene. He sat stone still in shock. An ice cube slid off his head and landed on the table.

"But Blaze, honey, you don't pour lemonade on anyone just because you're mad!" Mrs. Martin stated as she grabbed the napkins from the table and handed them to Mr. Greene

"Leah, sit down at once!" Mr. Martin shouted.

"No! This worthless —,"

"I said, sit down Leah and you better do what I said. As long as you're in my house, you'll do as you told."

Oh Daddy, Celeste thought as she shifted herself away from her sister.

At that, Leah picked up everyone's glasses of lemonade and flung them onto Mr. Greene and then the carpet. Thankfully, none of them broke.

Celeste watched as he got up and tried to dash away from the onslaught. Instead, he somehow tripped and landed on the carpet and with the last glass emptied on him Leah started to scream at him. Mrs. Martin had attempted to stop Leah, but her sister had reached the point of no return.

War erupted.

Leah and her parents started to scream each other, and Mr. Greene had a thing or two to say as he got up from the floor and began to loom over her.

The sound of the doorbell somehow made it through the din and Celeste got up and walked away from the battle and opened the front door.

"Salutations, Lady Martin. Or should I say, Lady Greene?"

Jacob Othello Westwood. His name had the ability to rip the breath from her body and send her pulse humming like a needle on a sewing machine. The sight of him only made it worse — her heart pumped faster, her face flushed with warmth, and her inner core burst with radiance.

He wasn't a tall man, but he stood a few inches over her head. Thick golden blond hair rested on a high forehead. Soft periwinkle eyes, an eagle-like nose slightly off center, and firm lips collaborated to form his handsome face. His shoulders were broad, and he had a lean, muscled physique attributed to a steady workout.

Lord Westwood — the only man she loved and could ever love. And he was her sister's fiancé.

She made sure her face didn't reveal her thoughts as she said in response, "Salutations, Lord Westwood. Unfortunately, sir, this is not the most opportune moment. My sister—,"

"What on earth is that noise? Is that Leah?"

Celeste wordlessly stepped back and allowed him to enter. She closed the door gently behind her and watched him as he walked further into the foyer. His back side, sheathed in a dark blue shirt and tan colored pants, was just as nice as his front. Instantly, she forced another mental image of ice to freeze the train of her thoughts and focus once more on the present. Since the foyer opened to the living room, it wasn't difficult to see the commotion.

"Leahgirl?" It was Lord Westwood's pet name for Leah.

"Jacob?" Leah's voice transformed from a banshee to an enchantress in three seconds.

"Why are you making all that noise?"

"My sister's husband is terrible!" She launched herself into his arms, and he held her close.

"Come tell me about it."

They walked away and went back out the door, which Celeste opened in time for them to leave.

In the sudden silence that ensued, her husband's green gold eyes flared once more as they looked at her, but they were filled with anger. With certainty, Celeste knew they would never again light up with desire when he gazed upon her sister. And why that little fact should mean something to her didn't deserve a thought.

BLACK LICORICE TWINE

Twines of black licorice were wrapped around his wrists and feet. They held him solid against the wall. Clothed only in his pajamas pants, Solomon fought against their hold in the small prison cell. The walls were gray brick, but the bars were also made out of the licorice. The difference between this and a real cell was there wasn't any furniture of any kind or locking mechanism on the bars. He pulled at his candied bonds, but they only tightened and glistened. His efforts were ineffective, but he continued to try. He had to.

He gritted his teeth and pulled at the twine, and his neck strained with the effort, the cords of his throat vivid against the red of his flushed skin. He had to get out there. A beautiful woman was coming, and he had to run.

"Justin Harper," a soft, light voice called out.

A bucket of paralyzing, frigid fear doused his body. The blood escaped from his head to his feet as the woman came into his line of vision. She was delicate as an Asian orchid. Soft skin like vanilla frosting meshed with silky razor-straight black hair. Long, curved eyebrows nestled above short lashed, almond shaped eyes. A snub nose rested above her lips tinged like the color of peaches. She wore a lacy black peignoir that shaped itself along her figure.

"No! Stay away from me!" Once again, he pulled at the black licorice twine but it held fast to his body.

She hadn't moved, but an instant later, she stood in the center of the cell.

"Justin Harper," she whispered. Her lips formed a smile.

"No! Stay away!"

She planted herself in front of him and stared at him as if she could bore a hole into his mind.

"I'll never go away," The wispy voice threatened.

She lifted her hand and pressed her forefinger against his mouth. She commanded, "Eat."

His head moved violently from side to side.

The woman tugged at his lower lip and despite his efforts, his mouth opened without resistance. "That's right, Justin. Eat!" She demanded once more as the smile left her face and an expression of intense concentration took hold. She placed her forefinger in his mouth. She used her other hand and forced his mouth close. He bit half her finger off but instead of bone and blood, just a licorice limb surrounded by a flimsy layer of skin.

"Now swallow!" she shouted.

He shook his head and pulled again, but it was useless. Her face wrinkled as her eyebrows drew close together, and she started to sneer.

"Do it now, Justin Harper. Swallow!"

"No!" he spoke. At that moment, she shoved the appendage down his throat.

Solomon woke up. He coughed and heaved. His fingers splayed on his chest and sweat-drenched his body. His heart thrashed against his rib cage like two wrestlers in a ring. He panted as if he'd finished a 100 meter dash.

He turned his head and saw the red light from the small digital clock on his nightstand — 3:14 a.m.

He waited until his pulses and heartbeat returned to normal. Then he uncovered himself from the bed and got up, walking to the door opposite his massive bed. He opened the door and flicked on the light switch.

Light flooded the bathroom. It was an opulent room swathed with luxury in the form of brilliant green marble floors and white tiled walls. A Jacuzzi, standalone shower, and a claw foot tub occupied various corners of the room. Under a large glass block window, a heated towel rack that ran the length of the wall hovered above a green marble vanity with gold fixtures. Although it had been five years since he was last in his suite, he barely gave his surroundings a glance. The dream still held him captive. Without taking off his pajama pants, he opened the shower door and turned on the hot water.

It cascaded down onto his thrown back face. The hot droplets stung, but he ignored the pain momentarily as he tried to wash away the dream. It had happened again; the woman wanted him to devour her in some way. Why? What did it mean? For a moment, his mind hovered over the dream, seeing the woman as she stood before him, missing a finger and the licorice limb gleaming dully.

After a few moments, he adjusted the temperature and allowed his thoughts to roam.

Solomon hadn't spoken to his wife in three days and hadn't seen her in two. He remembered the humiliating experience of meeting her family and thought that if he never saw them again, it would be too soon.

Yet, he could have handled that aspect of the visit if it hadn't been for his wife's actions — or rather, inactivity.

He sighed as he remembered the drive to the airport in the limo.

"I can't believe that your sister did that to me!" He had screamed at her. Dried lemonade stuck to his skin; his clothes were ruined.

Celeste had glanced over at him with that dead expression of hers.

"Leah has always had a volatile disposition," she'd said in the low colorless tone he began to associate with her.

"And you didn't say a word to stop her! I'm your husband, Celeste."

"In name only, sir."

"Celeste, I'm your husband," he'd repeated. "I would never allow anyone to treat you like that. I'd pulverize anyone who would dare do something like that to you."

She had stared at him, and the plainness of her face struck him anew.

"Meritorious sir. Yet unnecessary."

"So if my mother meets you and pours hot boiling coffee onto you because of something you said, I'm just supposed to hand you some paper *towel?"* He had used the illustration to make a point. He hadn't expected her to answer.

"If you so wish, Mr. Greene. Let me asseverate, sir, that this union is only bound by paper, not emotive regard. You can suppress any husbandly inclinations of protection."

Her response had stunned him into silence. A man had an obligation to protect his wife. Although his parents were two steps away from becoming citizens of Looneyville, his father had instilled in him a sense of duty toward any woman who became his wife. Although he had avoided matrimonial ties till now, he knew he carried the influence of his father into adulthood. He felt wounded. What was left of his sense of manhood fell to the floor of the limousine. He'd lashed out as he exploded.

"What kind of attitude is that? I know we married each other for our own reasons, but you're not even trying to make the best of this thing! I'm just to ignore you and act like you don't exist? I went to meet your family because I want us to have a friendship Celeste, not some kind of long distance business relationship. And you let your sister treat me like a piece of garbage! What is wrong with you?"

She'd stared right through him, her eyes like dried maple syrup, and never answered.

He turned off the water, walked out the shower and went over to the vanity. He picked up a towel before he took off his wet pajamas, threw them in the corner of the bathroom, and dried himself off. He opened one of the drawers, pulled out a pair of boxers and another set of pajamas. Dressed again, he flicked the light switch and back into the bedroom.

Strange he wasn't afraid to go back to bed now. Thinking of his wife had rid him of the effects of the dream.

Solomon dove back into the bed and stared up at the ceiling. After that explosion in the car, there had been silence all the way to the airport, the plane ride, the car ride to his family mansion in Rochester Hills. He wondered what she had thought of it when they came up on the circular drive. When they had arrived at the mansion Patrick Batcher, their household manager, opened the door and smiled, his brown face lit with greeting. Patrick, an Indian man, had a head of silky short black hair and bronze eyes that sparkled with intelligence. Clean shaven, he dressed in a pair of tan slacks and a hideous Hawaiian shirt. This fact told Solomon that his parents were gone. When they were in residence, Batcher was expected to wear more formal attire.

"It's good to see you, Solomon. Is there someone with you?" Patrick had asked as he started to walk toward them.

"My wife."

Patrick had stopped midstride and his eyes widened. "Pardon me?"

Solomon had given him a wry grin. "My wife, Celeste Greene. Celeste, this is our house manager, Patrick Batcher."

Thinking back on it now, it really shouldn't have been a surprise for what Celeste did next. He'd only known her for almost two weeks now and despite her plain face, monotone voice, and her costume dresses, she was unpredictable.

She got out the car and walked over to Patrick. 'It is a pleasure to make your acquaintance, Mr. Batcher."

She'd taken a handful of her voluminous skirts in either hand, spread out the fabric, and curtsied in an elegant manner, kneeling almost to the ground.

Solomon had grinned as he saw Patrick's face slacken with surprise and incredulity. The man was used to the pompous ways of his parents' behavior of him as a house manager. From time to time, they'd even called him a butler. But in one fell swoop, Celeste had shown him respect and deference in a way Patrick instantly understood.

"The pleasure is all mine Mrs. Greene," Patrick had spoken after a moment. "Welcome to the family."

Solomon watched as his wife bowed her head in a demure fashion. He asked drily, "I don't suppose you'd have any lemonade on you, do you Patrick?"

And for one brief moment, Solomon could have sworn he saw her eyes light up as she turned to look at him. The strangest emotion went through

29

him as their glances locked on each other for a brief moment. A hint of intimacy he'd never experience before as he knew they both remembered her sister and only they recognized his pun on words. Even now, lying in the darkness of his massive bedroom, he could feel the intensity of that connection.

Well, God had given him his wife, and he had hoped for the friendship between them. Maybe it had started.

He turned his thoughts to other things. Tomorrow, he would meet with Gonzo, his best friend and go hang out at the skateboard park. The life he had been leading up till now had lost its luster. He'd have to figure what he would do.

Then he'd have to go to back to church and reacquaint himself with his religious duties. That was, after all, the deal he'd made with God if He gave him his wife.

As sleep started to fall, Solomon thought, at least his wife had warm maple syrup eyes.

###

His green gold eyes had seared her, licked against her reserve like a tongue of flame. Despite her resolve, she couldn't escape the effects of that brief connection.

There couldn't be any intimacy between them. They were married, not lovers. And yet, there it was, a small bond being stitched together like chains from a crochet hook. No amount of icy control could loosen it. Celeste sighed and turned over in the massive bed.

So lonely, a tiny voice said into her head.

No, it isn't. This is exactly what I want, Celeste argued as she began to freeze up again, her emotions and longings she encased in ice. She allowed her imagination to run, created visuals of ice sickles that struck down all the wayward thoughts of longing and desire until she felt nothing but the comfort of numbness.

There now. All better.

###

"Mr. Batcher, may I speak with you?"

Celeste watched as Mr. Batcher rose from his chair at the desk in his office and went around it to pull out the comfortable leather seat.

"Of course, Mrs. Greene. Please sit."

She nodded as she took a quick glance around the room. Neat and clean, the tan walls were covered with shelving filled with curios and knickknacks. A desk dominated by a large scale computer monitor and a marked up calendar that covered the surface of it stood in the center of the room. There was a picture of a young girl on his desk and another of a woman not much younger than her host.

"How can I help you, Mrs. Greene?" he asked as he sat back down.

"I have several things I need to have attended to if I can utilize your expertise." Celeste said as she sat back and folded her hands in her lap. She wore one of her favorite pieces, a long 1770s French inspired shimmery day robe. It had ample quantities of lace at the end of the tight fitting sleeves of the forearms and opened at her elbows. Made of midnight blue taffeta, it flowed over her body. Underneath she wore a long high necked plain white gown that came to her feet with long sleeves tied at the wrists.

She noted the way Mr. Batcher eyed her attire as he said, "What can I assist you with, Mrs. Greene?"

"I understand from my husband that he is rich."

The man nodded slowly. "That's a direct way of putting it."

"I wonder then, if it would be possible, to have things from my apartment moved to the mansion, my rent paid, and all my other expenses handled. I did have a vehicle, as well. Is there some place to store it?"

She saw his mouth twitch slightly. "Yes ma'am."

"Also, I would like to have a phone installed in my suite. There is a particular phone I would like to have if I can show it to you."

"Well, well, well aren't you just falling into your role of a pampered wife easily," a voice said from behind.

Celeste turned and saw her husband for the first time in three days. Black shorts hung loosely on his hips. A plain green T-shirt drooped from his shoulder, and a helmet hid most of his head from sight, the straps hanging from his chin. Protective gear covered his elbows, knees, and hands. His foot pumped the tail end of a skateboard over and over without sending it fully vertical.

"Good morning, Mr. Greene," she greeted as she rose from her chair, while Mr. Batcher stood as well.

"Celeste. I see you've taken advantage of my wealth. One wonders, if we're just walking titles, why should you bother with using my resources?"

His green gold eyes narrowed slightly as they fixed on her. She held his gaze as she said, "If you do not want me to utilize your resources, by all means, do let me know. You must remember, sir, we married a week ago. We never went to my home. We neglected to discuss my interests, my work, or my education. You simply grabbed me once I said yes to our proposal and then touted me to a hotel where I stayed by myself before you came and got me the day we married. However, I happen to be on sabbatical from my modeling career, my rent was paid to the end of this month, and I have a Bachelor's degree."

"Modeling? Since when are you a model?" His voice filled with disbelief as the skateboard hit the floor with a thump as his foot went off it.

"I am a parts model, sir. In particular, hands." Resentment started to rise, but she quickly iced it down with her mind. His opinion wasn't important to her.

"Hands?" She saw him glance down at her hands folded neatly in front of her. "That explains the gloves."

Celeste didn't answer.

His foot fell hard on the tail end of his board. It leapt up, and he caught it in a fluid motion. "Patrick, do whatever Celeste needs. I'm off to the park."

She sat back down as did Mr. Batcher and continued her requests. "Mr. Batcher," she said as she ended with all the details, "Once this is complete, you may not see much of me except at dinners until my husband's parents arrive."

Mr. Batcher's eyes probed into hers as he asked, "Why did you marry Solomon?"

"I have my reasons." Unbidden, an image of Lord Westwood came to the forefront and with it a tsunami of feeling. Excitement, heart break, and desire all threatened to crash into her. The visions of his hair, thick, golden, and curled at the nape of his neck made her want to reach out and caress her fingers through it. His soft, periwinkle eyes arrested her, and she felt her breath catch. She could still feel his lips against her cheek and unconsciously, she put her gloved hand to her face. Lord Westwood was all that was good and kind and patient.

And her sister's fiancé.

With an iron will, she visualized ice on his face. The ice grew thicker and thicker until the image froze over, and she exhaled.

There now. All better.

HER SMILE

"Dude, that was sweet!" Gonzo exclaimed as Solomon executed a bone breaker.

Solomon grinned as he glided on his skateboard, breathing hard after the tricky maneuver. It called for him to pop the tail of the skateboard with his feet while he flipped it with his hand. Balanced on the edge, he landed on the truck — the axle assembly between the wheels — at the opposite end. After a few seconds, he flipped it back over and landed on the deck, the surface of the board.

The fact he could still do the trick amazed him. It had been some time since he'd been on his board but the moves were still there and for the first time in a long time, a sense of genuine accomplishment filled his mind.

The skateboard park, a few miles from his home, bustled with activity. There were both indoor and outdoor components, and he'd chosen to practice outside, feeling the deck under his feet reunite with the flow of his body.

He'd skated since childhood. Eight years ago, at twenty-three, he had participated in competitions and won awards for his skills. He'd even created some of his own tricks, but that was before . . .

"You still got it man," Gonzo said as he glided past Solomon on his own board. Effortlessly, he executed an Ollie. It was a basic move that lifted the board off ground. He then flipped the board twice, called a double flip, and landed on the deck once more.

Gonzo was as tall as Solomon with a slimmer build. He had crew cut black hair, black eyes, and a narrow nose. Dark hair covered his arms, legs, and chest thus one of the reasons why he had been nicknamed Gonzo. They'd been friends for years and had competed against each other. Although they hadn't seen each other for five years, they had kept in contact off and on during that time.

"Still see you still don't have it," Solomon quipped. He turned the board backward, called riding fakie. Then he picked up speed and performed a tre bomb. The move propelled him into the air while his board rotated 360 degrees. In perfect synchronization, as the wheels touched the ground so did he land on the board. It had been four years since he completed that move. He exhaled as he rolled forward while Gonzo whooped in the background. He felt alive again. Exhilarated. Years off his board and the old skills were still there.

"So what's been going on with you?" Gonzo asked as he prepared to do another Ollie.

"I got married," Solomon told him.

Gonzo turned into a statue and his eyes popped out in shock. At that moment, he had more resemblance to the Muppet than ever before. All he needed to have was a hooked nose. As Solomon watched, Gonzo continued to stare at him, and before he could warn him, his friend crashed into a bench. He fell to the ground as his feet left the board and it continued its trek rider-less.

"Don't act all shocked now," Solomon said wryly as he skated over to Gonzo sprawled over the lawn chair and jumped off the board to help.

"Sol, dude, are you serious! You got married!" Gonzo waved him away and straightened from the bench.

"Yeah. Last week."

"To who?"

"Her name is Celeste."

"Where did you meet her?" Gonzo asked as he folded his arms.

Here's the hard part, Solomon thought to himself. He rubbed his face. "At a museum in Denver. I saw a painting. The lady in the picture was hideous. I remember thinking, 'Woof!' Celeste looked at me, and I saw she didn't look any better than the chick in the portrait."

"Wait, wait, wait," Gonzo interrupted as he sat on the lawn chair. "You're talking about Celeste, your wife?"

"Yeah."

"The woman you married is ugly?" Gonzo's voice was full of incredulity.

Solomon sighed. "Well, she's not my type. She's really plain looking. Nothing about her jumps out at you except her clothes."

Gonzo gaped at him, his eyebrows arched so high they made him look like the furry Muppet he was named after. "What?"

"Let me start from the beginning," Solomon started as he sat on the ground next to Gonzo. The memory unfolded.

Solomon had gone to the museum to escape. He didn't often go to museums to pick up women but once or twice he had. A girl with pink hair who was into ancient Grecian art. The other, an older woman who liked younger men. He'd been happy to accommodate her for the brief period they were together.

But now he'd wanted to get away. The memory of the blueberry woman kept rearing her head.

He had gone toward the Renaissance section and stopped at a painting simply titled, "A Lady and Her Husband," artist unknown. He'd studied the painting. The woman wore some kind of old-fashioned blue dress with the thing around her head that had looked like a halo. The man stood next to her, clothed in a sparkly jacket with all kinds of jewels on it.

"Wow, not the prettiest thing, are you?" he'd asked the painted woman.

"At least she is married." He'd whirled around. A young woman dressed in an outfit not too dissimilar from the one in the picture stood before him. A quick glance had told him she lacked looks like the woman did. Her skin dark like cocoa — no, nutmeg.

"Oh, do you work here?" he'd asked, assuming the outfit was part of the museum's employee uniform.

"No, I do not," the woman replied.

"Sorry."

The woman had remained silent, her eyes focused on the portrait. A rare occurrence. Once they met him, most women wanted to strike up a conversation.

"What did you mean by at least she's married?" he'd prompted when the silence continued.

"Visual appearance is not a salient factor for a spousal partner. There are other qualities to be desired." Her voice had a bland tone to it, full of disinterest. Yet she continued to stand and study the painting.

"Yeah but a man's got to look at his wife when he's sleeping with her."

"Does he?" Her eyebrow had arched, but her face remained averted.

Solomon grinned, but it left his face as the woman didn't try to be coy with her remark. Another rare occurrence.

"So what are you saying?"

"There are other reasons why people marry."

"Oh," Solomon had stated, "like for money or position."

"And yet, still more."

"Not really," Solomon had answered as he'd turned toward her, "Either it's sex, money, or position."

"You seem so sure of yourself, sir. But there are factors to consider."

"Such as?"

"Protection."

Solomon froze as the word hit him. Marriage for protection? Instantly he'd understood what she meant.

"I see," he'd replied slowly as he turned to look at the woman. "Self-preservation."

She'd inclined her head in acquiescence, a graceful gesture that made her queenly.

The incident from a few weeks back had flashed through his mind and he gritted his teeth. The blueberry woman. He'd glanced back at the picture. It was the most radical idea that he'd ever had in his life but when he turned back to the woman next to him, he simply blurted it out.

"So if I asked you to marry me, what would you say?"

The woman gave no visible sign of surprise, but she'd turned toward him. "I would ask why?"

"Do you want me to be honest?"

"By all means, be candid."

"I need protection from beautiful women." He'd wanted to say more, but she interrupted him with, "I see. And as I am not a beautiful woman, I would be ideal to protect you from them."

"I didn't mean it like that," Solomon interjected, his skin flushed because she'd been dead on point.

"I have lived with my looks my whole life. I will marry you sir. What is your name?"

"And the rest is history, as they say," Solomon finished.

Gonzo stared at him for a long moment. Then he said, "Dude, if it was anyone else on the planet, I wouldn't believe you. But it's you, so I know you're crazy. And she just accepted the fact you married her for her looks?"

"Yeah. Weird, isn't it?"

###

It's nice to have money, Celeste thought as she surveyed her room. The space burst at the seams with her sewing machines, bolts of various material, her computer, television, books, and her other handcrafts she enjoyed. It would take some time to organize everything like she wanted it but for the first time in two weeks, she felt a sense of her equilibrium coming back.

Massive and luxurious, the bedroom was swathed in creamy white walls and orange accents. The canopy bed surrounded by netted curtains had a direct view of the gardens. The thick white carpet caressed her bare feet with gentleness. An archway separated the bedroom from the sitting area. Two oranges plush chairs bracketed a small glass top table with magazines arranged neatly on it.

She thought back to three days ago, the last time she'd seen Mr. Greene. In spite of her resolve, she found herself having an interest in his world. He was a skater, a world she'd never had any interest in knowing, but now it intrigued her.

Icy, keep it together. She closed her eyes, pulled his image and concentrated on freezing it in her mind. The ice grew thicker and thicker until she could no longer see it.

She opened her eyes and started to organize her debris.

Three hours later and with assistance from Mr. Batcher, Celeste had her suite as she liked it. Her crafts were in the sitting area, and her computer rested on a discarded desk Mr. Batcher had found.

Quickly, she turned it on and logged into her social media networks, her blogs, email, and her YouTube channel. It had been two weeks since she'd been online. It was tantamount to being without civilization. There were dozens of communiques from fans of her costume channel and questions from her crafts channel. Her agent had sent a plea for her to come back to work. She also received e-invites to two costume balls in the future.

She began to deal with these various issues when her Skype phone started to sound off, and a quick glance showed the icon of a daffodil on the screen. With practiced ease, she turned on the recorder and then answered the phone.

The video blinked as the call came on.

"What is that dreadful thing you have on, Celeste Martin?"

The feeling of irritation came up, and Celeste did nothing to dampen it. "It's called an original design, Daffodil Simmons. I'm sure your knowledge in that area is limited."

"Oh, please! Impress me when you can recreate a true work of art."

"After you."

"Darling, where have you been? It's been two weeks and no sign of you at all. I was beginning to wonder if God had chosen to do the world a service and rid us of you."

"God would do us a service if, by some happenstance, you'd swallowed arsenic. What do you want Daffodil?"

"I want to know where you've been. Our fans have been worried."

Celeste debated on what she would say as Daffodil's face filled the screen. The woman's facial features were a landscape of her mixed heritage. Thick, wooly dark brown hair contrasted with stormy deep blue eyes. Her upside down mouth and peanut butter skin rounded out her exotic appearance.

The woman shared her interest in costumes as a general study. Whereas Celeste instructed on how to make various costumes, how to wear them, the best materials to use, and other specific deals, Daffodil focused on generalities of the time period.

"My name is now Celeste Greene," she said finally.

Daffodil's eyes widened in surprise and gave a bark of laughter in disbelief. "Married? You?"

Celeste didn't respond.

"You must be joking." Daffodil laughed again.

Her face flushed with heat and her hands jerked on the keyboard. Daffodil's attempt to get a rise out of her was poorly disguised, but she continued to keep her silence.

"Oh, this is rich! How much did you pay him? You must have gone through a nest egg to accomplish that."

"You can burn, Daffodil," Celeste bit out as she did her best to retain icy control over her emotions. "He married me for my looks, if you must know."

"What looks? You haven't any."

"To my husband, I have the kind of looks he wanted in a wife." *That much at least was true.*

Daffodil came closer to the screen, her lips curled in a nasty smile, "Well, I'm intrigued. Is he blind?"

"Bite me, Daffy Duck!"

The instant the words were out of her mouth she regretted her lack of control. She'd learned some time ago Daffodil fed off rousing her anger. Even now, through the monitor, her face creased into a Cheshire cat smile.

"Are you upset, Celeste? You really need to control your emotions. That's not ladylike, is it? A lady is not rude to another human being."

Calmly, Celeste responded, "Quite true. Yet you assume I consider you among the same species."

An expression of irritation dominated Daffodil's face. "Now, as to why I contacted you. Are you going to Mabel's ball?"

"When is it?"

"Oh dear, you did receive an invitation, did you not? I should like to think Mabel knows an amateur like you."

"When is it?" Celeste repeated as she ignored the intended barb.

"Halloween, three months from now. The theme is the French court. I do hope you can conjure up something suitable by then. As you know, the winner at the end of the evening receives $10,000 as well as the opportunity to travel to Europe for the best design. However, this marriage of yours intrigues me. I shall include an additional wager to this. I will contact you again with the conditions of it."

"Very well."

"Good day, Celeste.

"Good riddance, Daffodil."

Celeste hung up the Skype and turned off the recorder before she began the task of converting the video and then uploading it to YouTube. They were rivals in the amateur costume arena and their spats had a following. Their rivalry had begun two years ago on a wager Daffodil had made to her. Their first wager had been for Celeste to create by hand and wear for a week a corset that resembled the whalebone counterpart of time gone by. Unfortunately for Daffodil, Celeste had already made one and wearing it was a cinch. That had been the start of a number of wagers and competitiveness between them. Some of their fans thought their conversations were

42

scripted and simply a web show. But Celeste knew the animosity between them was very real although she wasn't quite sure of the cause. After all, Daffodil had been the one to start it. Behind the beautiful face, her adversary had a vindictive streak.

The antique phone she had installed in the suite rang. She sighed as she reached over and picked up the earpiece. It had to be Blaze. She had texted her number earlier that morning.

"Celeste Greene."

"Icy, I want to apologize." Leah's voice screeched through the phone.

It wasn't often Leah apologized for anything. "Whatever for, Blaze?"

"For the way I treated Solomon. I don't know what came over me."

"Blaze, you must learn to control your temper."

"Icy, how can you marry a man who says you're ugly? It's not right. You're one of the most beautiful people in the world, sister mine."

Celeste sighed. "Thank you Blaze. You're very kind. Yet, I cannot carry a torch to you, dear sister."

For the simple fact that, in place of a stomach, an active volcano resides in you, Celeste thought to herself.

"Are you sure this is the right thing to do? You hardly know this man! I don't understand how you could marry a man you barely know. What if he's a wife beater or a serial killer?"

"It is for me to worry about, Blaze and for you to support me. Or pray for me if you'd rather do something spiritual about it."

"I have and will keep doing so."

"I suppose you'd like to come to my new home. We will have our wedding reception here."

"Yeah, Mom and Dad were talking about it. What's your address?"

Celeste spent several minutes making arrangements. As she hung up the phone, she decided to seek out Mr. Batcher to coordinate the event.

She opened the door and walked down the hallway. She started down the winding staircase when she froze. Her husband, balanced on a skateboard, slid down the banister. Before she could even think, he jumped over the edge of it and landed smoothly on the floor and kept rolling, laughing as a masculine voice whooped, "All right!"

Fright and indignation coursed through her veins as she lifted her heavy skirts to race down the stairs. *Of all the idiotic things to do!*

"Mr. Greene, what on earth are you doing? Are you completely insane?"

A movement caused her to turn her head. Ice-cold shock went through her and then she screeched in pleasure and ran down the stairs to fling herself into the newcomer's arms.

"My lord! I'm so happy to see you!"

Solomon had never seen Celeste smile and the transformation left him flabbergasted. She had a beautiful smile. The lips gleamed and softened. The even white teeth sparkled like white peppermint against her nutmeg skin. It was even more of a surprise to see her throw herself at Gonzo like a little girl at her father after a long trip. Her arms were wrapped around Gonzo's neck in a crushing grip. To top that off, Gonzo had a ridiculous expression on his face. His eyes were large with delighted surprise and his mouth open and laughing as he lifted and swung Celeste around in a circle before he set her down again.

"My lady! I never dreamed I'd see you again."

"Oh, my lord! I can't tell you how much it pleases me to have an opportunity to reacquaint myself with you."

"The pleasure is shared."

"Goijaart, dear Goijaart."

Solomon felt he'd done an Ollie into the Twilight Zone. The idea cemented more when Gonzo got down on one knee and clasped his hand over his heart. He could feel his eyebrows scamper back into his forehead at the sight.

"Am I still your knight, my lady?"

"That has never changed, sir."

Solomon watched as Gonzo took her hand and kissed it in a passionate way, and the strangest feeling came over him. It caused his eyebrows to draw together and made his lips flatten into a line. What the heck? He'd never seen Gonzo act like this before and yet, Celeste accepted this charade as if it was the most natural thing in the world. And why did Gonzo kiss her hand like that? He'd pressed his lips to her flesh as if he were a starving man and had just found nourishment. Solomon folded his arms as he stepped off his skateboard and leaned against the wall, staring at his wife and best friend gazing at each other.

Gonzo rose up and smiled down at Celeste while she smiled up at him. Her face lit as if from an inner glow.

"It's so good to see you Celeste," Gonzo repeated.

She giggled and wrapped her arms around him again. She leaned her head on his shoulder, her head turned away. Gonzo rested his head on hers and closed his eyes in a manner of contentment.

Solomon waited a brief moment to see if either of them would remember he was alive, but nothing happened as they continued to hold each other.

Deliberately, he cleared his throat, and they both jumped as if someone had thrown firecrackers down their clothes.

Good. Solomon thought derisively.

"Remember me?" he spoke into the silence as the two of them stared at him as he'd just stepped off the space ship.

"Solomon, however do you know Goijaart?"

45

"Gooyard," he mocked, as he glanced at Gonzo, "and I have been friends since the womb."

"Indeed?"

The smile dropped from her face, but her eyes had changed from warm, maple syrup to brown molten gold.

"Yeah. I'm dying to know how the two of you know each other." Solomon responded, his voice dry as he started toward them.

Gonzo's black eyes regarded him as he stepped closer. They were filled with some kind of emotion. He couldn't quite put his finger on it, but he dismissed it from his mind. He was probably just embarrassed.

"My grandmother lived near them and every summer before she died, I used to stay with her," Gonzo started to say. He then turned toward Celeste, "Wasn't it Granny who taught you how to sew?"

Celeste grinned as she glanced back at Gonzo. Again, Solomon felt his eyebrows draw forward. Why did she have to look at Gonzo like that? She gazed at him like she'd just found the secret to immortal beauty. "Yes. Such happy memories, Goijaart."

"Excuse me, Mr. Solomon," Patrick's voice said from behind.

Solomon turned. "Aw, Patrick, lay off the 'mister' while the old people are away, will you?"

"I'll try to remember. Speaking of which, your parents are holding for you in my office. They want to speak to you on the phone."

Inexplicably relieved, Solomon turned away. "Patrick, Gonzo's staying for dinner. Can you have Mrs. Houston make enough for three?"

"I'll see to it."

As Solomon strolled way, he could hear Celeste's voice behind him say, "Mr. Batcher, I do need to speak with you when you have a moment?"

"Mrs. Greene?"

46

"Come with me Goijaart," Celeste ordered.

Her voice trailed off, and Solomon turned his attention to his parents' phone call which was sure to be interesting.

THE VIRGIN'S GARMENT

"How could you do this to us?"

"Hello Mama," Solomon greeted as he settled in Patrick's chair and put his feet on the desk.

"Don't call me that! I've told you more than once." His mother hated being called 'mama'. It didn't match her persona as the Reverend Daughter of the Virgin. He had been twelve years old when she told him to call her mother and nothing less.

"Oh Mama, don't be upset. I won't call you that in front of your adoring audiences."

"They are our flock, Solomon."

"That's right Mama. Your little sheep and you are the Reverend Daughter sent by the Holy Virgin to lead them to the throne of heaven. I know the spiel, Mama. It's wasted on me."

"Hail Virgin, clothed in purity, help me not murder my son," his mother snapped out.

"And that would completely defeat the purpose of clothing me in the garment of the Virgin's purity."

"You be quiet! Why did you get married and not tell us?"

"You were out in the field, gathering the lost children of the Virgin urging them to grab her hem and be purified. Your son's wedding would have hindered your mission."

"Stop it, Solomon."

"Stop what, Mama?" His voice dripped with innocence even as he knew his mother seethed on the other end of the phone.

"Your disrespect toward the Virgin, your father, and me." She snapped.

He leaned further back into the chair and gazed at the ceiling. Why did he deliberately raise his mother's ire? She hadn't done anything to him. The answer came – the interaction between Gonzo and Celeste had disturbed him. He had to take out these crazy

49

feelings out on someone, and his mother happened to be convenient. He sighed and decided to stop. "Forgive me, Mother. I was wrong to disrespect your beliefs."

"Bless you my son," she responded, her voice full of relief. "Now, do tell me of this woman."

Celeste's face came into focus in his mind. What to tell them? He barely knew himself. "Her name is Celeste. I married her two weeks ago."

"Why?"

An easy question to ask, Mother. The hardest to answer, Solomon thought to himself as he sighed once more.

"She was the wife I asked God for," he said simply. "She restored my belief in God, Mother."

"She must be a remarkable woman to restore your faith, my son."

Unremarkable, Solomon thought. "You could say that, Mother."

"We intend to meet our daughter-in-law and her family. She does have family, I take it."

"Yes she does. Her parents and a younger sister."

A sister with an uncontrollable temper. He snorted at the memory. As he thought back on the incident, it came to him that although Leah's beauty had caused a spark of attraction to flare, after that display of her temper, he couldn't care less how beautiful she was.

"Good. Good. Of course, there is more for us to learn about her but that will happen in time. Why did you come back home after five years?"

The question was entirely expected and yet Solomon jumped in the chair as if he'd been hit by lightning. Snatches of his dreams rose up, and he fought the accompanying fear as faces of beautiful women made his heart beat frantically like a hamster in a cage. The memory of their faces came at him in a kaleidoscope of images, one after the other, after the other . . . long hair, short hair, braids, curly hair, straight hair . . . green eyes, hazel eyes, blues eyes . . . brown skin, pale skin, tawny skin . . . wide lips, thin lips. The images hurled themselves at him like a ricochet of bullets. Faster and faster, they came at him, swirled and taunted him. They were bullies of a sort, not with words but their memories that lingered in his mind. Beautiful women were to be feared.

Would they ever go away? Would he ever escape them?

"Solomon! Are you ignoring me?"

He winced at the sound of her shrill voice but glad for it as it broke the hold of his memories and dreams.

"No Mother. Forgive me I was simply lost in thought."

"Answer me. Why did you come back?"

He rubbed his hand over face as he sighed. They had no idea what the past five years had been like. He had no desire to enlighten them either. But he could answer honestly. "It was time to come home."

"We will be home in two weeks instead of three. Two days after that, we will have the wedding reception with the new family. Batcher will handle everything. We'll have servers, and I'll relate to Mrs. Houston the menu. And then we'll get our Swarovski dinnerware, the chair covers, the—"

"As you said, Patrick will take care of things." He felt like a fraud. Celeste and he were going to divorce in a few years so why bother with all the trimmings? But then again, no one knew this except for themselves. And they did marry rather quickly so their families, in a way, were entitled to splash a little on their reception.

"We'll talk later, Solomon."

"Yes Mother."

"Your mother loves you, my son. Grasp the hem of the Virgin's garment and allow her purity to wrap itself around you."

Solomon rolled his eyes as his mother hung up the phone. It was her form of a blessing as Reverend Daughter, and he shook his head.

51

He pushed the chair away from the desk and placed the phone back on the hook as he stood and turned to observe the gardens. At times, he had no idea what his parents' beliefs were. He could hear his mother's well-rehearsed speeches, see her on large platforms across the US, her eyes "brilliant and clear, almost shining with virgin light" as one enraptured commentator remarked.

"Touch her! Cling to her! Raise your mouths and open your heart to the Virgin's purity. If you touch the hem of her garment, she will make you pure. You shall be wiped clean, if you touch the hem of her garment." Solomon rubbed a hand over his face. He had never believed what his parents taught the masses. After his parents had left their church to create their own religious organization, he'd left his beliefs as well. But his faith in God was restored now. He had his wife, and it was up to him to make good his part of their deal.

He focused on the scenery in front of him. He saw the gardeners working it as they cut and trimmed the hedges. Two figures were off in the distance and his eyes narrowed as he recognized them to be Gonzo and Celeste.

What's their story?

He folded his arms and continued to watch them as they went further along the path. They had been so happy to see each other. For a while, they had been in their world that excluded outsiders, even him. A strange connection had been reestablished, and he wondered what the effects of it would be. They looked close as they walked side by side. As he continued to watch them, the strangest sensation flowed through his veins. He couldn't pinpoint exactly what made him feel that way. All he knew was his wife and his best friend had some deep connection, and it didn't sit well with him. He planned on finding out just how close they'd been. After all, Gonzo and she were looking a bit too cozy for comfort. Even from his position in Patrick's office, he could see Celeste leaning against Gonzo and his arm wrapped around her shoulders. Solomon decided to go get his wife.

###

Celeste sighed softly in contentment as she tightened her arms around Goijaart's forearm as they sauntered through the gardens. They were perfect for a stroll. Large hedges lined man made paths that flowed and led to different areas of the estate grounds. Dozens of flowers were clustered into sections divided by pathways. A series of apple trees in the distance loomed like sentinels at the entrance of a magical kingdom. Nature's perfume of plant life and wind rose and wafted around them pleasantly.

"Oh Goijaart! When I awoke this morning, I had no inkling you would be a quantum of my day."

"The same for me, my lady," he answered her.

"I had no idea you knew Mr. Greene."

Goijaart stopped midstride. Confusion mapped his face as he asked, "Mr. Greene? Are you talking about Solomon?"

"Yes."

Goijaart's tar hued eyes widened in surprise. "You call Solomon 'Mr. Greene'?"

"I prefer to address him as such in private. However, I would never do that in front of company but with you, I can be myself."

Goijaart stared at her for a few moments, and she took the time to study him, as well. He wasn't handsome like Solomon, but his dark, wild look had its own appeal. How many summers had they spent together as children at his grandmother's house? She allowed her mind to wander as the amiable memories resurfaced.

"You can always be yourself with me, my lady. I wouldn't have you any other way," he said after a moment, and he started forward again.

Truer words have never been uttered; Celeste thought to herself and wrapped her mind around the comfortable notion. No need to hide with her best friend. Steady, reliable, dependable, even though he could be stubborn and critical. She wouldn't have him any other way.

"Tell me of this marriage of yours, Celeste," Goijaart said quietly.

"Why should I, my lord?" she asked. The warmth left her voice.

They stopped once more, and he pulled his arm from her and she felt him gently grip her upper arms. His dark eyes peered down into her own "I've always been your friend, my lady. And we've always been honest with each other. Tell me—why did you marry Solomon?"

Celeste argued deep within herself as she held his scrutiny. Of course, he'd want to know why she'd married Mr. Greene. Even though they'd not seen each other in seven years the connection they held as friends was still there. She looked up at him and still saw the knight he'd always been in her eyes, and surely a lady can trust her protector with her secrets?

"Have I informed you my sister is engaged?" she started.

She saw Goijaart's eyes widen, and he squeaked out, "Blaze's engaged? To who?"

"His name is Jacob Othello Westwood."

"Does he know about her? The woman's crazy!"

"My sister has always been a recusant and not even my father could dominate her completely. It was only because of her belief in honoring 'thy father and thy mother' that my father had a modicum of control. Yet, Jacob Westwood has done what no other man can do—he tamed her. They've been engaged since February. She plans to join in matrimony with him around the same time next year."

"I don't understand. What does Blaze's engagement, extraordinary as it is, have to do with your marriage to Solomon?"

She dropped her eyes. "I am in love with Lord Westwood."

Goijaart's hands fell from her arms. She glanced up briefly at him. His body had stiffened as if a whip of static electricity zipped through his body. The bushy eyebrows rose into his hairline and the pupils dilated.

She folded her arms as she turned from him and targeted her attention on the rows of flowers. "Jacob Westwood met me first. We met at the library in the same aisle. I remember being so focused on extricating the book I wanted. I did not give heed to my surroundings until I found a white well-formed hand hovering next to mine on the book. I glanced up and saw Lord Westwood." She sighed as she faced Goijaart again. "He's very handsome, my lord. Tall with thick, blond hair and eyes the color of periwinkles. At that moment, I fell in love."

"Love at first sight, my lady?" Goijaart asked, his voice dripped with sarcasm and Celeste smiled with pleased remembrance. "Ever the skeptic, my lord?"

"I only accept the material, the physical, and the measurable my lady. As this you well know. With all due respect, spare me the illogical."

"Whether or not you believe as such is irrelevant. I am simply recounting to you what happened. May I continue?"

He nodded.

"We laughed and he allowed me to have the book. To this day, I cannot remember the title of the book, but it captured our mutual interest. We stayed at the library and talked. At closing time, I knew I was irrevocably in love with him. His conversation intelligent, casual and yet thought provoking. He's a minister and at the time, he was finishing seminary."

"Surely you jest, Celeste. Not a minister! This is even more fantastic."

Celeste glared at him even though her mouth twitched in amusement. Goijaart didn't like ministers as he'd had bad experiences with them. Or religious people in general.

"Pray, carry on," Gonzo responded meekly.

"For a few weeks, we met off and on. In retrospection, I realize Lord Westwood had no interest in me of a romantic nature. He simply spent his recreation with a friend. He used the time to work on his studies. But for those weeks, I imagined this was the commencement of an amazing affiliation. And soon, I would be Mrs. Celeste Westwood."

"What happened?"

"My sister nearly killed a serial rapist. That's what happened. She told me later that in the middle of her rage, Lord Westwood's voice cut through the red and calmed her down. Such as that had never happened before."

She didn't tell Goijaart about seeing the relationship develop between them. Or how often she'd spied on them in their moments together and saw the way he kissed her with passion and intensity or the sweet nothings she'd heard him whisper to Leah. She couldn't tell him the pain of realizing no man would ever see her the same way Jacob saw her sister.

And the great injustice of God had done to her for making her ugly.

"I still don't understand why this would cause you to marry a man you barely know," Goijaart's voice cut through her thoughts.

"I know," Celeste answered him. "And for right now, I don't want to discuss it anymore."

The memories, her dreams, her desires, stood in her mind's eyes like wooden soldiers. Viciously, she imagined an axe of ice, and it chopped the memories into woodchips. Over and over, she pulverized them with the fury of her mind. Happiness, love, and contentment were not meant for her.

"Celeste? Are you okay?"

The sound of Goijaart's voice startled her from her inward workings and the familiar numbness cascaded over her.

"I'm fine my lord I was simply lost in thought," she said slowly.

"You know you can place your trust in me, princess." Goijaart spoke softly as his hands rubbed her arms.

"Now I can truly appreciate your concern when you address me with such eminence. Rest assured my lord, I am well."

"Undoubtedly. However, it would be culpable of me if I did not insist upon your welfare."

Celeste reached up and hugged him. "My lord, now that I have found you again, I shall never let you go."

"How can you let go of a leech?" Goijaart countered as his arms tightened around her waist and lifted her off the ground. He whirled her around, and she felt laughter bubble up to the surface.

The warmth that always pervaded her when she was with Goijaart melted her insides. It was so wonderful to be with her best friend again. She laughed and then caught her breath. Mr. Greene watched them. His lips curved into a smile, but his eyes were narrowed.

"Mr. Greene is something wrong?"

He came forward slowly as Goijaart placed her back on the ground, removed his arm and took a step to the side.

"Not at all. I wanted to let you know my parents will be returning in two weeks. Two days after will be the reception."

"Indeed? Well, I had better prepare my family. Goijaart, come with me; unless you have things to do?"

"Actually, I have to talk to Solomon about something. I will see you later at dinner, my lady."

Goijaart lifted her hand to his lips and kissed her knuckles. As a child, she had always insisted he saluted her in such a manner when their playtime was over with.

"Oh Goijaart," she sighed happily. She walked away from him and inhaled the fragrance of the gardens.

CANDY CANE ROPE

Ropes of candy cane bound him to the chair while a giant marshmallow gagged him. A single light bulb hung from a thin wire in the ceiling, and the rest of the room was bathed in darkness. Tears stung his eyes as he fought against his candy cane restraints around his chest, arms, wrists, and feet — but they had the strength of marble. The marshmallow refused to dissolve in his mouth and remained even as he tried to bite down.

The doorway suddenly darkened by the curvaceous figure of a woman.

"Eric Blake," the woman's voice spoke, and it smoothed over him like frigid water flowing over rocks.

His eyes widened as she advanced, vibrant like an Irish rose. The light revealed her in phases, bottom to top. Long, dainty feet with strawberry colored toenails were hemmed by matching silk pajama pants edged with lace. Slim legs seductively clung to by the silk stretched the fabric. The hourglass waistline was accentuated by a V-neck halter top, and curly copper hair surrounded a long, elegant neck. Jade eyes edged by long curly lashes, an upturned nose and childishly pouty lips. Her arms were slender and sinewy and in her hands she clinched a coiled whip of candy cane.

A scythe of glacial, nipping fear sliced into Solomon's body, opened his chest and exposed his thudding heart. Over and over as each step brought the woman closer, fear flayed him. With renewed vigor, he fought against the candy cane rope. He twisted and tugged at his wrists in an effort to set him free. The marshmallow bulged and expanded until it overlapped the corners of his mouth.

"Eric Blake," the woman's mouth moved as her tongue darted out and over her lips.

The marshmallow gag muffled his scream.

"Oh yes! That sound!" The woman laughed as she rolled her eyes and neck in a movement of pleasure.

Solomon struggled violently. He wrenched at the candy cane ropes, twisted his wrists and grappled with his toes to move the chair. His face flushed with blood from his exertions. The chair rocked back and forth but never fell. The ropes tightened their hold; the candy cane glowed in the light. He had to escape. He had to try!

The woman purred. Her eyes darkened to the color of mold and the mirth vanished from her face as an expression of intent drew her eyebrows together and her mouth fell slightly open in anticipation.

The whip uncoiled; the red and white band twisted together and met at a point. She backed away until she was once again shaded by darkness and then silhouetted by light pouring in from the doorway. He saw the dark figure of her arm rise.

The tip of the whip cracked against his chest, and he flinched instinctively but there wasn't any pain. It fell again, this time on his stomach, and he jolted. The sound echoed in the air like a firecracker. Over and over, it touched various parts of his body. He didn't know how long he sat there as he shivered from response, felt no pain but was utterly trapped by his candied bonds and tormented by a beautiful woman.

Then it was over, and the woman walked back to him, hips swaying. She reached out and pulled the marshmallow gag from his mouth and threw it to the ground. It shattered like glass on the floor.

"No, no, no," he moaned, and once more struggled against his bonds.

"It's time to eat, Eric Blake." She panted harshly, the red lips wide open as she gulped.

"No, please, no! Get away from me!" he screeched, rocking the chair again.

"I will never go away," she whispered as she leaned over him. Her hair cascaded over him in a coppery waterfall. Her mouth opened over his shoulder, and her teeth sank into his flesh and left a gaping hole in his shoulder.

In horror, he gazed at his shoulder. It was marshmallow with a candy cane center.

Solomon jerked awake from his dream. He scraped at his shoulder fervently, expecting to see a marshmallow wound. A few seconds passed before he stopped and longer for his heart to stop its attempt to escape the confines of his ribcage. He pushed the covers away from his sweat-drenched body. The cool air rushed against his skin and he welcomed it. Darkness shrouded everything except for a pinprick of red light from his digital clock: 4:30.

"Dear God," he breathed into the quiet room.

He exhaled a long breath. Would he ever escape his past?

Moments later, he stepped into the shower and let the water cover him even his pajamas.

As crazy as his dreams were, as odd and bizarre they had been for a while now, that had never happened before.

The woman had bit him. What did that mean? What did any of his dreams mean?

"Don't think about it," he gasped under the gush of water, "don't think about it."

He forced himself to turn to other thoughts. Not a difficult task. He went over the conversation he'd had with Gonzo in the gardens over a week ago. He had, of course, in the end lied.

Solomon still remembered the look on Gonzo's face as he'd watched Celeste walk away. Again, that strange sensation he couldn't name had come over him and he squelched it down. Celeste had made it more than clear she wasn't interested in his husbandly sentiments.

"What in the world is wrong with you, man?" he'd asked the moment Celeste walked out of earshot.

"Nothing," Gonzo had stated as he folded his arms.

"Really? 'Sir Knight?' 'My lord?' 'Gooey yard?' Dude, I thought your name was Guy!"

Gonzo's face had flushed cherry red. "And now you're blushing like a little girl!"

"Solomon, I—I had no idea you knew Celeste Martin. When you mentioned her name, I thought, 'There's no way he's talking about my Celeste'." Gonzo had turned his back to him, and his arms dropped to his sides. 'I guess she's your Celeste now," Gonzo spoke quietly.

"Why didn't you tell me about her? You obviously are good friends."

"It's hard to explain."

"Try me."

Silence stretched, and Solomon could remember how the trees rustled in the fingers of a gentle wind. The flutter of birds as they flew overhead had mingled with the distant sound of the lawnmower.

"Celeste was my secret. I didn't want to tell anyone about her." Gonzo had answered finally, his voice full of resignation.

"How did you meet her?"

"I used to spend the summer with my grandparents. She and her family lived down the street. Man, I must have been seven years old then."

"So what happened?"

"It's kinda vague now, but I remember seeing this little girl walking down the street with her mom. Her mom apparently wanted my grandmother to give Celeste sewing lessons or whatnot. I don't know. Anyway, after that we started playing together."

"Look, dude, I know boys and girls can play together, but this is a whole lot different."

Gonzo turned back to him. "We created our own world. Our fantasy. I'm not sure how it started, but it did. I was her knight and she my lady. At first, I had to kill bugs or give her my toys when she wanted them. One summer I had to pull her in a red wagon for a week. I wanted to play my video games, but she insisted I carry her to my grandmother's house in a chariot."

Solomon had grinned at that. One thing he knew about Celeste—she could be a bossy woman.

"And you did it?"

"I am her knight," Gonzo had said, his voice matter of fact. "Every summer, I looked forward to seeing her and being her knight. I hated my name but she turned it into something dignified. 'Sir Goijaart, the Black Knight' she'd titled me. As we got older, it was still our world, but our interests had naturally grown. We began to confide to each other. We trusted each other with our secrets. When I told her about the girls I liked, about my mother and my uncle, she listened to me. And then she would take a small handkerchief she embroidered with our initials and would symbolically place our secrets inside of it. Although Celeste doesn't talk much and when she does, most of the time she's issuing orders, she rarely does anything without a purpose. Even the way she dresses has a meaning to it."

"Well, what happened?"

"Time, I guess. We got older, and Celeste started to become more and more remote. One of the last conversations we had, she made a remark about happiness not being hers. She told me she would never marry."

"Do you know why she felt that way?"

"I don't have a clue. But Celeste was my lady, and I did everything I could to make her feel better. We went to the museums, art galleries, craft shows, fairs. That last summer, when my grandmother died, she came to the funeral dressed in her mourning outfit. If I hadn't known her, I would have been upset, thinking she wanted to take attention away from my grandmother. Then I saw it. The very first handkerchief my grandmother had showed her how to embroider attached to this massive dress she wore and I knew. She dressed to honor my grandmother whom she loved just as much as I did. Later on, she'd given me a black silk handkerchief, sprayed with some kind of perfume, and she pressed it into my hands. Without her saying anything, I knew she gave me a final secret . . . a last goodbye. My lady left. I couldn't do anything to make her stay.

"The next time I saw her was today."

Solomon still remembered the feeling that washed over him as he listened to Gonzo's story about Celeste. They had a rare special friendship. He'd never had a platonic relationship with a girl in his life since he turned fifteen. Even before then, he'd been aware of women from a young age.

Girls, as a young boy, didn't have cooties but bubblegum scents or jolly rancher tongues. Sometimes they had glittery lipgloss when they pursed their lips, their mouths looked like flowers. They had glossy curls or neatly oiled scalps. Polished hands or feet and crooked smiles with all or some teeth. High pitched voices and pink and purple outfits. As a teenager, girls smelled like fruit or cookies. Their mouths still glistened with lipstick or gloss, but now their eyes were lined with eyeliner and shaded with eye shadow. They had developed from thin rail sticks or pudgy adolescence into girls with hips, thighs, and breasts. Sometimes they became beauty queens, gothic introverts, or insecure wall flowers. Most women were some of all, as he had discovered. Whether their hair was perfectly coiffed, spiked with gel or mousse, braided, or demurely styled, he had liked them all.

As a grown man, he enjoyed women even more. Tall, short, sophisticated, carefree, reserved, it didn't matter. He'd wanted them all.

To hear of Gonzo having a friendship with a woman that had no sexual contact was amazing. What would it have been like to have a girl as a friend and nothing more or less?

"Why didn't you try social media? Or get a background check?"

Gonzo had cut him a look out of narrowed eyes. "She's my friend, not a criminal. And I did try social media but I could never find her. Maybe she's under a different name. It's easy nowadays."

"Well, she is a hand model."

Gonzo had nodded. "That doesn't surprise me. She always had nice hands and liked to work with them. She has a natural aptitude for hand crafts — sewing, knitting, crocheting, embroidery, weaving, you name it. Knowing Celeste as I do, she would have wanted to earn the money to continue to create her costumes. She never wears anything else."

"Why didn't you guys ever — "

"Have sex?" Gonzo snorted. "Jeez, Solomon. Celeste is my friend. Why would I risk my friendship with her by having sex with her? She was — is — my lady. My princess. I am her knight, and I would protect her from even me. Besides, I could and did get it from elsewhere. She called it 'go a-wenching'."

"You are so lame! My lady? My princess? Give me a break!"

64

Gonzo's eyes had stared hard into his own. "What woman do you know would marry you when you told her she's ugly?"

"A desperate one," he'd replied.

"Does Celeste seem desperate to you?"

"No," he'd answered slowly.

"Once you understand why Celeste married you when you insulted her, you'll begin to understand her."

"Not interested in understanding her. In seven years, we're going to dissolve our marriage, and that will be that. According to her, I'm a walking title."

Gonzo had frozen in an abrupt way, and his eyes grew like saucers. "You're planning to divorce?"

"We both are. That was the deal when we got married."

"I see. And she agreed to this?"

"It was her idea!"

"I see," Gonzo had repeated. "Well, enough of this. Let's go to the park and practice."

Solomon changed into a new pair of boxers and pajamas and got back in the bed.

He had lied to Gonzo. Celeste did interest him. A husband should know the little quirks that made his wife tick. But the woman avoided him as if he were covered in lice. He hadn't seen her in a week. She took her meals in her suite, and the house was large enough to ramble in without seeing her. Most of his time he spent at the skateboard park.

A sudden thought made him sit up straight. Why did he have to play this her way? He didn't want to increase the distance between them. He wanted to get to know his wife. Not in the biblical sense, but if God did indeed give him this wife, he should get to know her.

What was she wearing? One of the long skirts with petticoats under it? Or a giant dress that cleared four feet in all directions? He hadn't seen her maple syrup eyes, nor seen the nutmeg skin in a week. Well, tomorrow he would go to her and make her spend time with him.

And on that pleasant thought, he fell asleep.

FIRST KISS

Celeste hadn't seen Mr. Greene in over a week. Of course, it wasn't possible to retain the distance indefinitely but if she persevered, her life would be what she wanted. She would glimpse her husband in passing, like ships that passed in the night as the awful cliché went.

The phone rang in her bedroom and she answered it.

"Celeste Greene."

"Hello Celeste dear, how are you?"

She leaned back on the chair. "I'm fine mother. And you?"

They exchanged social trivialities for a few seconds and then Mrs. Martin said, "Icy, did you tell Solomon about—"

"No, Mama, I did not disclose that information to him," Celeste interrupted. The familiar anger at God she kept banked under her icy control started to melt her reserve and clamored for attention. Being upset with God wasn't going to change anything and with effort, she focused on icing down her rage until numbness pervaded her body once more.

"I know why you did this Celeste. You're trying to get back at the Lord. My dear, you should have waited until God sent you the man that would love you just as deeply as He does."

As always, her mother cut through and hit the mark. Marrying Solomon had been a "take that" moment aimed at the Almighty. With this marriage, she'd told God she would be a married woman despite His determination for her not to be happy.

"Icy, your father has hired a private investigator."

"Admirable," Celeste answered in a clipped tone, not surprised her father had done such a thing. Her father hadn't like Mr. Greene from the start. No matter what his private investigator found out, short of any illegal activity, she'd remain in this union until the seven years were up.

She heard her mother sigh on the phone. "God loves you, my sweet. Don't let this anger at Him control you to such an extent you forget where your blessings come from. Solomon doesn't appear to be a man that will hurt you, but you do understand this scenario could have turned out much differently."

"Quite." If she kept her responses short, her mother would end the call. The anger fought against the bonds of her control. If she continued to talk about it, it could burst through. The floodgates of emotion she suppressed had to be locked.

"All right, Celeste, I'll let it be. Do you like your new home? I can't wait to see it. Since the wedding reception will be there, it must be large."

Celeste released a breath she wasn't aware she was holding, and the tension left the muscles of her body as she gave her mother an audio tour of the mansion. She hung up the phone a few minutes later.

Goijaart had been to see her twice, and she expected him today. Respectful of her position as Mr. Greene's wife, she made sure to relay to Mr. Batcher to let Mr. Greene know Goijaart was in attendance, but both times, she had been told Mr. Greene wasn't on the premises. For his visits, she found a small den in the massive house on the first floor to entertain Goijaart and limited her time with him to a half hour or less. Goijaart didn't mind in the least, and they spent the time reminiscing and catching up.

She decided to go to the den now. Five minutes later, she settled in the armchair and bent over the dress she was making for the wedding reception. The dress took up a lot of her time. Often, she stayed up late to work on it. She had all the undergarments she would need to make it work, and it would take a couple of hours to be fully dressed. She had gotten used to dressing herself in her costumes over the years and after altering some of the undergarments with front-closures as opposed to back, she indulged.

Celeste hadn't worn modern clothes in years. They had no appeal for her. How could she feel like a princess in jeans and a T-shirt? God had seen fit to make her unattractive, so she needed these outfits to look somewhat decent. When Grandmother Thomas had first shown her how to sew she'd run with it. She would never be as beautiful as her younger sister, but her clothes would.

The den overlooked the gardens, and the descending evening sun flushed the room with dazzling colors of red, pink, and purple. In the evenings when she worked, she kept the curtains opened so the moon's light could shine through. The décor was modern, hardly her taste at all but the potential to turn the room into the Elizabethan style she preferred would require a complete overhaul. Her mind began to churn with ideas.

"My lady?"

Celeste jerked at the sound of Goijaart's voice and then smiled as she rose and put the dress aside. "Good evening, my lord," she curtsied. She clasped her hands together.

He bowed his head, his hand hidden behind his back. "Good evening."

"Do come in. I'll tell Mr. Batcher to let Mr. Greene know you are here."

"I informed Patrick of my presence, and he stated Solomon was out," he said quickly, as he sauntered in.

"Oh, come in and sit." As they both sat, she asked, "Did you want anything to drink?"

He sat forward in the chair, his hand still hidden. "No, I'm fine. I ate before I got here."

Celeste felt her eyebrows draw together. "You are more than welcome to have dinner with us, my lord."

"Ah, but eating in the conviviality of three would diminish the pleasure of conversation with the intimacy of two," Goijaart stated.

"But you are my lord husband's honored friend sir." She didn't tell him she refrained from having dinner with her husband.

69

However, if he wanted to eat with them, she would tolerate her husband's presence.

"And yet, I remain *your* knight," he replied in a quiet voice, his dark eyes locked onto her face for a space of a moment and Celeste could have sworn she'd saw a scintilla of interest in his eyes. But that was utter nonsense, and she dismissed the wayward thought. The movement of his arm from behind his back drew her attention.

"For you kind lady," he said as he brought forth a beautiful bouquet of blue irises, white roses, and orange dahlias.

"Oh, Goijaart!" Celeste exclaimed as she clapped her hands in delight and took the flowers from him. "Our flower game!"

He flinched as if in pain and the smile slipped from his face.

"My lord, did I say something wrong?"

"No, my princess. Not at all. I'd forgotten about our flower game. This bouquet is a symbol of our friendship. Not our game." He glanced at her sheepishly but disappointment lurked in his expression.

"I've insulted and belittled your gift sir," Celeste moaned, stricken at the thought she'd diminished her knight in any way.

"Like I mentioned, I'd forgotten." He shrugged.

Goijaart continued to stare at her as the silence lengthened. Celeste allowed the silence to linger as she tried to think of something to say. Finally, "Are these from your grandmother's greenhouse?"

"Yes."

"How do you maintain it? Do you go to your grandmother's house?"

Goijaart sat back and began to tell her, and the awkwardness of the past moment became a vague memory.

She sat back and rested the bouquet in her lap as she listened to him speak.

Unlike the closeness she had shared with Lord Westwood, the bond with Goijaart had been forged in their youth. He had been her mainstay, and she looked forward to his visits every summer. And now, after such a long gap, their friendship renewed as if there had never been an absence. Where others may have questioned the silence, her knight did not.

"I take it Mr. Greene isn't privy to your horticultural aptitude?" Celeste asked as he paused in talking about his grandmother's greenhouse.

"No, he is not."

Celeste leaned forward as an imp of mischief egged her into teasing. "Oh? And what do you bargain for my silence?"

"You wouldn't say a word," Goijaart answered. A grin brightened his face and Celeste saw how handsome her friend looked.

"How can you be so certain?" She inched closer, feeling her mouth smirk on one side of her face.

He leaned in as well. His face so close it almost touched hers. "Well, my lady! Even a princess of royal blood can be strangled with silk."

They both laughed, and Celeste threw her head back in glee.

"I see you both are enjoying yourselves."

The laughter caught in her throat as the sound of Mr. Greene's voice broke through their melee.

Mr. Greene darkened the doorway, his face as unreadable as a blank sheet of paper and yet she sensed the anger emanating from him. It confused her. Why should he be upset? She hadn't seen him in over a week.

"Mr. Greene, I'm pleased you could join us. My knight and I were just—"

"Having a nice cozy chat," he finished for her, his voice clipped and in low tones as he came further into the room.

The sensuality that exuded from her husband struck her as potently as a caress. The spiky black hair, the green gold-flecked eyes, and the muscular frame made him pulse-leaping, mouthwateringly sexy. His charisma could have been an extra limb on his body and as tangible as flesh. Stonewashed jeans and a sleeveless T-shirt enhanced his looks, showing off the toned arms.

"I'll take my leave, my lady," Goijaart said as he got up from his seat across from her.

Celeste returned her attention back to her knight. "Thank you for coming to see me, my lord. I do hope you'll come again."

"Verily," Goijaart answered as he bowed. She noticed as he walked toward the doorway, Mr. Greene frowned at him. Goijaart met his gaze and then left the room.

"Is there something you require, Mr. Greene?" she asked as she took the bouquet from her lap and placed it in a small vase on the side table next to her.

"Why was Gonzo here?"

"He came to spend a few minutes with me. Is that a problem?"

"Yes." He ambled closer to her and stood next to her chair. His green gold eyes glowered at her from his not inconsiderable height.

"Why is that?" She picked up her dress and started sewing again.

"How many times has he been here?"

"Three."

"How long did he stay?"

"No more than thirty minutes."

"Why—"

"What benefit is this interrogatory, sir?" Celeste interrupted. She forced herself to restrain the nervousness rising in her. Tension radiated from him, palpable as breath. She could see the muscles of his forearms tighten, and his hands clench in fists.

"Why didn't you tell me he was here?"

"Mr. Batcher did not give you the message?" She jerked her head up in surprise.

"Patrick isn't here," Mr. Greene breathed out and Celeste noted his stance relaxed.

"Yes, Mr. Batcher always notifies you when Goijaart is here. The two other times, you were away."

"Oh." His voice had softened to its normal timbre.

"Did you require me, sir?"

"I wanted to see if you would join me for dinner tonight. I haven't seen my wife in over a week."

Celeste fought to keep from rolling her eyes. Hadn't she made it clear she did not want anything to do with her husband? Did he not understand?

"No, thank you." She responded politely.

"Why not Celeste? We're married for heaven's sake!" He waved his hand in agitation.

She put down the dress and looked up at him. "I do disdain repeating myself or answering ridiculous questions. But I'll do this for you. I do not want anything but the barest of contact with you. I do not want your company. I do not desire to be with you. All I have taken from you has been your name and that you gave to me." Her voice was at its driest, and she knew it.

"You are some piece of work, aren't you?" A note of disbelief underlined his words.

"Whatever do you mean?" She pretended ignorance although she understood.

The gold specks in his eyes flashed. "You tell me you don't want to have anything to do with me and yet Patrick gives me the bills of the money you've spent in handling your affairs. You don't want my company and yet I find you in here with Gonzo as cozy as lovers."

"Goijaart is not my lover sir. Neither are you."

Before she knew it, Mr. Greene reached down, gripped her arms, and pulled her against his body. His hands scorched her through her

73

layers of clothes. Her dress fell from her lap, and she gasped in surprise.

"What are you doing?"

His lips captured her mouth. Her first kiss – and the shock of it – rendered her immobile, and she stood stunned. He hadn't closed his eyes but gazed into hers while his lips moved expertly over hers. Weren't first kisses legendary for having rainbows burst from the air, and stars crash into the ground? None of these things happened. What did occur was a rise in the temperature of the room. Heat, long dormant under her icy will, began to diffuse through her body. This warmth differed from her anger. It cascaded over her limbs, transformed her muscles into mush. His lips were smooth and firm. They plied hers like boys in a playground, rough but teasing. Her eyelids began to grow heavy.

No, this can't be happening, her mind screamed at her. *My mouth belongs to Lord Westwood, not my husband.* How could she betray the memory of his lips upon her person?

With icy determination, she damped down the warmth growing in her and turned her body into stone. She stiffened until most of her was as malleable as brick.

Mr. Greene drew back from her, and she missed his lips in spite of her resolve. She had to admit it, if only to herself, he'd taken her for a ride.

"Don't you wish you were my lover now?" His voice spoke with confidence and male arrogance. There was even a hint of boredom with his tone, and she had the vague notion he didn't expect anything else but some sort of capitulation on her part.

"After that display of your skill, no." She would not betray Lord Westwood by allowing another man to touch her.

His eyes turned into saucers and his mouth went slack. "What did you just say?" His voice yelped in disbelief.

She turned away from him and sat back down in the chair. She picked up her dress and started to sew again. She ignored the fact her legs still wobbled.

Her husband exploded. "That's it! I want you out my home, and I'll send a lawyer to work the divorce. You can take you, your cracked up dresses, and anything else you have out of here."

Panic surged through her. She couldn't divorce yet. Not yet. So they couldn't do seven years but they had to remain together for two years at least. That would be long enough.

"Mr. Greene," she started, her voice modulated, "I can't understand what upsets you. If you do not wish to remain married for seven years as we discussed prior to our wedding, then I am willing to reduce the time to two years. If you no longer wish for me to utilize your funds for my daily expenses and hobbies, do tell me, and I will make other arrangements. Goijaart is your friend and I will not meet him in this house if it upsets you. If you no longer wish for me to live here, then I will find a place to stay until the two years are up. But understand me well, I will not give you a divorce until two years are up."

She looked at him. He gazed at her as if she'd grown three heads. *Let him think what he will. As long as he can't see the effect of his kiss on me.*

"You are some piece of work," he muttered after a moment. But his shoulders slumped in a gesture of defeat. That puzzled her. Why should he feel defeated?

"I take it you agree to my proposal?"

"On one condition: we spend time together. You are my wife, Celeste. I do not want this distance you created. So we won't be lovers. Fine, but I want to be friends."

"I do not desire your friendship sir. I have my knight." Especially after that kiss, all she wanted was safe, calm, Goijaart.

"But I desire yours. Just see me as, your knight's squire."

Celeste's heart hammered against her chest. Her hands jerked in response to his statement. She swallowed the pin cushion that suddenly formed in her throat. This man desired to be friends with her. He had said so in the past but now, at this very moment, he wanted to be close to her in a way similar to Goijaart's. A platonic association not hampered by feelings of possession or emotional ties. Even though she was hideous to look upon, he wanted something from her.

See God? See what I can do? Take that!

Thinking of her words, she knew she had been cruel to him. And though she would not allow any form of physical intimacy between them, she could at least apologize. What way could she show the depth of her apology?

It came to her the next instant, and she put aside her dress and rose and smoothed out her skirts.

"I will be pleased to join you for recreation in the evening, Mr. Greene. I beg your pardon for my careless words."

Then she did it—the Texas dip. A formal curtsey, it had a degree of difficulty to it. She crossed her ankles and began to sink to the floor. She bent her knees as she lowered herself completely to the ground. As she neared the skirt of her dress, she turned her head to the side. Typically, the action helped to prevent any makeup she had on her face from marring her dress. Celeste didn't wear makeup, so the move had more of a ceremonial purpose to it than actual necessity.

"Celeste! What are you doing?" Mr. Greene said from above her.

"Apologizing to my squire."

A LITTLE TASTE

"After that display of your skill, no."

The words played over and over in Solomon's mind for the past three days as he started his workout.

The gym room, like most of the rooms in the mansion, implied wealth. A wide mirror ran the length of the wall from top to bottom. Two sets of weights occupied one corner of the room, while several fitness machines of various disciplines hugged another corner. The treadmill flushed against the back wall since it was closer to the entrance.

Solomon gripped the barbell in his hands and began to exercise his pectorals. With each repetition, he endeavored to rid his mind of her words. Usually he lifted between 75 to 80 pounds. Today, he increased the weight to 105 pounds. Perhaps the extra weight would be sufficient to clear his mind.

He'd never, in his young teen and adult life, had any woman give negative feedback on his prowess. Talk about a blow to his tattered manhood. How could this woman who wasn't attractive say something like that?

"That's not true," he contradicted himself as he continued his workout.

Thick curly short lashes hooded her maple syrup eyes. They were amazing. Each time he noticed them, they became even more so. Her smile perfect and the white even teeth beamed against delicately full lips.

And her laugh . . .

Three days ago was the first time he'd seen her laugh. It had been a wonderful sound, high pitched and free. The sound had caused an image to form in his mind of pushing her on a swing and watching her smile and laugh as she went higher and higher in the air. And her eyes would turn from maple syrup to molten gold like they had for Gonzo.

Gonzo. He let the barbell fall to the padded floor and exhaled sharply. The proverbial fly in the ointment. Celeste was so friendly with him. Gonzo had given him no reason to wonder anything but the closest friendship between them. Yet, he felt in his gut there was more to it than just a friendship renewed. He'd seen the way Celeste completely relaxed around him and saw their byplay between them. When he'd seen them lean toward each other, their heads so close Gonzo could have kissed her with little effort, he wanted to do violence.

Solomon reached down, fixed a tight grip on the bar, and started his repetition once more. His mind split between the count and remembering his actions with Celeste. The kiss he gave she didn't even react to it.

Definitely a first!

He knew how to kiss. It wasn't the first thing he learned how to do well. He developed the skill thanks to the countless volunteers and first time orientations granted to him over the years. Kisses weren't special, simply the first step to the inevitable lovemaking sure to follow. Even one-night-stands started with a kiss and he'd had his shares of those as well. Why people made such a big deal about them was beyond him. Yet even the women from his one-night-stands liked the way he kissed. Hadn't he been told what a great kisser — even a better lover — he'd made?

And his wife responded to his kiss with all the fervor of a wax model.

He dropped the weights once more to the floor. He lost track of his count and didn't care. He walked over to the bench, picked up the fifty pound dumbbells, and started to work on his biceps.

"Everything about her is cold, dead, dull," he lied out loud to himself.

I want more, the thought made itself heard.

"Argh!" he exclaimed as he switched the weight to his other hand.

That small voice whispered what he consciously tried avoid. In spite of his experience, the feel of her mouth under his made him crave more. Even admitting that tidbit to himself made his skin flush. How in the world could he be affected so much by a tiny, hardly passionate kiss from a woman who didn't want anything to do with him in the first place?

He snorted and let the dumbbell fall to the floor and ran his fingers through his hair and sighed.

The whole point of the deal he'd made between himself and God was he would have a wife to deter him from his needs. All because of the blueberry woman. In order to make good on their deal, he had to go back to church. He'd been putting it off. He wanted to rid himself of the past and the beautiful women that haunted his dreams. Beautiful women were his Achilles' heel, his Kryptonite, and his weakness that gagged him and made him helpless as a prisoner. Solomon had no control when it came to being around them. His instincts kicked in, and he would do whatever it took to get them in bed, one lovely woman after another. Some had played hard to get but . . .

"That's it," he spoke to the empty room, "She's playing hard to get, so my ego is forcing the usual tactics to try to get her."

A swell of relief came over him. It wasn't the kiss. Just the same old male conquest drive.

"What a relief!" he breathed and with renewed vigor began his exercises again.

Now that he had solved the problem, his mind turned to the past three nights in her company. They could hardly be called scintillating. It was easier to pull out little bits of meat from between his teeth with his tongue than try to spend time with his wife. That first night flashed before his mind, and he remembered it vividly. She had worn some kind of white lacy dress. It had a long skirt, which trailed behind her for several feet with long tight sleeves with lace at the end of them and her white gloves. Even the bodice of the dress covered her, with the neck of it coming under her throat. She looked uncomfortable.

Dinner had been stilted and the conversation the barest of social entreaties. He'd felt like he had been talking to a stranger. She'd said nothing about the food, asked him to pass the salt and generally made herself as quiet as possible.

Afterward, they went to the media library on the first floor. The entertainment center housed the flat screen T. V. and crammed with DVD's and other media. Celeste sat down on the couch and adjusted her dress. She'd wrapped the skirt around her ankles and then clasped her hand together on her knees. Although she hadn't said much, he recognized the invisible chasm between them.

"I have a ton of movies here, Celeste. What movie do you want to watch?" He hadn't really wanted to watch a movie. He'd rather take a walk in the gardens, but maybe a movie could bridge the gap between them.

"I don't watch movies."

His eyebrows had arched into his hairline. Sure, he had met people who weren't moviegoers, but he hadn't expected to marry one.

"I find that hard to believe, woman. Isn't that dress you're wearing from a movie?" A small straw but a straw nonetheless.

Her eyebrow arched. "It is. Are you familiar with it?"

She called my bluff! He'd thought.

Outwardly, he'd fought to keep his face calm. "Oh yeah. The one with that actress with the red hair." He hoped she'd fill in the blanks.

"Gillian Anderson." Celeste had nodded.

The name had sounded familiar, but he couldn't place it. He'd gambled again. "That's the woman from that old show."

"*The X-Files.*"

"And she played the woman who liked that one guy."

"The House of Mirth. You are correct sir. I did fashion this dress from the movie with some minor alterations."

Sending a quick prayer of thanks to God he hadn't been found out he said, "There Celeste. You've shown you watch movies."

"I shall revise my statement. I do not watch movies for entertainment. I watch them for study."

"How do you mean?" He didn't really care; as long as she kept talking and opening up to him.

"I often get my costume ideas from period films."

"Wow. So you can just look at a dress or whatever and make it by hand?"

"Not quite so simplistic but I can determine the basic style of the dress. I do have a degree in costume design after all."

"Well, why aren't you in Hollywood, working on movies?"

Celeste gave him such a derisive look his toes curled in shame. "Do I appear to be a woman who wants to go to Hollywood?"

No, she didn't look like a woman from that gilded cesspool. She belonged there as much as he belonged in a monastery.

He rubbed his hands on his pants. "Okay, that's fine. I've got some T. V. shows over here. Anything catch your interest?"

"I don't watch television for entertainment."

He'd slapped his hand against his face. "What exactly do you do for entertainment?"

"Sew."

"It's tempting but I'll pass. C'mon, Celeste, we have to do something together."

"Why this need for recreational time with me?"

The question, asked in her neutral tone, stopped him. Why did he have this overwhelming need to spend time with his wife? In the beginning, he just wanted to be friends. Now, it was more than that. But he couldn't tell her what he barely understood himself.

81

"I want to get to know you," he answered.

"I have given this some thought, and I believe that it's not probable for us to be friends. Not like Goijaart and myself. Therefore, we shall be acquaintances."

"Acquaintances!" His voice squeaked. It sounded like a dirty word from her mouth.

"I will join you for dinner, but my recreation shall be my own. Good night, Mr. Greene."

Before he could even move, she'd left the room. He let her go. So they only had dinner together, but it felt more like eating rations with a prison cell mate.

"Master Solomon?"

The voice cut in on his thoughts, and he threw the dumbbell down and jumped up. He wiped his face with the towel wrapped around his neck. "Patrick, please! Save it for the Reverend Daughter and the Exalted Son."

"Your mother and father called and relayed they will be here by Sunday which is the day that's prepared for the wedding reception."

"This already spells trouble."

Patrick inclined his head. "Perhaps. But I shall endeavor to ensure everything runs as smoothly as possible."

"Thanks Patrick."

Patrick left and Solomon went over to the treadmill, set the machine and started his jog. Soon he would have the honor of seeing his in-laws again. Perhaps this meeting would go better than the other. He had invited them to stay in the mansion—they had enough rooms to house them but they declined preferring a hotel. Good old lemonade Leah would be there. He hoped nothing went wrong.

Just a little taste of Leah's temper was enough to set his teeth.

Just a little taste of Celeste wets your appetite.

The thought came out of nowhere. Somehow he tripped on the treadmill and his feet wobbled under him as he tried to maintain his pace. His hand landed on the display and without knowing it, he pushed the button which increased the speed. The belt of the treadmill went faster, and he struggled to keep up. His left arm grasped the bar while he tried to slow down the belt with his right. Before he could regain his rhythm, his foot slipped once more, and he fell on his backside and flew back off the machine, his hand hitting the bar.

"That woman!"

THE WAGER

"Daffodil, do not record this call. I wish to converse with you privately." Celeste spoke deliberately and distinctly. Her voice gave no indication of the icy rage at rest in the pit of her stomach.

"Well, this is a first," Daffodil answered as she leaned back in her chair on the other side of the monitor. Her eyebrows lifted in surprise. "We have nothing to hide from our followers or each other."

"Daffodil, I insist." Celeste answered. The three words articulated in a deceptively peaceful tone were a command.

Her rival shrugged, and Celeste saw a quick movement of her arm. "There. We are not recording. What did you wish to converse with me about?"

"This farcical wager," Celeste said.

"What makes it ridiculous? It is no different from our other bets in the past."

"You comprehend very well this sort of gamble is not in our usual sphere of competition."

"I disagree, Celeste. This is very much right up our alley."

"I must obtain a fructiferous condition by this time next year?"

"It's funny how the angrier you get the bigger the words you use to explain yourself. And yes, you have to be pregnant by this time next year."

Celeste glared at the screen as she studied Daffodil's attractive features that dominated the screen. Of all the insidious, manipulative things to do! The wager was made all the more fantastic because Daffodil was dead serious.

"Construe your rationale for this ante. This is the 21st century, not the 15th."

"Oh?" Daffodil tilted her head to the side and smirked.

Celeste felt her eyebrows draw together in a V. "What do you mean, 'Oh'?"

"Look at us, Celeste. You are wearing a 15th century day gown complete with bum roll, corset, layers of petticoats and a long trailing robe. I am wearing a post Napoleonic era gown from 1807."

"1810." Celeste corrected. A momentary satisfaction pervaded her as she saw the smirk drop from her opponent's face. Yet, the gratification she felt was short lived. Daffodil obviously knew she could not have made this sort of gamble unless she had something Celeste truly wanted.

"The point is," Daffodil continued, "we are two grown women who play dress-up. We have leisure time to imagine ourselves princesses, queens, and high-born ladies of days gone by. We live every day in our fantasy, Celeste. The modern world has no appeal for either of us except for its technological advances. Neither of us works, but we dress every day in our costume. I gamble at times that you wish you had been born in the fantasy of yesterday. Yet we both know that if we had been born yesterday, you'd been a field slave, and I would have been the mulatto mistress of a plantation owner."

Celeste felt her teeth cut into her cheek as she recognized the insult for what it was. Daffodil knew where to hit to make it hurt. Once more, the rage against God welled inside her. He made her ugly. His hand took leftovers, threw it together, and named it Celeste.

"You really know where to hit, don't you, Daffy Duck?" she asked, her voice low.

Daffodil leaned forward until her whole face filled the screen. "I don't like you, Celeste."

"Why, Daffodil? You started this opposition between us. I didn't even know who you were until you started betting with me, attacking my expertise and my acuity for my art of costume design. I did go to school for this, you understand."

"I did as well, just in a different direction. But that's not the reason why I have something close to hatred for you." Her lips had curled in a snarl.

Celeste knew her face mirrored the confusion inside of her. "You have some sort of personal vendetta against me? To my recollection, I have never done any harm to you by word or deed. The only interaction I've had with you has been virtual and any antagonism between us has been initiated by you."

Daffodil stared at her, for once silent. As Celeste met her gaze, she saw an expression of sadness quickly cross the woman's face before she masked it with her normal haughty demeanor. What had she to be sad for?

"As to my reasons for my dislike, I will tell you when I am ready."

Celeste decided to come back to the matter at hand. She knew the woman well enough to know that if she lingered on the topic, she would take pleasure in aggravating her. "However, Daffodil, I refuse ingression into a gamble which hinges on my maternal state." The very idea reeked with preposterousness.

"Yes, you will," Daffodil affirmed in an arrogant manner, "because I know for certainty your marriage is a farce."

Celeste did nothing to betray her shock, but her body flushed with heat. What did she know?

"My marriage is not a farce," she responded.

"Oh, I don't doubt you're married. You would never lie about something like that. Where's your ring? Why haven't you encouraged your husband to meet me via video call? Why not let your fans see you are happily wedded? Why didn't you tweet and say, 'Got hitched.'? Why didn't you say anything?"

'I do not have to apportion my personal life to anyone." Her fans and followers knew certain things about her. It was necessary due to the virtual environment of the Internet. The idea of sharing every aspect of her life online to people she didn't know face-to-face hardly appealed to her.

"Very true. But you are married, Celeste Greene. Certainly it's not a state you wish to remain hidden. I've yet to see a married woman hide the fact, unless for adulterous pursuits. If I hadn't pressed you about your sudden sabbatical, you would have never said a word."

Celeste could feel her face harden as her lips tightened. Carefully she said, "I will not enter into this wager with you."

"You will, and this is why," Daffodil responded, a smirk creased her face as it filled with arrogance. "Next year, around this time, Valencia Short will be holding a ball. Not just any ball but a maternity ball. Of course, no one has to be pregnant to attend. But the ones who are will have the opportunity to enter a contest. The contestant will design a maternity dress to be used in a period film piece going into production around that time. Furthermore, the winner will have a walk on role and will assist in the costume production of the movie."

"Daffodil," Celeste's breath rushed out in surprise. Any amateur costume maker would chomp at the bit for the opportunity. It would be the beginning of a career in film costume design for those who wanted it. Hollywood had little appeal to her, but it would be absolutely spectacular to see a gown she created on the lithe figure of some well-known celebrity.

"But you have to be pregnant."

Celeste jerked. "That's discriminatory!"

Daffodil shrugged dismissively. "I know. We're not as liberated as we think we are."

She stared at the screen. Daffodil's face showed assurance she would accept the wager. Celeste knew she would. It would be a dream come true to create a dress for a period film. But it was more than that. Finally, she'd carve a name for herself. Once she and Solomon divorced, she could be gainfully employed. It could possibly mean commissions from all over the world in the movie industry or for large scale costume parties, theater plays, and other opportunities.

But she couldn't get pregnant, not by her husband. She couldn't allow Solomon to touch her. His kiss had been wonderful, but any further intimacy was out of the question.

"Fine. By this time next year, I'll be pregnant," Celeste lied.

"Hmph," Daffodil scoffed, "We'll see."

The screen blacked out as the call ended.

Celeste got up and prowled her room.

She couldn't have a sexual relationship with her husband. When she first met Mr. Greene, the thought of kissing him made her gag. Now, it was no longer repugnant. When he had kissed her three days ago the icy shield she'd built over her emotions cracked. And a little taste of that had her wondering what more would be like?

"Oh, why did I agree to this wager?" she shouted to herself and ran her fingers through her waist long hair.

She knew she would lose. Her husband didn't want her. The rage she kept carefully controlled threatened to heat, to explode and with a sheer force of will, she contained it. Even if he did, God wouldn't let her.

REVEREND DAUGHTER AND EXALTED SON

The peal of the doorbell rang throughout the mansion. At this, Patrick smoothed his features into a bland mask and tugged the edge of the hated butler suit. He cleared his throat, reached forward, and opened the door of the mansion.

As always, Patrick assessed his employers with keen eyes. Mrs. Cordelia Greene, also known as Reverend Daughter of the Church of the True Virgin of the Washed Saints walked inside. The rigid stance of her posture indicated her emotions were on a tight restraint. Her arms were folded across her chest in a defensive way while her mouth compressed into a straight line.

If her emotions were ragged, that could hardly be said about her appearance. Cordelia was as highly trained as a Rajput warrior in that regard. All aspects of her person could be used as weaponry in a sense. Clothes were her defensive shield with every item meticulously chosen to enhance. The teal blue suit she wore showed off the petite slightly boyish figure. An hourglass silhouette or a voluptuous figure would distract worshippers, but a hint of innocence in the undeveloped body of a woman added to the purity she sought to portray. Her beauty was a sword, flawless and sharp. Its perfection, her armor. Clear, sugar white skin shone with an ethereal quality. Chestnut brown hair glimmered with vibrancy on her shoulders.

Her eyes were a peculiar weapon she gave to her son. The power she wielded with them varied. How often had worshippers knelt at her feet, arms outstretched, entranced, enthralled? "There is something about the Reverend Daughter that makes one feels as if she is not of this world, but from the womb of angels," Patrick remembered reading once in a news article. "She has the capability of using her eyes to grip you in a web of exaltation. Without a single word, she binds you to her with a singular look. Her magnetism draws the worshipper in because she compels you. As a Washed

Saint of the True Virgin church, it is blasphemy to not say 'Hail Cordelia, full of grace.'"

Patrick had been with the Greenes for years now. She had sent money to his sister's village and would continue to for as long as she lived. The village had been able to build a health clinic—which Cordelia staffed—a school, and help with irrigation efforts. A church of the True Virgin had been erected there as well. It wasn't nearly as massive as those erected in the States and other parts of the world, but it housed a large painting of a Middle Eastern version of the Holy Virgin wrapped in yards of fabric.

From what his sister had said, everyone revered Cordelia as a goddess.

Right now, the Reverend Daughter looked less like a goddess and more like a woman fighting to keep her emotions in check. The muscles in her cheek ticked.

"It is good to see you again, Mrs. Greene."

"Thank you, Batcher," Cordelia cooed and patted his hand.

Patrick kept his eyes from flinching at the way she said his last name. Only Cordelia could make him sound like a pet and treat him like one.

"Ah, Batcher, good to see you, old boy," Theodore Greene greeted and patted Patrick on his shoulder.

Patrick wanted to bare his teeth and snarl. Old boy? Did he really look like a basset hound?

Yet Theodore Greene looked like a man no one wanted to cross. He had the body of a wrestler. Massive shoulders two small children could sit on comfortably, a broad chest strained against the fabric of his clothes, meaty hands that occasionally cracked walnuts, and muscled legs resembled tree trunks. Bald, he had a crinkled rectangular forehead, long haired black eyebrows that were a sharp contrast to his light gray eyes, a long narrow nose and thin lips. Theodore Greene, in contrast to his physique, was congenial and quite easy going. He was harmless, but no one knew that.

"Where is Solomon?" Cordelia asked as she came further into the mansion and allowed Patrick to close the door.

"He is at the skateboard park," Patrick stated.

"How could he do this to me? Doesn't he know we have guests coming within the hour? It's his wedding reception for the Virgin's sake! What kind of son is he to make our guests wait?"

"Mrs. Greene, he did say he would be back in time for the reception. And also, Celeste, your new daughter-in-law apologizes for not meeting you but she is getting dressed and will be down presently."

"Good. At least she has some manners," Cordelia sniffed and without a glance to Theodore, made her way upstairs to their suite.

Patrick waited for some form of instruction from Theodore, but the man said nothing, just stared at the departing figure of his wife and then exhaled a long drawn out sigh.

"Patrick, see to the luggage, will you? I'm going into my throne room. Can you bring coffee in about ten minutes, old boy?"

Patrick knocked once on the door and then entered the throne room, or rather a luxurious 'man cave'. The waning sunlight filtered into the room from the large window and brought his profile into stark relief. The Exalted Son had a resigned look on his face as he sat in his throne chair, as he called it.

"Where would you like me to set it, Mr. Greene?"

"Set it on the table, old boy."

He hated being called "old boy" by Theodore as much as he detested the patronizing way Cordelia treated him. The coffee set rattled slightly as Patrick fought a knee jerk reaction to dump the coffee set on top of the Exalted Son's head. Instead, he placed the coffee set on the glass top table with a lion's head foundation underneath

"Anything else, Mr. Greene?"

"Patrick, sit down," the Exalted Son ordered with a casual wave of his hand.

Of course the chair's smaller than his, Patrick thought as he obeyed.

"How have things been since we've been gone?"

Patrick cleared his throat and rubbed his hands on his thigh. He wondered exactly what Theodore wanted.

"Everything has gone smoothly since you left," he answered.

"Did you know Solomon was getting married?"

"No, I didn't. I did not meet the new Mrs. Greene until he brought her two weeks ago to the mansion."

Theodore didn't say anything for a few moments. Patrick saw his gaze focused on the windows, but he had the distinct impression the man didn't see anything in front of him.

"How should a father feel when he finds out his own son, estranged from him for five years, comes home married to a woman he never had a chance to meet?"

Patrick remained silent, knowing the question had a rhetorical quality to it. He thought about Solomon's wife, a unique woman. She had a quiet nature, very reserved, but he sensed she had heat under her calm exterior. The way she dressed made for a delightful distraction. Every morning, he had no idea what kind of outfit she'd have on, so it kept one guessing. She treated him with respect and deferred to him on manners of the estate. What he really like about her was that she called him Mr. Batcher. Her formal manner presented a nice change as well.

But he would have to be a fool not to notice she and Solomon slept apart. When Celeste had first requested separate bedrooms, he'd been hard-pressed to contain his astonishment and pretend her request was as common as asking for a drink of water. Over the past two weeks, he saw she avoided her husband and spent as little time as she could away from him. Solomon spent most of his time at the skateboard park or in the gym room. Curious as he was about their arrangement, Patrick remained respectful of their privacy.

"You know old boy," Theodore spoke again, pulling him away from his thoughts, "Some time ago, I can't remember when, I saw the most interesting nature show. Have you ever heard of zombie ants?"

It was the last thing he expected to hear. His eyebrow arched as he said slowly, "Yes."

"They are a very interesting phenomenon of nature. They are ants attacked by a specific parasitic fungus that controls them, kills them, and feeds off their dead carcass."

Patrick waited, hoping there would be a point to this waste of time.

The Exalted Son said nothing for a few moments and then, "As of late, I can't determine whether or not I'm the parasitic fungus or the host ant." He gave a hard snort of laughter. "I used to know Patrick. You know what my wife and I really are. In the beginning, I could handle this knowledge of my place in the world. Then, when I began to waver in indecision about whether I was the parasite or the host, I tried to ignore it." He sighed. "You know, when the fungus takes root in the ant, it leads the ant to a leaf and forces the ant's mouth, or mandibles, or whatever you call them, to grip the vein of a leaf so tight they can't release it.

"They die with their mouths shut."

Patrick shifted slightly in his seat. He wondered when the nature narration would be over. He also tried to avoid the resurgence of memories he had long suppressed brought on by Theodore's little speech. Despite his efforts, a pair of penny brown eyes flashed in his mind, and he stiffened at the wealth of emotions that swelled inside him. He did not want to think about her.

"I cannot continue in this indecision, Patrick. Eventually, I need to determine what I am."

Patrick looked at him. Theodore's eyes probed into his own.

"What will you do when you determine what you are, sir?" he asked in a low tone as he fought to close the door on the vision of those limpid eyes in his head.

"I'm not sure, old boy."

The sun's light dimmed and cascaded the room in murky pink light.

Abruptly, Theodore cleared his throat and rubbed his hands together. "Also, I'm raising your salary by $500. With an additional person to care for, that's more work for you. I know you'll do a great job, old boy."

The Exalted Son reached over and patted his arm and Patrick jumped up swiftly and stepped away.

"Thank you sir."

He closed the door behind him and leaned against it. His eyes closed. True, he knew what Cordelia and Theodore were. It was the reason they kept him. Subsequently, they also knew what he was which is why he stayed.

Kishori, his mind whispered.

The very name made him flinch, and he inhaled a shuddering breath. A face floated behind his closed lids, almond-hued with black, waxy eyebrows lifted over those penny brown eyes. Almost white teeth chewed nervously at a pair of fine lips. Violently, Patrick scrubbed at his face and gritted his teeth. He pulled at his hair as he forced his mind to stop thinking about Kishori.

A few moments later and discipline once more mastered his body. He exhaled slowly.

At the end of the day, everyone had their secrets.

NINE FOR DINNER

"Oh my gosh! Patrick Batcher's an Indian!"

The greeting Patrick almost uttered scrambled back down his throat on dog's feet. His eyes widened.

"What did you think he was — an alien?"

He trailed his eyes from the bright-eyed black hobbit woman obviously Celeste's mother to the plump female figure at the back of the group. The sight of her caused a masculine appreciation for her beauty to pervade him.

"Well no. Just that Patrick Batcher doesn't sound like an Indian name," the hobbit woman said again.

"What is his name supposed to be, Chewbacca? Leave it alone, Mama. It's not that big of a deal."

"Hello Patrick," a rumbly voice greeted and he connected his eyes to meet the dark brown eyes of Celeste's father, a middle-aged football player.

"It's nice to meet you," her father continued, "Thank you for arranging for the limo to pick us up. It was unexpected."

Patrick started to breathe a small sigh of relief. Here at last was some gratitude.

"Don't ever do it again. I don't need to have my daughter's in-law's wealth thrown in my face. We're not a charity case nor do we wish to be treated as such."

"I'm sure Mr. and Mrs. Greene didn't intend to convey that," another masculine voice interjected. Patrick swiveled with shock to face a blond haired gentleman.

"Who are you?" Patrick asked bluntly, surprise negating social niceties.

The plump girl smiled up at the blond man who smiled back down at her. "My fiancé. We knew Celeste wouldn't mind, and she'd love to see Jacob again."

Patrick ticked off a mental list of the past minute. Obviously being an Indian man in a butler suit was a surprise, he'd been compared to an alien form of Bigfoot, he'd been berated for being kind, and he now had to prepare for an uninvited guest.

Yeah, that's about right, he thought.

"It's a pleasure to meet all of you," Patrick lied as he fought to keep himself impassive and bland. He definitely would earn the raise he'd been given a few moments ago.

Deftly, he took inventory of their packages as he closed the door. He walked in front of the family, hearing the bags they carried rustle behind him. He led them to the small dining room. It was a minimalist room with modern flair. Bright colors, sleek lines, asymmetrical shapes, and of course, the tables and chairs were designed for artistry, not comfort. Patrick hated the room. It had been set up with appetizers. Sausage rolls, celery stalks filled with cream cheese, crackers topped with yogurt cheese and salmon, and stuffed mushrooms. Lemonade and iced tea were in two glass vertical pitchers. Celeste had refused anything alcoholic to be served, her one input into today's dinner.

"Please feel free to sit anywhere. I'll let Mr. and Mrs. Greene and Solomon know you're here." He motioned for them to set their gifts down and made a mental note to bring the gifts to the living room during dinner.

Leah had sauntered over to the appetizer table, and Patrick watched her covertly, helplessly drawn to her. Celeste's sister had an aura about her that immediately captured a man's attention. It blazed as she walked by. The russet curls bounced with vitality. Her face, with its youthful hue and mature lines, caught him in a web of longing. She had small, pouty, bow-shaped lips made to be kissed and a curvaceous figure a male would die to caress. If he were just ten years younger . . .

"This stuff is awful! Who made this?" Leah exclaimed, and Patrick went rigid as his admiration crashed like a Corvette into a brick wall.

"Leah, you are a guest here," Mr. Martin admonished.

"Daddy, I may be a guest but I don't have to eat slop. What? Did the person who made this look at the expiration date on the container of cheese? It tastes like just this side of the moldy green valley! This is Celeste's wedding reception for Pete's sake!"

"Blaze, really! Keep your opinions to yourself," Mrs. Martin reprimanded as well, her voice filled with dismay.

"Mama did you taste this? I'm not making this up. It's awful."

"Leahgirl, be quiet now. If you don't like it, you don't have to eat it. You don't have to ruin everyone else's experience. After all, it is Celeste and Solomon's wedding reception dinner," Jacob countered in a mild voice.

"But J-hun, look at the salmon. It's curled and dried up like a squid. And they put it on Ritz crackers! Are you kidding me?!"

"Leah, be quiet!" Mr. Martin bit out at his daughter as he stalked over to her, his eyebrows drawn into a V. His eyes were dark and glittered with censure.

"But Daddy, it's awful."

"Leahgirl," Jacob interrupted as he put an arm around her and hugged her close, "No one cooks like you do. So anything less than your cooking deserves to be treated with sensitivity."

Patrick watched as Leah closed her mouth and then smile at Jacob. "The sausage rolls are good. A tad soggy, but it doesn't detract from the taste."

"Ah, well, let me try a couple."

Patrick left and walked to the small dining room. He took deep breaths for a full minute and then straightened, tugged at the monkey suit and started toward the kitchen when the doorbell rang. It was going to be an interesting dinner.

###

"Ah, Gooey baby!" Leah exclaimed before Patrick could open his mouth to formally introduce the second uninvited guest for dinner.

"Blaze," Gonzo said as he brushed past Patrick into the room, "I didn't like it then, and I don't like it now."

"Oh, but Gooey baby, no one but my sister can pronounce your name. And seeing you again is like seeing an older brother."

"Leahgirl," Jacob intervened, "be nice."

Leah looked up again at Jacob and Patrick saw Gonzo's eyes widen with surprise. "All right, Gonzo. It's good to see you."

"And you too Blaze," Gonzo said as he came further into the room. "Mr. and Mrs. Martin."

"Hello, Gonzo dear," Mrs. Martin greeted and Gonzo bent to give her a hug. "So very nice to see you again after all this time. I was just asking Celeste about you a couple of months before she got married."

Conversation began to flow in a normal fashion as the Martins and Jacob crowded around Gonzo. Patrick breathed a small sigh of relief. Maybe, just maybe, the evening would go smooth. After all, this was a meeting of the in-laws and yes, although their respective daughter and son had married in an unorthodox fashion, at the end of the day, it could be much worse. Gonzo was the common factor between the Martins and the Greenes and maybe that would be the glue to bring a new cohesiveness to an expanded family.

A discreet cough behind him caused him to turn and see the Reverend Daughter and the Exalted Son standing side by side. The Reverend Daughter, glorious and ethereal, dressed in a simple white dress with a square neck. A mother of pearl pendant adorned her chest and her hair flowed down her shoulders. The Exalted Son stood out in a gray suit and gold shirt and gray crocodile shoes.

"Go ahead, Batcher," Cordelia nodded to him.

"Could I please have everyone's attention? I'd like to present Solomon's mother and father," Patrick began.

"Oh my gosh! That's that psycho cult lady!" Leah burst out as she leapt up.

"Leah dear, what on earth are you talking about?"

"Mama, that's the lady with the churches! You know, the buildings with the Virgin tugging on her clothes."

Four pairs of startled eyes turned toward the Blessed Dyad of the True Virgin. Silence pervaded for long moments and grew uncomfortable. Patrick decided to intervene once more. "Theodore and Cordelia Greene, Solomon's parents."

"Oh my gosh! Celeste married into a cult family," Leah said.

UNEXPECTED

Solomon shook his head, a novel experience for him to knock on a woman's bedroom door before he entered, and stranger still to have to obtain permission to enter his wife's room.

"Who is it?" Celeste's voice called, slightly muffled by the barrier of the door. He rolled his eyes. How many other men were banging down the door to get to her?

"It's me." He turned to the knob to find it locked. He called out, "Celeste, open the door."

"For what purpose?"

For what purpose? He repeated silently to himself. What did a man usually want when he went into a woman's room? Not her knitting needles, that's for sure! He blew out a breath and pinched his nose and tried again.

"Celeste, we have guests down stairs. Not just any guest but our families. Open up so we can go down together like real newlyweds."

"No."

Solomon felt his eyebrow arch as he stared at the white surface of the door.

"Why not?"

"I believe I have been pellucid about our marital contact. I will meet you downstairs in a few moments along with everyone else." Her tone of dismissal came through loud and clear.

Solomon stared at the door, felt his mouth go slack in surprise. Yet a moment a later, he barked out a reluctant laugh. This bossy woman never kept life boring. A spark of admiration ignited in him. Celeste wouldn't be easily run over by anyone. For all her reserve, she was a steamroller in her own right.

He smirked. What she didn't know was that he'd chew nails to a pulp before letting someone lock him out of a room in his own home. He respected her privacy but when it came to a united front, she wasn't going to play him for an idiot.

Celeste glanced back and forth between the portrait of Queen Elizabeth and her reflection. She thought back on her husband's audacity to try to enter her suite and twirled around the mirror. She would go down stairs in a few moments. Once again, he presumed too much. And it had been a simple matter to dismiss him.

Besides, she had avoided him ever since they had their small talk about being her knight's squire. Why this constant need for her companionship? She thought she could handle a platonic association between them. Before he kissed her.

Despite her self-discipline, she could not forget the memory.

An audible click sounded in her room like a bomb, and she swirled in time to see Mr. Greene saunter into her domain, a Cheshire cat smile on his face.

"I beg your pardon!" she screeched out in shock. "Why have you entered my chamber?"

His green gold eyes locked on to her. "I have respected your privacy, Celeste. I have given you your space. But there's something you need to understand. Woman, this is my house and no one keeps me away from what's mine."

A little thrill went through her, but she squelched it. Why did he have to say "woman" like that? It made her feel like a girl getting a mock stern talking-to from her sweet heart.

I wonder if I'm included in what's 'yours,' Celeste thought as she sniffed, strangely mollified by his attitude. She concluded she wouldn't have her way in this, so she didn't try to sway him.

"Celeste, what are you wearing? Is that a dress or a tent?"

Celeste whirled back around to the mirror. The color of the dress was a dark emerald green with two layers of gold-netted overlay. The sleeves were puffed wide at the shoulders and then narrowed at the wrist, edged by gold lace. The matching emerald gloves were overlaid with the netted material. A gold cord edged around waist and hem.

It wasn't as heavily ornate like the queen's dress that had dazzled with pearls, rubies, and other precious stones. She decided to forgo showing any part of her chest and so the dress came up to her neck with the ruff under her chin in gold lace. The matching cloak layered with the gold-netted material flowed nicely around her and fell to the floor in a graceful manner.

"I'm not quite sure what you mean," Celeste said finally after a few moments.

"Celeste," Mr. Greene said as he walked further in the room, "it looks like you have a table attached to your waist under that tent."

"Very good," Celeste said, pleased. She wanted to make sure the dress was as accurate in style as possible, if not detail, with the portrait of Queen Elizabeth.

"Let's go Celeste," Mr. Greene said as he took her arm. His cologne wafted over her, a pleasant scent.

Of course, God would make Mr. Greene devastating, Celeste thought with some irritation. Only His perfect hand could sculpt a man with such precision. The Almighty had apparently seen fit to grace his son with bronze skin exuding vitality and smoothed the broad shoulders that beckoned a woman to rest her head there. It could only be by divine intervention the man would have a face most women found sensual and arresting. The spiky coal black hair contrasted the green gold-flecked eyes that looked at her with a measure of triumph. The dark gray suit only enhanced his physical appeal. He appeared exactly as one would expect him to appear. A suave, experienced playboy.

And you, dear God, left me with nothing, Celeste thought as the resentment she kept hidden began to heat and melt away at her reserve. The dull brown skin, the skinny body, the face only her mother could love — all given to her by the so-called loving God. Plus the other . . . no, it wasn't good to think about *that*. It was all she could do not to shake her fist to the sky. Leah *always* had men chasing her. There wasn't a time in her memory when she hadn't seen the way men gobbled her sister with their eyes.

All I have are my clothes.

"Celeste!"

Celeste jumped, startled. "Mr. Greene, forgive me."

"Where were you, Celeste? You weren't even here."

"I was ranting at God, Mr. Greene," Celeste found herself saying. She ignored the voice telling her to be quiet. For this brief moment in time, the truth seemed prudent.

He stilled and took his hand from her arm, staring down at her.

"Why were you ranting at God, Celeste?"

If Mr. Greene had laughed at her or said something derisive, she would have immediately clammed up. Yet, his voice had been soft and quiet, and he looked down at her as if he wanted to know. The icy voice in her head screamed to hush, but she ignored it. "God chose to make you handsome. He chose to make my sister lovely. And me, he made ugly. Isn't that why you married me? Wasn't I the answer to your prayer?"

"Celeste, I—"

"Well, Mr. Greene, you have the answer to your prayers. What about mine?"

Solomon had never seen this side of Celeste. Her maple syrup eyes held him in a vise-like grip. They were naked, vulnerable. Her face bereft of her usual stoic expression pleaded with him, the mouth open slightly as if to say more. Gone was his distant, eccentric, temporary wife. In her place, stood a young woman, exposing her need for answers.

"Celeste," he started and stopped, not sure what to say.

Suddenly, her eyes hardened, and the supplicated look vanished as if a hand had wiped it away. Although she hadn't moved, he felt a gulf suddenly separate them, and he sighed softly. Celeste was the one who kept him away. For whatever reason, she refused to trust him.

Yet he wanted her to trust him. He had married for his protection but what if she needed him in some way? How could he help her?

"Let's go, Mr. Greene. We do have guests waiting and it is, after all, our wedding reception."

A dead body would have sounded more ecstatic.

MARTINS' MERCURY

Only the Blessed Dyad of the True Virgin could turn a nine person family dinner into a bloated, over the top affair.

With horror, Solomon glanced at the great room. Their wedding reception had been spared no expense. The great room, already opulent with its French inspired décor resembled the hall of royalty. Green and gold ribbons graced the ornate chairs around the marble dining table, covered by a golden table cloth. The dinnerware glistened under the chandelier.

"Is that the silverware?" he heard Mrs. Martin whisper to Mr. Martin.

He could understand her astonishment. The 14-karat-gold cutlery embedded with Swarovski emerald glittered next to the dinnerware of the same design. Heavy crystal glasses shaped like goblets twinkled next to satin napkins artfully folded into hearts.

The room glimmered. The walls gleamed. The table sparkled. The dishes glinted.

Solomon stifled a groan. What he wouldn't give to drive up to McDonald's and order a Big Mac.

"How lovely," Mrs. Martin said a few moments later as they were all seated at the table. Patrick had hired servers dressed in uniforms of black with gold or green vests to oversee the dinner preparations.

Celeste sat at one end of the table with himself at the other. Both sets of parents were to his right and Jacob, Leah, and Gonzo were to his left.

"Why thank you, Brenda," his mother replied. "It was the least we could do."

"Seems rather extravagant to me," Mr. Martin grumbled as he looked around him.

"Yeah," Leah agreed, "'over the top.' 'Pompous.' 'Ridiculous.'"

109

"Ever the tactful one, right Blaze?" Gonzo spoke as he glanced at her.

"Really, young lady. Your attitude is quite offensive," Cordelia said as her eyes narrowed at Leah.

Quickly Solomon glanced at Leah's glass. Great, it was still empty.

"At any rate," Jacob intervened, sliding his arm around Leah's shoulder, "this room looks fantastic. A nice wedding reception for the newlyweds. Although Leah and I are planning to have a big affair, there's nothing quite like a small gathering with those closest to you. Knowing Celeste, this type of thing is right up your alley, isn't it my lady?"

Solomon took a glance at his wife and could tell something bothered her. Her gloved hands were tightly clenched together. She had avoided his eyes ever since they left her bedroom, and he wondered if she was still upset over her remarks about ranting at God.

"I do prefer intimate affairs," she conceded with a bow of her head in Jacob's direction.

"I second that," Gonzo interjected with a small smile at her that Celeste responded to with one of her own as her hand unclasped and he saw her shoulders relax.

Smiling at Gonzo again, Solomon thought with irritation. He was the only man in the room that received that reaction. Without being too conceited, Solomon knew he was attractive but Celeste acted as if he had swapped faces with the Elephant Man. No woman had ever treated him like this before. She wasn't impressed by his money, moved by his kiss, or aware of his appearance. If Gonzo walked into the room, her face radiated joy. When he entered in the same vicinity, she'd acted as if he'd come down from the bell tower.

Ever since that danged blueberry woman, things hadn't been the same. He wondered if he'd lost his appeal. Since when did any female on planet Earth ever prefer Gonzo Thomas over Solomon Greene?

"Doesn't that sound like an innuendo," Leah remarked with a sly tone in her voice.

Celeste's smile left her face, and she stared hard at her sister while Gonzo shifted uncomfortably in his chair, glancing around quickly as if searching for an escape. For a moment, Solomon could have sworn he looked guilty. But what did Gonzo have to feel guilty about?

Were his suspicions true?

"Blaze, really! Stop being childish," Mrs. Martin admonished from across the table. Unlike her customary peaceful expression, her eyes had narrowed, and the corner of her lips turned down. She meant exactly what she said.

Obviously Leah knew what that look meant because she dropped her eyes to her plate and pressed her mouth shut. Glancing between both of them, it made him wonder where exactly did Leah get her temper from?

By sheer force of will, Celeste kept the mayhem on the inside from showing itself.

How could Lord Westwood be here? Why did Leah bring him? Did she do it to taunt me?

Immediately she dismissed the thought. Leah had no inkling on how she felt about Lord Westwood. Knowing Leah, she probably considered Lord Westwood to be part of the family as soon he would be.

Surrounded by the gilded room bursting with gold and green, it only seemed to enhance his physical beauty. Lord Westwood could have been the mythical Eros, golden haired with delicate wings, a simple toga embracing his frame, belted by a cord of gold and feet shod with gold sandals. His periwinkle eyes were soft and smiling with inner peacefulness as he gazed down at her.

And she would be Psyche. Beautiful, with her long hair braided to her feet. Her skin would be a vibrant brown, her arms outstretched to receive him, her butterfly wings golden in the sunlight. He would adore her because of all the obstacles she had endured to be worthy of his love. Butterflies and birds would surround them and he would lift her and they would fly to Mount Olympus and —

"Icy!"

The sharp grinding sound of Leah's voice jolted her from her fantasy, although she didn't react to it.

"Yes, Blaze?" Celeste said calmly.

"I asked you if we can eat. I'm starving. Patrick is waiting for you to give the word."

Mr. Batcher stood by her side, and she nodded to him and then stayed him with her hand as she turned to her mother-in-law who watched her. "If you wouldn't mind if we start dinner now, Mrs. Greene?"

"I find that agreeable," she said, bowing her head slightly.

The servers began bringing in the food. Broccoli soup, red skin potatoes cubed and mixed with thyme, baby carrots steamed and lightly salted, fluffy, airy biscuits, lemon chicken and rump roast. As the smells wafted in the air, Celeste admonished herself for her flight of fancy. Eros and Psyche, birds and butterflies! She had really deviated from the realm of reality. God would not give her a fairytale life. She was not going to have Lord Westwood as her husband. Ferociously, she allowed her imagination to form a long handled scythe with its curved edge. With it, she cut down her dreams. No man would want her or love her. The most she could have was a dead marriage. She allowed her gaze to fall upon her husband and was surprised to find him watching her.

Why had she opened up to him like that?

"My lady," Goijaart spoke softly to her as the clink of cutlery and murmured conversation dominated the dinner table.

With relief, she tore her eyes from her husband and smiled at her knight. He had saved her once again.

"Sir?"

"I wanted to see if I can take you to Granny's house next week sometime. I know you'd like to see the greenhouse."

"I haven't traversed there in some time. Thank you for the invitation, sir."

"I can drive you there."

"No, that's quite all right. I'll just make sure to let Mr. Greene know about it and see if he'd like to join us."

"I did let him know," Goijaart said as he glanced away from her to take the napkin from his holder, "He said he didn't have a problem with it. He had other things he was doing."

"Very well. I shall meet you Tuesday of next week."

"So Celeste," Mr. Greene, Solomon's father spoke, and she turned from Goijaart to him, "tell me about yourself. I see you like to dress in costume. Did you make that yourself, child?"

"I did, Mr. Greene." It shouldn't have surprised her that her father- in-law was tall as well as big. He looked like an old-fashioned prizefighter. She would hate to be on the wrong end of his hands. But his eyes were gray like steel and as gentle as a soothing rainy day.

"Really? That's some talent you have there. I hear Gonzo's grandmother taught you to sew?"

"Yes sir. She gifted me with her knowledge of everything she knew. I am grateful to her.

"Without her, I would not be the woman I am today."

"What a nice thing to say. I was just speaking to —"

"Everyone, please place your utensils down. We must give grace to the Virgin," Mrs. Greene interjected loudly, her voice carrying over the din of everyone's conversations.

More curious than anything, the table quieted. Celeste noted her father-in-law's jaw clenched, and his son merely looked bored.

"Holy Virgin," the Reverend Daughter began. "Let this food nourish us with purity that flows from your garments. May it wrap us in warmth and flood our hearts with your perfection. Thank you, dear Virgin."

It wasn't the prayer that bothered anyone as much as the actions that accompanied it. Mrs. Greene, as she prayed, lifted a square piece of purple cloth tattered around the edges and kissed all four corners. Then she held it between her hands as she prayed.

Of course, Celeste thought, *Blaze isn't going to let that go.*

"What in the world—" Leah began when Jacob suddenly interjected. "Thank you for sharing your faith's blessing. I would like to follow up with a prayer of mine own to Almighty God."

"Is not the prayer to the Virgin sufficient, Jacob Westwood?" Cordelia challenged him as she sat back, her green eyes focused on him.

"No, it isn't," Lord Westwood said bluntly but without aggression.

"Please, please," Mr. Greene said as he glanced at his wife, "do say your little prayer."

Jacob did so readily, and the room relaxed and the servers moved again.

"I can't believe you call that a prayer, Mrs. Greene," Leah said as she lifted her fork, "It seems very strange to call upon any god—or goddess, rather—by kissing a napkin."

"Leah, be quiet!" Mr. Martin shouted across the table.

"No, it's quite all right Samuel," Mrs. Greene said softly. "Please, allow Leah to speak her thoughts."

"Now, really Cordelia, must you?" Mr. Greene started to say when Leah interjected, "Thank you, Mrs. Greene. As I was saying, I think it's very strange you would call upon your goddess in the manner that you did."

"Not at all. This cloth is a piece of the Virgin's holy garments. As I've told countless others, we do not worship a goddess."

"You don't?" Goijaart asked as he began cutting into a sliver of rump roast.

"Of course not. Gods and goddesses have a habitual propensity to disappoint."

"What exactly do you mean?" Lord Westwood asked as he ate a forkful of carrots.

"Really? We're seriously going to talk about religion at my wedding reception?" Solomon's voice cut through the discussion.

Celeste glanced down at her husband. His face scrunched into a scowl as his mouth thinned to a straight line. His nose flared in aggravation. Frankly, she was glad to be talking about religion. A far better subject than the origin of their relationship.

"I see nothing wrong with such a dialogue as long as it's conducted respectfully," Mrs. Martin said, "I for one find it fascinating to be breaking bread with a cult leader."

"It's not a cult," Mrs. Greene said, "but as I was trying to explain, worship of deities only leads to disappointment. Prayers go forth, and prayers go unanswered. As many unbelievers can attest to. Only believers struggle with keeping their faith. The True Church of the Virgin of the Washed Saints does not adhere to a deity. We venerate the Virgin and strip her from miraculous connotations."

Celeste sat mesmerized. Mrs. Greene had a melodious voice. It flowed like honey over chocolate. No wonder the Washed Saints was the fastest growing new faith in the past fifteen years.

"Who made this lemon chicken? It tastes like citrus acid times a million!" Blaze's voices broke the trance Celeste had found herself in.

Leah had taken the sleeve of Mr. Batcher. "Patrick, tell the cook the recipe calls for lemon *chicken* not chicken *lemon*. We want to have a hint of lemon not drink lemonade from the chicken!"

"Leah! Do you have to be so grotesque?" Goijaart said.

"I'm not being grotesque. The chicken is."

"Blaze, hush," Mrs. Martin spoke again, her voice deadpan and the expression that Celeste rarely saw on her face was there again. Leah realized she had once again crossed a line and clamped shut. She put the chicken on a napkin and rolled it up.

"I can agree with that assessment, Mrs. Greene," Goijaart stated as he ate around his food, "Deities disappoint because they've a lot on their shoulders. I choose not to wrap such a noose of belief around my neck."

"As such Gonzo, the Church is not a religion in the sense of worship of the spiritual. In the same way that followers of Christ touched his garments and were healed, the Virgin's garments will lend purity to their lives. They will be freed from all negativity and hopelessness. They shall grasp her garment and purity shall flow through them."

"What are you basing this foundation of faith on?"

"A vision I had nearly twenty years ago. The Virgin appeared to me and told me the truth of herself and her place in our lives."

"That's very interesting," Lord Westwood replied, "What makes your vision more valid than anyone else's?"

A jerk went through Mrs. Greene. Celeste noted she looked shocked. "What exactly do you mean?"

"Exactly what I said. What makes your vision more valid than anyone else's? Many people have had visions over the years, all professing to have some form of truth or some kind of enlightenment. Why would your vision of the Virgin telling you anything be more acceptable than anyone else's? And, by the way, the woman who did touch the Lord's garment was healed because of her faith, not his clothes."

Goijaart laughed at the confused expression on the Reverend Daughter's face while the Exalted Son looked as if the food on his plate was the most fascinating thing he'd ever seen. "Methinks the Blessed Dyad don't answer probing questions of faith frequently."

"Can we please talk about something else?" Solomon pleaded with a hint of a whine in his voice.

Celeste could see the frustration her husband's face. He obviously wasn't a Washed Saint.

"Where are you going for your honeymoon?" Mrs. Martin asked as she took a spoonful of broccoli soup.

Celeste felt her face flush with heat as she looked down the table at her husband. His eyes probed into hers for a moment and then he smiled that Cheshire cat smile he had earlier when he unlocked her door.

What was he contemplating?

Talking about God had made Solomon lose his appetite. It had been a while now since he made the deal with God about giving him a wife. He'd made mental plans to go to church, but each time he allowed something else to come up.

He thought about Celeste and what she said about her prayers. Why had God answered his prayer but not hers? Why did some prayers get answered and others didn't? What *was* her prayer?

Thinking about his mother's words about the propensity of gods to disappoint, Solomon thought he could agree with that to some extent. Prayers went unanswered daily forcing people simply to take matters into their own hands.

Did they ever get far? Solomon wondered. He'd give anything to take away his past and the ramification of his actions. If he had a machine that could erase the last ten years of his life, he'd be free from his past. As always, the images of beautiful women from his past began to float before his eyes—mouths open, limpid eyes, skin soft and supple. His heart started to beat faster as the wave of cold dread began to take over his body.

Swiftly, he glanced at his wife. Seeing her face, the images began to recede into the dark abyss of his mind. His heart slowed. His hands warmed.

As he focused on Celeste, he was struck by her majestic appearance. If her chair were any higher, she'd be sitting on a throne.

Her gloved hand moved gracefully as she said something to Gonzo. The calmness fell over him. What was it about his wife that instantly relaxed him? He thought it was her appearance he initially responded to. After all, she wasn't one of the beautiful women of his past. Yet, what was that about her drawing him? Her eyes were gentle even in their remoteness. No makeup in the world could make her skin any smoother and clear.

Maybe her self-control fascinated him. When she spoke, words were never wasted. No effort was made to be talkative or fun. Even her bossy demeanor added to her appeal.

Solomon couldn't pinpoint why his wife had the ability to affect him so.

Gonzo had leaned toward her again, and she smiled at his best friend. Solomon felt his eyebrows draw together. He hadn't seen much of his friend lately. Earlier in the week, Gonzo didn't join him at the skateboard park. Unusual for him since he'd returned.

"Where are you guys going for your honeymoon?"

The word had the effect of static shock. Honeymoon? He hadn't even thought of that.

As he caught his wife's eye, the answer came to him, and he smiled.

"Well, we weren't going to tell anyone but in about four weeks, I'm taking my wife to Arcadia."

"You're going to Greece?" Mr. Martin asked.

"No, Samuel, Arcadia. Our villa in Florida," his mother interjected with a slight smile. "It's our home away from home in the summer. I love going there when we're not busy with our children.

A darling residence in Tampa Bay with a private beach and surrounded by the lushest palms trees."

"It sounds absolutely heavenly," Mrs. Martin said as she turned toward the Reverend Daughter.

"That's why we call it Arcadia. Imagine a 7,000 square foot house with six bedrooms and five bathrooms. We have a giant pool in the back of the house and next to it is a patio area with a statue we had sculpted of the Virgin. We've had the kitchen updated with stainless steel appliances and—"

"And a room full of hot air where your bloated head resides," Leah inserted with a voice that clipped at the occupants in anger.

"Leah!" Mr. Martin shouted across the table as Mrs. Martin and Gonzo said at the same time, "Blaze!"

"Oh, come off it! All of you!" Leah started as she stood and addressed the table, "I'm to sit quietly and meekly while this psycho cult chick starts spouting off the glamour of her house while she makes money off deluded people sucked in by the bull! Give me a break! I have to eat cruddy food and deal with the fact this marriage between my sister and that pathetic excuse for a man," she jerked her head toward Solomon, "is a farce! She married into a cult family for goodness sake! Don't expect me to ignore it."

Solomon felt his own anger rise and as pandemonium rose from the voices of everyone at the table except for Celeste and his father. The servers were standing off to the side, wide eyed with shock. Patrick simply stared off into the distance.

"Shut up Leah," Celeste's voice cut through the din. All conversation stopped as they turned to look at his wife.

"Icy, I won't—" Leah began.

"I said shut up Leah," Celeste repeated, her voice quiet but the impact of it resounded like shattered glass. Solomon studied his wife and saw the rage. Her hands were clasped together and her whole body rigid. A muscle ticked in her cheek. Her maple syrup eyes were narrowed on her sister.

119

"You have forgotten yourself, Leah." Her voice quivered in anger. "These people are my in-laws. That man, my husband. I will not assent to your incessant harassment of these people. Incontestably, you are beleaguered in some fashion. Lord Westwood," she addressed Jacob, "out this room and down the hall is a modern version of what I'd like to call a drawing room. It has the loveliest landscapes my in-laws have collected over the years. Take your fiancé and be good enough to show them to her. Perhaps the serenity of the art will sweep in and calm her aggravated spirit."

"An excellent idea, Lady Greene," Jacob said, as he pushed away from the table and grabbed Leah.

"Icy, c'mon—" Leah started.

Celeste's head darted in a quick fashion, her maple syrup eyes darkened to the color of molasses. Leah closed her mouth. "Leave. Now. Leah."

Jacob took Leah's hand and led her out of the room.

Silence pervaded the room.

"Ah, Martin's Mercury, eh, Icy?" Mrs. Martin asked a moment later on a sigh.

"Martin's Mercury?" Solomon asked as he watched his wife. Her rigid posture gave the impression if someone touched her, she'd splinter into pieces.

"It's what we refer to when we talk about our tempers. All of our tempers eventually shoot up to 90°, some quicker than others. But my darling Celeste, when she gets angry, she gets very quiet and very cold. Like ice."

"Goijaart," Celeste interrupted her mother, "would you show my mother and father the library? Mr. Batcher told me there were some excellent books in there on Internet marketing as well as some autobiographies my father would be interested in. In about a half hour, we'll all meet in the drawing room along with my sister and Lord Westwood."

120

Solomon saw Gonzo squeeze her hand and then her mother and father got up and walked out with him. Before they left, they bent and kissed her on the cheek.

"Mr. and Mrs. Greene, would you mind leaving Solomon and I alone for a half hour? We will meet you back in the drawing room as well with the others. Mr. Batcher, would you see to it that tea and coffee are brought in a half hour?"

Patrick nodded, and the room emptied.

HER HUSBAND

It had been a perfect day to travel to Grandmother Thomas' house. The warmth of the sun cascaded over her as she drove three hours into Ohio. The scenery had burst with color as the vibrant green trees melded against an eye-piercing blue of the sky. Little white clouds moved against the horizon. Due to the warmth of the day, she dressed as an American pioneer with the light tan skirt and gauzy blouse. It had been some time since she'd been out the mansion. The distance would give her some perspective over her situation.

Soon, she found herself wandering in the greenhouse and inhaled the fragrant and earthy scent. Her mind flooded with memories of Goijaart and herself as children.

They walked the small aisle way in the greenhouse in contented silence in the familiar surroundings. The workbench at the back reminded her of when they used to plant flowers under Grandmother Thomas' direction. Each evening toward the time she had to leave to go back home her knight would be forced to give her a flower and declare his homage to her.

"Do you remember the vows I used to demand of you?"

He laughed. "Oh, my lady, do I? As I recall every evening at precisely 5:14 PM."

"You know why it had to be 5:14 PM, don't you, sir?"

He slanted a glance at her. "Of course! Five minus one equals four and you had to 'forgo' our time together!"

"Oh my lord, were we ever so corny!"

"And I was forced to come to the back of the greenhouse, pick the most convenient flower, wait as you sat on the bench and then declare, 'Upon my honor as Knight of the Triangle Table upon which owes its fealty to yonder princess of the Royal House of Martin, I do so pledge my undying loyalty.' How did you ever get me to say all that every day for the summer?"

Celeste laughed along with him. "I abused my position as princess and yours as knight and made you. Do you recall how many times I used to make you do my bidding?"

Goijaart raised his arm and clasped her closer to him. "How many times did I pull you in my red wagon, give you my snacks, open the door, pull out your chair, and a dozen other menial tasks you harped upon me?"

They were silent, and Celeste sighed in contentment. Goijaart would always be her friend. His presence never caused her any discomfiture or awareness of him. Not like her husband.

Mr. Greene disturbed her and she didn't know how to handle it. She'd become aware of him. The looks he'd given affected her in a way she didn't want to acknowledge. All of this happened in a single moment when she told him about her rant with God and acted as if he really wanted to know. But perhaps it was before that: when he'd unlocked her door, pushed his way into her bedroom, and stamped his presence on her domain.

And later, when he declared he wanted to go on a honeymoon with her.

But it's Lord Westwood I'm in love with, whom I've given my heart to even though he doesn't know it. My husband will never have access to me. A familiar ache for him came to the surface as she thought of her sister's fiancé, but it wasn't as sharp as it has been before. What did it mean?

"What's on your mind, my lady?"

Goijaart's voice jerked her from her thoughts. "My lord, it's hard to explain."

They stopped at the workbench and sat on it.

He held her gaze and reached into his pocket and pulled out the black handkerchief she had given him at Grandmother Thomas' funeral. Her heart constricted as she thought of the woman who helped mold her into the craft woman she was today. Grandmother Thomas had taught her everything she'd known. The happy hours she'd spent in her workroom learning with dexterity and photographic memory had been some of the happiest of her childhood. She'd always be thankful to her.

"Oh Goijaart, I'm so sorry."

"No need, my lady." He placed the handkerchief between them and then looked at her. "Tell me what is on your mind."

"My husband," she blurted out and wrung her hands in an uncharacteristic release of emotion.

His eyes drew together. "What do you mean?"

"Sir, when Mr. Greene and I joined in matrimony, we understood our marriage was to be formal, platonic, and distant. In seven years' time, we would divorce. Yet, my husband constantly seeks my presence and attention. I have made it clear to him that I do not seek these things with him. All I have ever taken from him was his name."

"And what did he take from you?" Goijaart's voice had taken on a dark quality.

"My protection as his ugly wife," she spat out. The insult of those words hit her. In the past, she'd been numb to their effect. Even this had changed. Her ice shield slipped away from her moment by moment. With her reserve intact, she couldn't be hurt. She had remained unaffected when he proposed to her. Now, her defenses were melting, and the exposure of her heart to emotion grew with each passing day.

"You are in no way lacking in beauty, my lady," her knight said softly.

"But Sunday, something happened. When Blaze began her tirade at my husband . . ." Celeste paused as she stared blindly out the window.

"Yes?" Goijaart prompted.

"I was furious with her," she responded.

"One can understand that sentiment, Celeste."

"No, my lord, you do not understand." She turned her face toward him. "I had told her of Mr. Greene's reasons for marrying me. This upset her. The first time my husband met my sister, she poured lemonade on him. She even broke one of mother's crystal glasses. I did nothing. I felt nothing. And Sunday, she merely spoke to him and I wanted to maim her with a hammer. I thought, 'How dare she speak to my husband this way?'"

It went deeper than that, however. When Leah had insulted Solomon, she had also insulted her. A Bible verse flickered in her mind. "The two shall become one." Could she possibly be bonding in some way to her husband? More than once, at odd intervals, she'd been aware of the affinity between them. Did that have something to do with becoming one flesh? Did she just call him Solomon in her mind? Where was the familiar, distant Mr. Greene?

"I fail to see the problem."

"Since when did I become possessive of my husband? When did it matter how my sister or anyone else treated him? He was simply to be a title, not a man."

Celeste got up and rubbed her arms, the sound of the gloves against the fabric loud to her ears. She strode down the aisle. In spite of herself, she had *liked* his highhandedness when he barged his way into her chamber and even later, for all her protesting of their honeymoon, it *thrilled* her that he wanted to spend time with her.

And later, when they went to the drawing room and sat down to a strained atmosphere between their families, and opened the gifts presented to them, she had felt a connection with him.

This man was her husband.

Was it because she had glimpsed a side of him when he asked her about her rant with God? When she looked into his eyes, she had seen concern and a genuine desire to understand her feelings.

But she'd clamped up. The desire to tell Solomon all that resided in her and, in turn, share *his* thoughts was hard to ignore.

"I'm not meant to be happy, my lord. God took care of that some time ago."

"You said those words seven years ago, my lady," Goijaart said as she heard him get up and walk to her. "I don't understand why you said them then, and I don't understand why you are saying them now."

What to tell him? she thought. Even her knight hadn't known his lady's darkest secret. She decided to tell him part of the truth.

"I know you do not believe in God, my lord. But I beg you to oblige me while I try to share with you why I know that God has caused my discontentment."

He glanced away from her, his expression pensive. "It's not unbelief, my lady. Rather, a doubt as to whether or not any deity interferes with the affairs of men."

Celeste nodded in understanding. She knew Goijaart's secrets.

"My lord, I am ugly. Look at this face. It's the face only my mother could love. This body, skinny as a rail, bony hands, ankles and hips you can break eggs on. No one has ever looked at me twice." The words tumbled out like buttons from a jar. "Do you know how often my sister has been pursued by the opposite sex? My word sir, I've seen old men with arthritic backs try to stand straight when she walks by. Of course, no one knows what she's like until they get to know her, and then she is divested of her appeal. But to be admired at first glance." Celeste sighed as she walked away from him to go to the other side of greenhouse and stared out the moisture covered window. "Lord Westwood fell in love with her. At her worst. When the rage monster took her over and she nearly killed that serial rapist. Lord Westwood wanted her at her worst. And no man wants me. Or, so I thought.

"When Solomon asked me to marry him at the museum, he said it was for protection. He needed a wife to protect him. From what vice, I do not know. I wanted his name, to protect me from the fact no man would ever want to marry me at all. To protect me from the sight of seeing my sister marry the man I love. To get back at God for making me look like this.

"Yet, I feel as if in my heart, God created me this way so I would never get married." She whirled around on Goijaart, her face a mask of brewing hysteria and anger. "Why? Why did God make me this way? Why did I have to be the ugly one? My sister and I are from the same womb and yet, we're completely different. Why did Lord Westwood fall for my sister? How could he love someone with such a capricious nature?

"I did what I had to do to protect me. I became phlegmatic and dull. I deadened my hopes, my dreams, and my desires. I only lived for my costumes and my virtual followers. When I married Solomon, I told God, by my actions, that He didn't have any control over my destiny. I may not have a happy marriage, but I was wedded nonetheless.

"And now, Solomon wants to be with me. I'm scared."

"Why Celeste?"

"Don't you see it? I think Solomon wants me. I never expected that."

Goijaart turned away from her, and she noted in an abstract manner he seemed tense. "Isn't that what you want? A man to love you no matter what?"

"But God won't allow that for me. And for Solomon to start taking some kind of interest in his wife, then God would be even crueler to me."

"Why do you keep saying that?" He whirled around, his voice full of anguish.

Celeste saw the despair on his face, and she sighed. How so like her knight to be so concerned about her welfare. "I'm sorry, my lord. I'm babbling when I should be enjoying Grandmother Thomas' garden."

"Celeste, if you wanted to marry anyone, why didn't you marry me?"

Her body jerked in shock. "I beg your pardon?"

"Why didn't you try to contact me? If you were going to marry *anyone*, why not me?"

"My lord I—"

"Celeste, I am, your best friend. How many secrets have we shared over the years? I would have been the best husband for you, the one man who knows you better than anyone. You have never been unattractive to me—far from it. I've seen you grow up and change into a woman I admire. And then, after Granny died, you left me. When I called your cell, it no longer worked. Your mother and father said you had taken 'a job' in another state, and you didn't want to be contacted by anyone.

"I looked for you Celeste for almost a year but I couldn't find you. I gave up. And then, seven years later, I find you married to my other best friend and the years apart didn't exist. This," and he grabbed her gloved hand and held it in both of his. The black eyes glittered as they snared hers, "this bond we have is stronger than ever. Why didn't you trust me, Celeste?"

What could she tell him? That she would never make her knight unhappy by being married to her. She cared about their friendship too much to make him miserable.

"Can you forgive, my lord, for not trusting you?" She spoke finally, head bowed.

Goijaart sighed, and he grabbed her closer to him. She became enveloped by his body. Her head rested on his shoulder, and she breathed in the combination of his body as it mixed with the scent of plant life that surrounded them. "Of course, my lady."

They were quiet, and then she heard his voice speak into the stillness. "After seven years, what will you do?"

She exhaled as she continued to lay her head on his shoulder. Goijaart only stirred feelings of content and familial affection. Safe.

"We decreased the time to two years."

Goijaart jerked violently, and Celeste lifted her head. "What's wrong?"

"Nothing my lady," he croaked out. "Nothing at all. Suddenly, everything is right in the entire world."

HIS WIFE

This would probably be the first honeymoon in the history of man where a wife would rather knit than sleep with her husband. Solomon found himself satisfied with spending time with his wife bereft of sexual gratification. A concept he never expected.

"That man, my husband."

The words repeated in his mind and became more powerful.

Celeste had defended him. It blew his mind. A little over a month ago she had made it quite clear to him there was to be no matrimonial sentiments between them. Yet, two nights ago, she had defended him against her sister. With her defense, she acknowledged them as a unit.

He took a breath, lifted the barbell, and began to do his curls. He could see his reflection but didn't concentrate on it.

When everyone had left the room, she'd lifted her face toward him and started to speak, her eyes narrowed with anger and her voice like chipped ice. "Mr. Greene, how dare you arrogate to yourself decisions that do not belong to you!"

"What are you talking about, Celeste?" What did arrogate mean? He'd thought.

She'd risen and glided toward him, her gloved hands clasped in front of her. "I find it hard to comprehend you even had the temerity to announce a supposed honeymoon to our families."

Solomon had barely heard her. Her appearance had transfixed him. The gold lavishness of the room created a backdrop for her. It contrasted with her dress and reminded him of a queen. Celeste's chin jutted out in a stubborn manner. Her eyes had darkened to the color of molasses and shot out sparks. Instead of any sense of apprehension she may have hoped to evoke, he only saw an alluring woman.

"Why shouldn't we have a honeymoon, Celeste?"

"You know exactly why, Mr. Greene. I have been fastidious in elucidating what type of relationship this marriage is to be. However, you have defied every measure I have established to thwart the boundaries of this arrangement. I will not be a party to your artifice. I refuse to go anywhere with you."

Her little speech, delivered with a quivery, school teacher voice had been strangely appealing.

"Well, well, aren't you ripping me a new one." He hadn't been able to keep the amusement out his voice. All she needed was a ruler in her hand and a chalkboard behind her.

"Do not try to disparage me."

"The only reason why you don't want to come to Arcadia is because you are afraid." As soon as he said the words, he'd known they were true.

"I? Apprehensive?" Her face had reflected her confusion.

"No," he'd answered as he started walking toward her, "I didn't say apprehensive. I said afraid." He'd stopped in front of her. "You are afraid to be alone with me."

"Preposterous!" she'd exclaimed.

"Then why won't you do it?" he'd challenged and watched the expression of her face take on a hint of unease.

"I have already told you why."

"Oh, but my lady, I know that is the reason. Think of it. We'll be alone, just you and me. You won't be able to hide from me."

Solomon finished his set and rested the barbell on the floor. She denied that in her prim and proper fashion he found attractive. Maybe she started to see him as more than a title.

He had to admit he'd begun to see her as more than protection against beautiful women.

Exasperated with the admission, he picked up the barbell and started doing his next set.

When had that happened? At what point did Celeste begin to transform from being a woman whom he married to protect himself to being a woman he was starting to become fascinated with in a way he'd never had before with any other woman?

Mentally, he reviewed some of his past relationships, if he could call them that, from the time he turned eighteen.

There had been Vanessa James, his first hook-up in college. What did she look like? He could barely remember her face now. Had she been the one with the short curly red hair or was she the one with the blond hair? Dropping the barbell, he wiped his forehead and tried to think but her face didn't come up in his mind. At least he remembered her name.

Then there was Latisha Williams. Solomon remembered her distinctly because she'd been the choir girl who had watched him for a while before approaching him by the end of the first semester. Nice girl, nice body. He'd never heard her sing though, and they ended their fling about a month later.

After her were five drunken one-night-stands with girls whose faces he could barely see, much less remember.

He frowned as he went over to the dumbbells. He took two twenty pound weights, stood in front of the mirror, and started his squats as he lifted the dumbbells to his shoulders. With each move, he exhaled and balanced himself.

Next had been Tabitha—no, Tasha Long, the science girl. She had been a lot of fun, he thought in retrospection. She'd been the one with short curly red hair. Her focus had been in physics, and she used to spend hours talking to him over the phone about scientific things that sailed completely over his head; sleeping with her had made up for it. After a while, he'd grown bored with her and ended it.

Elizabeth Pepperwood was one of the women he'd regretted ever having a relationship with. Her purple hair and nose ring had added to her looks in a punk rock meets princess hauteur. She'd been manipulative and a liar although he'd didn't have any idea until she tried to make him marry her because she became pregnant. A paternity test solved that problem.

133

Breathing hard, he stopped doing the squats and wiped at the sweat on his neck. Come to think of it, just those few women had been in his first year in college. Staggered, he sat down on the bench and stared at his reflection. He'd slept with so many women and then later on, things had really gone downhill.

Solomon shook his head. There was the one woman he would never forget. Her face floated in his mind as the last time he'd seen her. The bloodshot eyes, a runny nose, and a quivering mouth that screamed at him.

He would never forget the blueberry woman.

What made Celeste different from every other woman he'd known?

Going over to the treadmill, he set the machine and then started to run.

Celeste did not have the drop dead gorgeous looks he gravitated to over the years, but her face was fast becoming the only one he wanted to see. She covered herself from head to toe in yards of fabric so he had no idea what her shape looked like, but that didn't matter. She went out of her way to avoid him. At first, he thought his growing interest was a response to a feminine ploy of playing hard to get. But it wasn't that. He liked the way she talked, nice and intelligently. A smile was rare but whenever he saw it, it lit her face. His wife was a mystery to him.

His wife.

Could the very fact that being his wife made all the difference?

Wasn't there a Bible verse about that? It had been years since he'd even seen a Bible much less touched one. Was having Celeste as his wife the major reason for his growing fixation on her?

His mind went back to Sunday night.

She had protested their honeymoon but in the end, he'd simply told her what he had told her earlier. "Nothing keeps me from what's mine, woman. And a honeymoon with my wife belongs to me."

At that, she had stilled and gazed into his face for a long moment, and he studied her back.

Quietly she'd spoken, "Are you going to constrain connubial rights upon me, sir?"

"What? No! What kind of man do you think I am? I've never had to force a woman to do anything in my life. I'm certainly not going to do that to my wife!"

"Very well, sir. If you see to the arrangements, I will make myself agreeable to your wishes."

"Celeste," he'd called out as she started to turn, "if you really don't want to go, we won't."

She turned back to him. "No, Solomon. I believe there are times when a husband gets his way, and his wife allows him to."

Then it happened, and the memory of it warmed him as it did two nights ago. She smiled, not at Gonzo, but at her husband. And she said his name and the sound of it on her lips was sweet.

LORD WESTWOOD

"Mr. Westwood is here to see you, Miss Celeste."

Celeste jerked up from the crocheting video she was recording for her YouTube channel and knocked it about. She pushed the stop button, and eased it away from the small desk.

"Please allow him entrance, Mr. Batcher," she told him as she stood from the chair in the den.

Lord Westwood sauntered through a moment later, smiling at her. Her eyes drank in his handsomeness. His hair shone like spun gold and the periwinkle eyes were filled with serenity and warmth as he came closer to her.

"My lady. It is good to see you. How are you?"

"I am well, my lord," Celeste answered and hoped the lump in her throat wasn't visible.

"That's good to hear," he responded. He came closer until he stood in front of her, leaned down, and wrapped his arms around her in a hug that enveloped her. Her breathing escalated.

It was torture. To be wrapped in his arms, inhaling his masculine scent, feeling the hard muscles through the fabric of his cotton clothes, and knowing that this man did not belong to her.

Lord Westwood pulled back, his face creased by smiles. Celeste glanced up at him before she turned and sat back down. She gestured to the armchair adjacent to her.

"Mr. Batcher," she addressed as he lurked in the hallway, "would you be so kind as to bring orange juice as well as the muffins Mrs. Houston made this morning? They were decadent."

Mr. Batcher nodded and turned from the doorway.

"So Celeste, how do you like your life as the wife of Solomon Greene?" Lord Westwood asked he sat.

I wanted to be your wife. I wanted to live my life as the wife of Jacob Othello Westwood. But you chose to fall in love with my sister. She could hardly say that though.

"I've become a lady of leisure," she said instead.

"What do you mean?" His brow furrowed.

"Well, Mr. Batcher is an excellent household manager. There is a cleaning service that comes every day. Mrs. Houston coordinates all the meals. A lawn care service is contracted to maintain the gardens. I've no need to leave the premises as I make all of my clothes. So, I have a lot of time to pursue my interests in full scale. I've never done such before."

"I hope to be able to provide the same kind of life for Leah," Lord Westwood stated as he sat back in the chair. "Of course, it won't be as nearly leisurely as you currently experience but she won't have to work. As a matter of fact, I just bought a house for her as a wedding present. I have the contractors making repairs on it and some updates, especially to the kitchen as you well know."

"What a wonderful present," Celeste spoke, as she tried to infuse joy into her voice while her heart broke.

"I haven't told her yet. I'm waiting until two months before the wedding so she can get all the decorating done or whatever. I'm glad the Lord has made it possible for me to do this for my soon to be wife."

"Indeed." Her throat constricted.

"That's an interesting dress you have on, Celeste. You look like Mary the First. Much prettier. What year is that from?"

"It's a replica of a 1521 gown I saw in a painting a few years ago." She glanced down at it. The blue velvet overdress contrasted with the underskirt in a vivid orange pattern doused with various colors. Gown sleeves covered a set of false sleeves underneath were ribbed with silver threading. As with most of her gowns, she didn't let any part of her chest show, so it came up to under her neck. The matching diamond shaped hood framed her face.

"I'm always amazed by your skill with a needle, Celeste. You truly are an artist in your own right."

The compliment warmed her, and she ducked her head shyly. "You are most kind, sir."

Lord Westwood cleared his throat and leaned forward. His arms rested on his legs. "I wanted to talk to you about last Sunday."

Celeste stood and went toward the window and clasped her hands in front of her. "What about it?"

"Leah is hysterical. You have not returned her calls at all, and she wants to apologize to you for her behavior."

"Martin's mercury is cold, Lord Westwood," Celeste answered as she continued to look out the window.

"I know you're upset with her. Leah's temper is always quick, volatile, and shorts out like a fuse. You know she feels awful for her actions."

"I understand Blaze very well, sir. After all, she's been my younger sister for all these years. However, Blaze needs to realize she cannot continue to give whim to her temper on account that a situation doesn't agree with her. She cannot always say the first thing that comes to her mind." Celeste swirled around. "She insulted my in-laws. She insulted my husband at my wedding reception. Does she really think a quick voicemail will absolve her?"

"Do you think your continued silence is going to make it go away, Celeste?"

Her eyes widened in shock. "Do you imply I am wrong?"

"Yes Celeste, but not in the way you mean."

Heat flushed through her. "I beg your pardon."

"Hear me out Celeste. It's true what Leah did was wrong but it's also true by not speaking to her, you are prolonging a conflict between the two you. You are only making things worse."

Celeste walked until she loomed over him. "Sir, you are cognizant my sister possesses a temper sorely in need of restraint?"

"I do."

"Have you been apprised of her conduct when she met my husband?"

"I was there."

"Then pray sir, why are you here?"

Jacob put his hands together under his chin and stared at her. His periwinkle eyes that had only moments ago been the catalyst for making her ache with unrequited longing were filled with a patronizing expression.

"I would expect this type of attitude from Leah, Celeste. Not from you. Both of you can't act like children, and I believe it is time for you to revert back to adulthood."

After he had finished speaking, Celeste stared at him. What had happened? In an instant, his hair did not seem nearly as close to spun gold as she thought. The color was too pale. She preferred Solomon's inky spiked hair. The periwinkle eyes were too soft and calm, placid like a lake hidden in a forest. Her husband's eyes flared with vibrancy, the gold flecks igniting like fire.

Suddenly, he was no longer Lord Westwood. The title she had given him became absurd. All he would ever be from this moment on was Jacob. And Jacob had ticked her off.

Mr. Batcher entered the room with the orange juice and muffins arranged on a small cart and prepared to set it between them.

"I'm sorry Mr. Batcher to put you through all the trouble, but Jacob was just leaving."

Jacob's eyebrows arched in his forehead. "Excuse me?"

"Mr. Batcher, will you see Jacob out?"

"You're upset."

"Get out Jacob," Celeste spoke quietly.

She turned around and faced the window again. She heard the dishes tinkle behind her and the rustle of fabric as muted footprints brushed against the carpeted floor. A moment later, an arm wrapped itself around her.

"I'll come back some other time, my lady."

And then Jacob Westwood kissed her on her cheek, his lips firm against her skin and soft but lacking the effect they had the last time they touched her face.

She said nothing to him and then she heard him leave.

"Do you need anything else right now, Miss Celeste?"

"No, Mr. Batcher. You can leave the food."

The door closed behind her, and she turned around. She just showed Jacob Westwood the door. The man she had been in love with for over two years. Celeste sat down in the chair and stared at the yarn on the table, but her thoughts were elsewhere.

Jacob Westwood had been the man of her dreams. The one man she wanted to marry and become his wife. She knew as a minister, he would accept her and maybe God would give her what he wanted in the form of him.

She leaned back in the chair and allowed her mind to travel back to the day before he met Leah and her dreams came to an end.

They had been at the library. She had pretended to look at an old book showing antique knitting designs, and he worked on a paper for one of his classes at seminary.

The sun had made guest appearances on that cloudy day. The trees had started to change colors and gold, brown, and red leaves were as vibrant as jewels as the wind rustled them gently to the ground. She had been happy as she basked in Jacob Westwood's presence while he explained some theological point to her. It didn't matter what he said; she'd agree with anything as long as he stayed with her.

"You know Celeste, I'm so glad I met you," Jacob had whispered suddenly, his eyes fixed on her.

"Why do you say that, sir?" She'd felt as if she were about to fly through the ceiling.

"You've been such a great help to me these past few weeks. I appreciate it."

"The pleasure is mine, Lord Westwood."

Lord Westwood had laughed and threw back his head. She could remember the way his neck looked, strong and masculine.

"You don't have to call me that, Celeste." He'd told her, his eyes filled with mirth.

"I know and I only do when it's just us."

"Why?"

"You remind me of someone who was very close to me."

"An old boyfriend?"

"No, just a very good friend."

"Ah, sweet Celeste," Lord Westwood had said. Later on, as they left the library, they'd stood off to the side of the door. The view had been glorious. The hazy sun had started to dip behind the clouds and the color of the leaves was muted by the setting sun. The wind blew softly. It had rustled her medieval gown and sent the corded belt at her waist swaying.

"I'll see you in a couple of days," he'd said and then he leaned down and kissed her cheek and she nearly burst from joy. It was possible that this man cared about her. He didn't find her ugly or strange, and he just kissed her right in public.

And then the next day, it had all changed.

Jacob met her sister and the rest was history.

Almost a year later, Leah had come bursting into her room, her eyes shooting off sparkles of delight. Celeste had known instantly before Leah opened her mouth.

"Icy! Icy! Jacob asked me to marry him!" Leah had squealed as she ran, grabbed Celeste in a bear hug and jumped up and down.

At that moment, the sun's light brightened the room to a flaming gold and Leah had jumped away from her. "Oh look, Icy! The sun's shining so bright I can barely see! God must be happy for me too! Yippee! I'm getting married! I'm getting married!" Leah had run out the room before Celeste could say anything. Not that she could have spoken; she had turned to a pillar of ice.

The sadness didn't leave her for weeks as she watched her sister bask in her pre-martial arrangements and saw the increasing number of visits Jacob made to their home. She had spied on them, tortured herself even as she listened to them whisper to each other. Once, she had come upon them kissing so passionately she was sure that had she not "happened" to bump into them, it would have gone further.

So she had taken more modeling jobs — pulling apart bread rolls, holding lotion bottles, dialing cell phones, typing on laptops, untwisting jars of peanut butter, showcasing jewelry and anything else. The rivalry between Daffodil and herself had started to escalate by then and despite the fact she didn't know the source of that woman's animosity toward her, she allowed herself to be swept by it. Invitations for various shows, fairs, and balls had started to come through, and she began to attend them all, showcasing her costumes. She did almost anything to keep from thinking about Lord Westwood and her sister. Her anger at God grew with each passing week, almost like bile collecting at the back of her throat.

A modeling job had sent her to Denver, Colorado that fateful day. A friend of her agent had asked for her to model some antiques for a silent video auction, and she'd acquiesced. She'd often gone to museums to get more ideas for her costumes, and that day had not been any different. Besides, Denver was gorgeous, and she'd like the city whenever she traveled there. When she'd seen the man studying her favorite portrait of a married couple from the 16th century, she had no idea she would leave the museum an engaged woman.

She came out her thoughts and picked up a muffin. She bit into as she relished the softness.

After all this time and with just this one incident, Celeste realized she didn't care for Jacob like she thought she did. Especially since he had the audacity to come to her home and tell her she needed to make up with her sister. His kiss had meant nothing.

What had changed?

She continued to eat as she pondered this thought, going over it around and around in her mind. And then it hit her. God had answered her prayer in one fell swoop. Her desire, her longing for her sister's fiancé disappeared. Two years of hopeless longing for a man that did not belong to her. Just moments ago, he had been the epitome of the man she wanted to spend her life with. A kiss on the cheek had turned her into his worshipper. Yet, how well did she really know him? She hadn't spent much time with him. After he fell for Blaze, she'd limited her interaction with him and yet held on to the fantasy. On Sunday, she had likened him to the god Eros and Tuesday, he was just Jacob. A man she'd just kicked out her home.

Finally, one prayer answered.

A knock on the door broke in on her musings, and Mr. Batcher entered a second later.

"Mr. Thomas is here to see you, Miss Celeste."

At his words, Celeste realized what had changed. And she smiled, "Show him in, please. And tell Solomon, won't you?"

No sooner had Goijaart entered the room than Celeste leapt up and threw her arms around his neck. An instant later, his arms clasped her to his body, and he peered down at her from a bemused face.

"Oh Goijaart! I am no longer in love with Jacob."

Her knight's arms tightened around her waist. "Well, my lady, a 'good morrow' would have done nicely but this is infinitely better. And you seem to be radiant with the knowledge that you are no longer in love with your sister's fiancé."

"I'm free of him! I'm free of him, sir!" Her arms clutched him around his neck as she squealed in delight. Free of the fantasy of Lord Westwood!

Goijaart lifted and whirled her in the air and set her down again. "You are so slender, my lady," he murmured in a low tone as his eyes drifted to watch his hands. They encircled her waist and caressed her sides.

"Fie on you, sir!" Celeste laughed, "You are well acquainted with the fact I am skinny as a toothpick."

"Really? I hadn't noticed," Goijaart stated. His eyes probed into hers with warmth. "All I see is a slim Nubian princess that sparkles like dark sapphire. A princess I have given my homage to countless times on many occasions." He bent his head further until his face blocked out everything else. In a distracted manner, she noted if Goijaart came any closer, his lips would touch hers. The knowledge of how close his mouth was to her didn't penetrate too deeply, and she dismissed it.

"Of course, a knight must please his lady," Celeste spoke as she smiled up at him.

"A knight? No merely a man longing for the heart of —"

"Gonzo, get your hands off my wife!"

RIVALS

Volcanic rage rushed through his body at the sight of Gonzo's arms wrapped so intimately around his wife and his mouth mere centimeters apart from her lips. Solomon barely kept a restraint on his temper as he stepped further into the room.

"Solomon, is something amiss?" Celeste's eyes were wide and guileless.

"'Is something amiss?'" Solomon mocked in a falsetto voice. "You bet there's something amiss, woman." He bit out, his gaze focused on his best friend as he removed his arms, slowly, from around her waist. His stomach churned. Celeste acted like the Ice Maiden from the coldest pit of the underworld but Gonzo all but kissed her, and would have if he hadn't shown up.

"Gonzo, what are you doing?" Solomon asked in a low tone as he folded his arms across his chest.

"Why nothing, Solomon," Celeste answered before Gonzo could respond.

Solomon studied his wife. Their very positions when he entered the room should have condemned them as lovers. But as he drowned in the open sincerity of her maple syrup eyes, he knew his wife had no idea how suggestive their embrace had been. All she'd seen was her best friend from childhood.

His temper died a little. For all of her eccentricities, Celeste wouldn't go behind his back and play loose.

As he shifted his gaze to Gonzo, his anger returned. On the other hand, Gonzo knew *exactly* what he did.

"Celeste, I need you to leave now," Solomon told her as he held Gonzo's gaze.

"Whatever for? Goijaart was here to see me."

"Gooey yard," his voice dripped with sarcastic accuracy, "and I have some things to discuss."

Gonzo stepped away from Celeste and Solomon saw his best friend held his scrutiny with a challenged expression of his own. It wasn't a competition on their skateboards. This was a declaration of intent.

"But Solomon," Celeste began once more and Solomon saw the confusion on her face.

"Just for a few moments, Celeste." It won't take too long to break both his arms.

"Please, my lady," Gonzo added his voice, "just for a few moments. This won't take long."

"Very well," Celeste said as she threw her supplies in a basket near her chair and glided out the room.

After she had left, Solomon exploded. A snarl erupted from his throat and the rage he'd barely kept in check unleashed. He wanted to pulverize Gonzo, rip his hands off his arms. Why did he have to hold Celeste so close to him? The way he'd caressed her waist and stared down into her face made Solomon want to beat the tar out him.

"What do you think you're doing?" He stalked toward Gonzo and grabbed a handful of his shirt. He twisted the material around his fist and started to choke him. He watched as the red flooded into his face. His lips had almost kissed his wife!

Gonzo struggled against his hold, his hands clawed at their grip. Finally, through significant effort, he unlatched his hand and shoved him, breaking his hold. He gulped in air as his eyebrows were drawn into a V. "Staking a claim," he gushed out after a few moments.

"On my wife?"

"Your temporary wife, Sol. You said yourself you don't want her. She's not pretty enough. And we both know pretty is all you want."

Solomon's teeth were clenched so tightly he felt the pressure would soon crack his jaw.

"Dude, she's still my wife!"

"Really? Your ugly wife?" Gonzo snorted and jammed his fists into his pockets. "You don't care about Celeste. But I do. I have every intention of taking your wife from you."

"I can't believe this. You sound like you're in a soap opera. You're going to take my wife from me? Dude, are you freaking kidding me?"

Gonzo stared at him and then turned away. He walked over to the window and ran a hand through his hair in an agitated gesture. "Sol, I had no idea it would come to this. When I saw Celeste again, I saw this girl who I grew up with, who knew all my secrets, all my bad, all my good, all my crazy and I could barely breathe! I didn't even know I felt this way until I saw her again. I'm in love with Celeste."

Solomon arched his eyebrow at the word 'love'. "So you just want to sleep with her? Man, you can sleep with anyone, not my wife!"

Gonzo whirled on him, his lips curled in disgust, his eyes narrowed and his nose scrunched like a ball of paper. "You don't get it, do you Sol? It's not about sleeping with her. I used to think love was just another word for sex. But the moment I saw her again, I knew it had to be more than that. If she lost both her legs, and her arms, and her face was cut up with a knife, I'd still want her. If she got into a car accident and became mentally unstable, I'd be with her. You think I'd feel that way about any woman?"

Gonzo folded his arms. "I tried to fight this, Sol. After all, you're my best friend. But when she told me you both planned to split anyway, I saw my opportunity."

"That's why you haven't been coming to the park. You've been schmoozing with my wife while I'm gone!" Solomon's fist curled at the idea of Gonzo touching his wife.

"I knew Celeste first, Sol! Not you! That gives me every right to go after her. And no, I haven't been schmoozing with your wife. Even after three months of knowing her, do you really think she'd do that?"

No, Celeste wouldn't. Hadn't she told him Gonzo wasn't her lover? Neither her husband?

Solomon stared at his best friend and a wave of helpless anger almost swallowed him. It would be almost too easy for Gonzo to take Celeste from him. He had the years, the relationship, and the perspective of understanding his wife. Hadn't he seen that on the day they had reconnected? The little fantasy world they created would be part of their lives, connecting them closer and closer until they were one unit with two parts.

Further, Gonzo had been around with other women but not to the extent Solomon had. Those women wouldn't form a barrier between them. They wouldn't haunt his dreams like lingering spirits.

This love thing. Gonzo affirmed it wasn't sexual desire. But love had to be physical. It couldn't be more. Could it?

But Celeste had smiled at him. She did say his name. They were going to go on a honeymoon. Could it be maybe she'd begun to warm up to him? Did his wife see him as more than just a walking title? Did he want to do what it took to find out?

Gonzo was going after his wife. Did he want to go after her too?

The idea startled him. When was the last time he'd have to go after any woman? Had he ever? Since age fifteen, every girl, and then woman he'd been with gave themselves to him. He'd never had to exert any kind of effort to get a girl to sleep with him. At one point in the last year or so, he had a different woman every night for a month.

Celeste was the first woman who had plainly stated she didn't want him. What would it be like to try to make her actually want him? What would he have to do?

A sense of anticipation went through him as he sifted through various scenarios.

He pulled himself from his thoughts. "All right Gonzo. Since you want to do this, we will do this. I'll even let you keep coming over here. I'm going after her too. And since I'm married to her, I guess I have the home court advantage."

Solomon turned around and walked out the room, calling over his shoulder, "You should have stuck to skating."

REANNE

A week later, Patrick put the last touch on the breakfast buffet in the small dining room. Tension crackled like lightning between the Exalted Son and the Reverend Daughter as they sat at the table.

The Reverend Daughter radiated her usual loveliness. She had chosen to wear her hair in a bun and adorned herself with a simple pink sheath dress that came just below the knee. Her slender arms were bare except for a pink pearl bracelet and a thin gold watch. The Exalted Son dressed in a black suit with a silk gold shirt and tie. The suit jacket hung on the back of his chair. His wedding ring glistened under the light, and he had a titanium watch on his left wrist.

Patrick sensed they were disgusted with each other.

"Do you want to serve yourselves?" Patrick asked in an effort to diminish the strained atmosphere.

"Yes, old boy. Thank you." Theodore said as he placed his napkin on his lap.

Patrick started to leave when the Reverend Daughter's voice stopped him. "No, Batcher. I want you to serve us. After all, that is what you are here for, isn't it?"

Patrick bit back a response as a wave of anger flushed his system. Only Cordelia could make him feel so low. He knew the reason he was there. Again, Kishori's image floated into his mind and with it came a tsunami of emotion. Determinedly he squashed the memory. If Cordelia wanted to use his service as a constant reminder of what he did to her, then he would not give that woman the hint that what she said affected him.

"Now why did you have to say that, Cordelia? Just leave the old boy alone. Don't take your anger out on him."

"You'd rather I allow myself to rant and rave against Reanne?"

Patrick's mouth almost dropped open. Reanne Listner was Cordelia's right hand in the Washed Saints organization, aptly titled

'First Daughter'. As executive assistant and priestess, she often researched and developed the Reverend Daughter's sermons. A devout follower, Reanne had refused a salary for her services and in return, the Washed Saints paid her expenses.

He knew of very few others in the Washed Saints hierarchy as slavishly devoted to the Blessed Dyad.

What did she do? Patrick thought.

"You better not say a word to her. I think you know exactly what would happen if you do." Theodore's bushy eyebrows had drawn so close together they could easily resemble a "unibrow."

Cordelia's alabaster face flushed. The rose hip color only added to her beauty.

"So I'm to ignore the fact you're sleeping with one of our devotees?"

"I don't care what you choose to ignore or not. What I want you to do is keep quiet. Reanne is innocent in all this, and I will not have my indiscretion give her any reason to doubt her faith."

Reanne and Theodore? Patrick fought to keep his facial features void of expression.

"Batcher, give me a waffle, two sausage patties, two bacon strips, hash browns, and fried apples," Cordelia ordered as she fixed her gaze on her husband.

Patrick turned to dish up the food. His mind still reeled from the idea Theodore was sleeping with Reanne.

"The same for me too, old boy," the Exalted Son added.

Five minutes later as he placed their respective plates before them and then poured orange juice in their glasses, the doorbell rang.

"Remember what I said," warned Theodore.

"I can lie very well, Theo. Just not as well as you it would seem."

Patrick walked out the room to the foyer. As he reached the door, he schooled himself to keep his features to show polite indifference.

"Good morning, Ms. Listner," he greeted.

As the Exalted Son had fallen into sin with this woman, Patrick studied her covertly as she greeted him in her wispy voice.

There wasn't much particularly remarkable about the woman. Her hair was carrot bright like Pippi Longstocking and poppy hued spots were scattered across her cheeks. Sky blue eyes rested in a face that would be nondescript without the freckles. An average nose, thin lips, and serviceable clothes added to a woman a man would quickly forget about.

This woman tempted the Exalted Son? Patrick thought as he closed the door and allowed her to walk in front of him where he could see her shape.

Nothing fantastic about that either.

As they entered the room, Cordelia looked up. She smiled what he secretly termed as the Barbie grin. Her lips stretched tightly over the brilliant white teeth but her eyes were devoid of emotion.

The Reverend Daughter stood as the woman came forward and knelt before her.

"Bless me, Reverend Daughter. Hail Cordelia, full of grace," Reanne intoned. She reached forward and lifted the hem of Cordelia's dress and placed it in her mouth.

"O pure Virgin," the Reverend Daughter started as she placed her hands on the redhead, "release your cleansing power, release your purity. Flow from the garment into your First Daughter." Reanne shuddered as she prayed.

He flicked his gaze over to Theodore. The man watched the proceedings with his hands clasped under his chin. His gray eyes seemed to bore a hole at the woman's supplication before the Reverend Daughter.

"Thank you, dear Virgin," Reanne said as she stood once more.

"Would you like to eat with us at the table?" Cordelia asked as she sat down.

"No, Reverend. It would be an honor but I am ready to do whatever you need me to do."

"Just as you would for the Exalted Son?" she replied as she raised a forkful of hash browns to her lips.

"I would do whatever you ask of me, Reverend." Reanne promised.

"What a faithful and obedient follower," she answered back. "What is on the schedule today?"

Patrick went forward and pushed the chair under Reanne.

Theodore got up from his untouched plate. He put his jacket on and tugged at the lapels.

"I have to go to the church to prepare today's sermons."

Reanne turned toward him, and Patrick watched as unobtrusively as possible as he gathered the Exalted Son's dishes.

"Exalted Son, will I be seeing you later this evening?"

Theodore smiled as he strode over to the First Daughter and placed his hand on her shoulder. "I'll be there."

Reanne kissed his hand and turned back to the Reverend Daughter.

Patrick saw Cordelia hold the fork tightly in her hand like a knife as she continued to smile the Barbie grin.

"I shall see you soon, my dear," Theodore said.

Reanne had to be a great actress. She talked business to the Reverend Daughter as the woman finally began to eat again. He saw the green gold flames in her eyes each time she looked up, which was probably why she kept her head down most of their conversation.

Patrick placed the dishes on the small cart he had on the side of the breakfast buffet and then stood while Reanne and the Reverend Daughter talked business for about a half hour. In all truth, he could have left but he was more than curious to see how Cordelia handled herself as she conversed with her husband's mistress.

That wasn't pure at all.

###

Celeste finished the edit on her latest video on embroidery and uploaded it to her YouTube channel. While she waited, she clicked open her email and browsed through her inbox. A few of her followers had sent questions and videos for her advice, and she prepared to answer them when the daffodil icon dominated her screen.

She sighed as she turned on the recorder and answered the phone.

"What do you want Daffodil?" she said without preamble.

"And good day to you too, Celeste," Daffodil answered mockingly.

Celeste didn't respond as she waited for Daffodil to give the reason why she had called.

"So Celeste dear, how long has it been now since you joined in holy matrimony?"

Her body stiffened in alarm. Daffodil had deliberately decided to call her out on the wager and in front of their followers no less.

"Three months as you are well aware," Celeste stated.

"That's a long time in today's world, don't you think?" Daffodil's image froze for a split second and then moved again. She rested her head on her thumb and forefinger. Once again, Celeste became painfully aware of her beauty. Today, she'd tamed her wild hair into ringlets on either side of her head. Dressed in a late Regency gown hued in a coral color added a sense of delicacy to her image.

Celeste remained silent as she waited for the woman to say her piece. She didn't have long to wait.

"I remember the last time we talked you said you were planning to start a family."

It took every ounce of control not to groan in frustration. Now she would be inundated with emails from their respective followers who would wonder about her state of maternity. And for Daffodil to make it public was a stab in the back. She had sent the wager to her privately and for all intents and purposes, Celeste had meant for it to stay that way.

"No, not yet Daffodil," Celeste ground out between her teeth as she attempted to sound normal. "Though I can hardly believe you would care."

"Oh but Celeste I do. Just think, if you get pregnant by this time next year, you'll be able to attend the maternity ball Valencia is holding."

And with that, Daffodil had successfully put all the pieces of their wager on the open channels of the Internet. Celeste's body chilled as she struggled with the anger that threatened to turn her into an ice sculpture.

"So, what do you say? If you're pregnant by next year, are you going to enter the contest at Valencia's ball?"

"Yes," Celeste bit out.

"Splendid!"

Her hand tingled with the desire to slap the smirk off Daffodil's face. The woman thought she had all the cards in her hand. Slowly, Celeste smiled as she said, "You won't be seeing me for a few weeks Daffodil."

The smirk dropped from her face. "Why is that?"

"My husband and I will be going on our honeymoon in Florida. His family owns a villa on Tampa."

The look that came on Daffodil's face surprised her. She'd expected annoyance or even amusement. What she saw was an expression of rage.

"You! Going on a honeymoon? You must be joking."

Celeste arched her eyebrow. "Why would I jest about something like that? Most newlyweds *do* have honeymoons."

"You can stop lying now, Celeste. No man would want to be seen dead with your ugly self."

Celeste knew she should be startled by the vehemence of Daffodil's verbal attack. Indeed, she should be shouting back at her. But something prompted her to stare deeper into Daffodil's face. Beyond the beauty, beyond the arrogance she saw something blazed through her eyes. Instantly she recognized it. She'd experienced it herself many times before as she stood in her younger sister's shadow.

Daffodil Simmons was jealous of her.

The idea seemed preposterous, but Celeste knew it was true. For all her looks, there existed something in Celeste she envied. What it could possibly be, she had no idea. Why hadn't she been aware of it before? Had her icy defense numbed her to all feeling, not just hers?

"Regardless to what you believe Daffodil, I am going on my honeymoon."

The woman curled her lip grotesquely even as a sob escaped her lips. Her eyes filled suddenly with a bright, moist sheen. A quick motion of her hand and the screen went blank.

Celeste sat back in the chair stunned. What in the world had just happened? This side of Daffodil had been a bombshell. What about Celeste could she possibly desire?

A WALK IN THE TWILIGHT

"Hello Mr. and Mrs. Greene," Celeste greeted her in-laws as she sat at the table in small dining room.

It had been three weeks since she'd seen them. They had been in residence, but it became apparent their religious duties took them out the house for hours on end. The mansion's size made it easy for them not to see each other for days. Except for quick snatches of conversation and social trivialities on the go, she had very little interaction with them.

"Hello, Celeste. It's good to see you today. Sorry we're eating late," Mr. Greene said as he sat down across from her smiling. Her father-in-law reminded her of a wrestler, but his kind eyes seemed to have more impact on her than his size. "I see you're wearing one of your costumes again. You look like a princess from the fairytales. It looks nice."

Celeste glanced down at her attire as she thanked him. It was an attempt to mimic the dress from the painting of The Arnolfini Portrait. She had of course changed the color of the dress to match her taste. A deep hued purple, it was lined with yards of black faux fur she had found at a party store some years ago. White faux fur underlined the white underdress. The most difficult part had been the dagging—folding the material, sewing it together, and then cutting it to make it fray as decoratively as in the portrait but she believe she'd done a good imitation. She didn't make the horn headdress the same as the portrait. She preferred to match her dress with a divided black hennin, the conical shaped halves to the right and left of her head with a purple linen veil coming to the end of her forehead.

"I don't know how you do it. Your talent is extraordinary," He continued, leaning back as Mr. Batcher put a plate of food in front of him.

"Thank you Mr. Greene. Grandmother Thomas often remarked she believed me to be a prodigy in regards to hand arts."

"Gonzo's grandmother was very good at those kinds of things," Mrs. Greene interjected as she placed a cloth napkin on her lap. "I'm glad she was able to pass her talent on to you. Gonzo would have died of boredom."

"Is that why you always wear gloves? To protect your hands?"

Celeste waited while Mr. Batcher put the plate in front of her and she thanked him. "I am a parts model."

"A parts model?" Mr. Greene inquired as he took a sip of water.

"Specifically, I am a hand model. I'd be most pleased to show you my portfolio when you have some time."

"Wonderful! I've never met a hand model before," Mr. Greene said with pleasure and Celeste found herself warming up to her father-in-law.

Suddenly, her skin became charged, and she knew Solomon had entered the dining room before he called out, "Sorry I'm late," as he took the seat next to her.

"Hello my sweet," he greeted, the pet name completely unexpected just as the kiss he placed on her cheek. His lips were firm and warm. An electric current went through her at the pressure. She fought to control her reaction to him. After all, he had to be doing it because his parents were with them for the first time since the wedding reception. The last three weeks had been the strangest she'd experience with her husband.

Somehow, without being quite certain how it happened, she had been persuaded to take a walk with him every morning at precisely half past seven. The first time it had happened, she had opened her bedroom door to see her husband standing outside of it, dressed casually in a long sleeved shirt and loose fitting pants.

"Good morning, Celeste," he'd greeted her, a wide smile on his face.

"Good morrow, sir," she'd responded. Surprise had mastered her body as she stood stone still in the doorway.

"I was hoping to catch you. Would you like to take a walk this morning? I usually don't get up this early, but I wanted to talk to you about our honeymoon."

"Our honeymoon?"

"Yes. Would you walk with me Celeste?"

As she thought back to that time, she had no idea why she allowed herself to agree with his suggestion, especially after his manner with Goijaart the day before. She had wanted to keep her distance from him and eradicate the closeness she began to feel toward him.

Perhaps she acquiesced because of the way the morning sunlight from the window in her bedroom touched his coal black hair and gave it the texture of black satin. The light had also turned his skin to bronze. Or maybe it was how he gazed at her, the green gold eyes steady and warm. Once more, his handsomeness threatened to overwhelm her.

It turned out they didn't speak at all during that first walk. The mansion sat on several acres of land, and the gardens were designed with walking paths. It had been a beautiful morning, and the dew sparkled like miniature diamonds in the sunlight. They strolled side by side. She was dressed in a 1908 tweed walking suit, the jacket long as it came past her hips. The long skirt trailed behind her. The walking stick she had brought with her was fashionable for the time, of course. Her hair was tied in a loose braid and stuffed under a hat. What a contrast it had been to Solomon's modern attire with well-abused gym shoes as they made muted footsteps on the path.

Yet, it had been a good walk. After an hour, they returned to the house and Solomon left her to attend to his own pursuits and she had breakfast in her den.

Since that day, they'd walked every morning. Solomon always met her in front of her room. Sometimes they talked about trivial things and other times they strode in complete silence. She now anticipated her morning constitutionals with her husband.

The last three weeks had also caused him to spend time with her. He would come upon her suddenly as she worked on her numerous projects or recorded learning videos for her YouTube channels. Slowly, she began to share parts of her life with him. He had been surprised at the number of followers she'd had online and how many invitations she'd received from balls and amateur costume functions.

Solomon fast became a fixture to her days.

"My lady?"

Solomon's voice roused her from her inner thoughts, and she turned to him. The green gold orbs assessed her with interest even as they lit with amusement.

"Yes Solomon?"

"Mother asked you a question," he answered as his lips lifted in a grin. Her heart throbbed in her chest.

Swiftly she turned to Mrs. Greene, "Forgive me for my wayward thoughts."

"I asked if you had plans for the weekend. I figured we'd go to a spa for some much needed mother and daughter-in-law time. I've been so busy with the Virgin's tasks I've scarcely had time to meet and get to know my new daughter. And I'm sure you've never been to a spa before; it'll be a treat for you."

It wasn't the first time Celeste noted how her mother-in-law had the propensity to mix a kind gesture with a condescending attitude. It made for a frustrated exchange. Yet, Celeste managed to restrain herself and not respond. Quite possibly, the woman had no idea she was like that.

Don't delude yourself. It's also quite possible a worm can knit.

"No, I do not have any plans, Mrs. Greene. I am honored with your inclusion of me in your recreation."

"I just love the way she talks, don't you Solomon?" Mr. Greene said around a piece of meat.

"It's one of those things I find amazing about her, Dad," Solomon answered and Celeste felt her face warm again. He *had* to be saying that for his parents' sake. He didn't really mean it.

Dinner became a leisurely meal. Tilapia fillets with jasmine rice and asparagus. Not the most imaginative meal she'd ever eaten. Admittedly, after a few months of Mrs. Houston's cooking, Celeste was inclined to agree with Leah. The food left a lot to be desired. When Leah turned sixteen, she had taken over all the meal preparation for the family. When it came to cooking, she became fanatical about its perfection. Leah refused to serve any meal unless she deemed it perfect. Having been exposed to such standards, eating less than that was tough to swallow. Literally.

The thought of her sister reminded her she had yet to speak to her. Since Jacob's visit, her sister hadn't called, and Celeste realized it *was* time to make up with her. After all, she couldn't stay mad indefinitely. What would be the purpose?

"I'd like to invite you to come to the church some time, Celeste. I want to broaden your mind and expand the narrow-minded focus you've undoubtedly had as a Christian."

Her father-in-law sighed. "Cordelia, really. Do you have to bring up religion at the dinner table?"

"I was talking to Celeste. It's our duty by the Virgin's command we bring the lost ones into the fold."

Celeste studied her mother-in-law as she analyzed how she felt about the statement. In truth, she had been brought up in a Christian home but didn't necessarily align herself to her parents' belief. She believed in God, but He had disappointed her with her unanswered prayers. But that had been before she married Solomon.

She thought she would never marry, but she did, unorthodox as it was. She thought she would never have a man show interest in her, but her husband did. The idea of having a home of her own had been

165

a dream but now she lived in a mansion. Even more amazing was that Solomon was the only other man outside of Goijaart who would allow her fantasy world she lived in. The love for Jacob vanished in a single instant.

So, in truth, God had answered her prayers. Just not in the way she thought it would be.

Perhaps there was more to this faith than she thought. Maybe, just maybe, she could delve deeper into this.

She thought about her mother-in-law's invitation to see her church. The fact her in-laws were cult leaders had been one that didn't bother her. It would be interesting to see.

"I'll let you know, Mrs. Greene," she answered finally.

"Good. So tell me, when do you leave for Arcadia?" Mr. Greene responded quickly as if he wanted to get on another topic as soon as possible.

"Next week," Solomon replied as he played with a few grains of rice on his plate. "We plan to stay there for about two to three weeks. It depends. Morayo said she was getting the bedrooms ready."

"Morayo?" Celeste asked.

"Morayo Hernandez. She's our household manager in Florida," Mrs. Greene responded. "A very capable woman from Cuba. She'll see to all your needs while you're there. Batcher, bring dessert."

The distance between her mother and father-in-law could almost be seen tangibly. They conversed with each other, but the conversation was so stilted it reminded Celeste of two very poor actors in a stage play.

After they had eaten the travesty of an apple pie, they began to leave the table. Celeste found her pathway of escape blocked by Solomon.

"Celeste, I know it's getting late but will you take a stroll with me in the gardens?"

"Is there any particular reason why we should walk now?" Celeste inquired. She wasn't sure if she should take an evening stroll with her husband. Especially when her heart beat like a steady drum. The rhythm increased as she stared into his eyes.

"Yes." It was as much of a command as a declaration. His eyes gleamed with challenge.

"Solomon, I'm sure Celeste would prefer to stay indoors. It's almost nine and will be getting dark soon."

Perhaps if her mother-in-law hadn't spoken, she would not have deigned to go out with him. True to Celeste's contrarian nature, she said, "Very well."

A warm wind met them as they started down the trail ten minutes later. Celeste sighed, content for the first time in her life. It was the most natural of past times to walk with her husband surrounded by an orchestra of sight and sound.

The sun set and the clouds were tinged by a dark hued pink, which accentuated the coming nightfall. The moon began its ascent and brilliant, vibrant light illuminated the world below. Silhouettes of trees rustled gently, and the cacophony of night rodents and insects filled the air.

Celeste inhaled deeply the perfume of the many flowers as they continued to traverse on the path, a comfortable silence between them. If a perfect moment existed, this was it.

The walk continued and then she felt Solomon grab her arm and gently tugged her down a path hidden from the main trail. Nonplussed, she followed him. The short detour led down a small walkway nestled by large bushes and then opened up to a clearing lit by several large lanterns.

A breathtaking view met her astonished eyes. A small manmade pond was surrounded by smooth stones made wet from a recycling waterfall. Not too far from it loomed a gazebo, white with vines and ivy wrapped around its posts. As Solomon drew her nearer, rose bushes lined the stairs and they ascended into the interior. Two white wicker benches, wide enough to seat two were angled toward each other while in the midst of them rested a tiny table covered with green cloth lit by two candles and between them a box.

Solomon guided her to one of the benches and sat her down while he sat on the other. The shadows of the candlelight danced on his face.

"Oh, Solomon!" Celeste exclaimed, her voice full of surprise and wonder.

He loved the way Celeste said his name. It didn't make any sense, but his name on her lips became an expression of art.

Since he started to pursue her, he found she allowed him more headway into her life. In a short period of time, he realized the day didn't have any significance unless it started with her. Despite competing for her against Gonzo, he found himself *wanting* to see her at some point in the day. Every time he glanced upon her or saw her or talked with her, the moment became etched in his mind.

Finally, he began to see glimpses of Celeste the woman, not the distant wife in these few short months. She smiled more at him and each time, he felt something inside of him constrict with pleasure. *Idle hands do the devil's work.* Celeste took that adage literally, so she constantly had some form of hand craft with her. She liked old-fashioned knickknacks as he discovered one day when she mentioned it in an offhand manner. Although she kept a barrier between them, slowly it started to come down.

He wanted to make tonight special for reasons he still couldn't quite formulate. If there was no such thing as love or if love was merely a synonym for sex, then why would he go through all this trouble for a night of lovemaking?

Even as the thought formed, he immediately dismissed it. Tonight was about doing something special for Celeste just because he wanted to.

"How do you like it?" he said finally.

"This is splendid. I can now deduce why you desired my company. It would be enjoyable to spend the evening in this slice of paradise."

"I want to give you something, Celeste."

In her customary manner, she didn't respond to his statement but turned to him and waited for him to act.

Taking the box from the table, he went and held it out to her as he sat down beside her.

She took it, and he noted the way she studied it. The dull antique silver sheen was inlaid with an intricate design. Minute pearl legs were at its base, and the small clasp opened when she lifted it. She was silent as she stared at the object nestled on the interior velvet. Then she flung her gaze upward.

"Solomon, this is not necessary," she said.

Pleased he had anticipated what she would say, he replied, "You're quite right. But necessity had little to do with this."

Celeste stared at him, and he scooted closer to her, feeling the yards of material touch his legs. The draw of her eyes trapped him. The maple syrup eyes looked like drops of golden butterscotch.

"Sir?" Her breath was wispy. Perhaps she felt the tug between them.

"I want to give you this, Celeste," Solomon murmured as he took the box from her, pulled out the ring and placed it back on the table. Set in an old-fashioned setting, it was a two carat diamond surrounded by emeralds that glinted in the light.

He took her left hand, sheathed in her gloves, pulled at each finger until it came off, and he glanced down.

In the candle light, he could barely see but her hands were warm and soft and the feel of them in his own sent a slight shiver through his body. They felt like flower petals. He'd never seen his wife's hands before nor felt them upon his body.

"With this ring, I thee wed again," Solomon grinned as he spoke. He took the ring and placed it on her finger. A perfect fit.

"Solomon," Celeste breathed as she glanced down at her hand and tilted it just the slightest way to watch it glint in the candlelight.

"I know I didn't give you a ring before, Celeste. I was determined our marriage would strictly be a friendship between us. But you wanted to make this a business relationship. In the past weeks, I have begun to look forward to being with you. I love our walks in the morning, with just the birds and the trees and wind. I like how quiet you are and yet when you speak, you tend to say much with very little. I like how we spend time together, and I like the way we are getting to know each other."

He leaned in closer to her. As he loomed over her the veil from her cone shaped hat fell back as she looked up at him. Shadows danced on her face.

"I've never known any woman like you, my wife."

Her mouth parted, and her breath blew across his chin.

"I lied sir," she whispered.

"About what?" He glanced down at the mouth so tantalizing close.

"Your skill. I would like to know more about you in that manner."

What more could he do but bend his head and kiss her? Softly and gently. He took his hands and caressed her cheeks with his fingertips. The smoothness of her skin had a luxurious quality to it. The way her mouth met his hesitantly gently amused him. An innocent. That was . . . different.

"Oh Solomon," she breathed into his mouth and the sound caused him to deepen the kiss, his lips forcing hers apart.

He went to put his arms around her, to draw her closer to him when she suddenly jerked away from him. She stood, gathering her dress in front of her.

"Celeste?" He felt bereft.

"Are you trying to seduce me sir? Have I not made it clear I am your wife in name only? What sort of subterfuge is this?"

He would have believed she had been unaffected by their kiss, but he saw the way her chest heaved and how she averted her gaze. Not to mention the way she said his name while he kissed her.

"I'm not playing at some kind of game, Celeste," Solomon answered as he got up and walked toward her.

"Yes you are!" she suddenly screeched. "You are trying to muddle the situation by using seductive acts to cloud the boundaries of this arrangement."

"I'm not Celeste."

"Happiness is not meant for me, sir." Her voice quieted. She whirled on him and dropped the folds of her gown until they landed on a puddle on the floor.

As he stared at her in the candlelight, he suddenly saw behind the icy mask, behind the clothes, behind her reserve. Celeste wanted a Prince Charming. A man to give her happily ever after. Why hadn't he seen it before? Was that why she wore the old-fashioned costumes? Did she use them to hide herself from the idea she would not have a prince of her own?

"Were you happy just now?" he asked her.

She remained silent as she met his gaze. Finally, she whispered, "Yes."

"Then why do you say happiness is not meant for you?"

"Disregard that statement, Solomon. I do believe it's getting late, and I shall retire now." She picked up her dress. She held the fabric against her stomach in front of her.

"Oh no, woman," he jumped in front of her, blocked her path. "It's not going to be that easy to get out of this."

"I would ask that you drop this subject."

171

"And I refuse. Not until you answer me. Why do you think happiness is not meant for you?"

"Solomon, look at me. Look at this face. Look at these clothes. Do you really think any man would want me? By your own admission, you married me to protect you from beautiful women. I'm ugly. Hideous. God's leftovers He threw together and used to make me. I have allowed myself to be swayed by your gentle attentions these past weeks. Our morning traverses in the gardens, our *tête-à-têtes* throughout the day. And tonight, when you gave me a wedding ring, I thought for one instant God had . . ."

She broke off, and Solomon finished for her. "Answered your prayer."

"Yes. But I am delusional."

Her face had retreated behind the cold mask of indifference. Her voice was at her most bland.

Solomon felt guilt for the first time. How, in all of creation, could he have told this woman she was ugly? In fact, she became more and more attractive to him by the day.

Tell her, a voice said.

Solomon stood in front of her and gazed down. "There is nothing about you unattractive, Celeste. Far from it. This skin," He lifted his hand touched her cheek with the tips of them, "reminds me of nutmeg and the petals of flowers. This nose, so slim and straight but just slightly turned up at the end." He leaned and kissed the tip of her nose. "Your eyes remind me of maple syrup. Rich, sweet, maple syrup. I can drown in them. I nearly did the first time I saw you. These lips," he rubbed his thumb over her lips, parted them slightly and pressed them gently against her teeth, "Just a taste of them from a month ago made me crave more. Tonight, I felt as if I'd tasted a little bit of heaven. Woman," he breathed as he stood closer to her, charged by her presence in a way that wasn't sexual but just as intense. "I gave you the ring because I want you to be my wife, in every way. But I will never force you to do anything you don't want to do. When we

172

go down to Arcadia, I want us to have a real honeymoon. With you in my arms and on red satin sheets."

DECISION

It amazed her as she sat in the darkness of her room, how the ring had been so ornately woven into its intricate design and yet, upon her hand, it felt as heavy as a boulder. The silver metal could have been shackles and the diamond a massive rock.

She stared at its brilliance as if the significance of it weighed her down. A part of her noted it had substantial value, but the knowledge made little impact on her. Solomon could have given her a curtain hook and the symbolism behind it would not have escaped her.

Before last night, she could have continued to lie to herself. She could have simply accepted their marriage was simply a business arrangement between two people for the mutual benefit of each other. Hadn't she said that in so many words?

Yet now, after last night, the ring became a glaring reminder of her place in life as a married woman with a husband that wanted her. Desired her.

A tear fell down her cheek, and she wiped it away.

She couldn't determine if the tear was one of sorrow or joy. More aptly, the ice from the inside of her melted and leaked through her eyes.

A man wanted her for the first time in her life. The joy coursed through her like a gush of fire, a flow of lava.

How long had she prayed for a man to want her? How long had she been ugly, unloved, and hopeless? A girl skinny, odd, and eccentric?

The doors on her memory opened and she could remember walking next to Leah while they went to school. She'd hear the boys whistle after her sister as they tried to hit on her. She saw Blaze go berserk as one boy in particular touched her behind, and she nearly broke his finger. She could remember the talent agent who came to visit her mother and father about signing up Leah as a child model.

He ran away when he very gently suggested she cut her hair, and she nearly screamed down the house in protest. When Leah became homecoming queen for her senior year, she glowed and sparkled. Then she'd almost lost her crown when she pushed the homecoming king down the stairs because he tried to get fresh with her.

Vibrant, fiery, insane Blaze. For all her temper, was normal.

Cold, demure, calm Icy. For all her control, was abnormal.

And now she was being treated like a normal woman with a husband that wanted to sleep with her.

Celeste cried in earnest now, tears of rage, sorrow, and happiness all rolled up inside her. God had answered her prayer and then slammed the door in her face. It didn't matter what she or Solomon wanted. God would not let her.

Her hands rolled up in fists as her nails made deep grooves in her palms.

Last night had been the most amazing night of her life. The feel of Solomon's fingers on her person, the touch of his lips and his declaration of intent had been unexpected. Never in the fantasy she created of Jacob had she ever felt the pull of desire between them like yesterday. His words had titillated her senses, and she imagined, just for one brief moment, it was possible. They walked back to the mansion in a contented silence. The twilight canopy glittered with stars. The moon had shone its light on the path, and she had been swept away by night sounds. When they arrived back at the mansion, he turned toward her, lifted both her hands to his lips and kissed her knuckles, holding her gaze.

"Thanks God," she whispered sarcastically into the silence of the room. A sense of loss weighed on her as she made the decision not to go any further with her husband. If he knew her secret, how would he react?

No, she refused to do it. The wife of Solomon Greene was all she could be, not a partner in his bed. Grasping at straws was not going to allow God to let her do anything more than look at the mirage of an answered prayer before it evaporated into thin air. Slowly, she took off the ring and put it on the dresser. Then she lifted the gloves she'd placed on her lap and put them back on.

Dawn's light filtered into the room. She sat in the chair in her bedroom and knew what her decision would be. It was the only course she could take.

Solomon whistled as he dressed for his morning walk with Celeste. She definitely would give into him now. He looked forward to being with his wife. He had meant every word he'd said last night, and he wouldn't take them back now. What had started off as a competition between himself and Gonzo was now a desire to be with his wife.

It didn't take long for her to capitulate though, and he anticipated his honeymoon with excitement. But when had it ever been difficult when it came to getting a woman into bed? It wasn't as if sleeping with his wife would be any different than sleeping with any other woman.

He contemplated his reflection in the bathroom mirror. He had to acknowledge that. Making love to his wife would be no different. It wouldn't be special.

The idea caused him to frown. He wanted it to be special, unique somehow. To be a union of more than just bodies. But he didn't think it was possible. It had taken almost a month before Celeste had succumbed, but she had just as every other woman and he would reap the benefit of that.

He left the room and walked to the other side of the mansion and knocked on her door. She would probably throw her arms around him and kiss him. Maybe she would even pull him into her bedroom, and they could begin their honeymoon a little earlier than thought. That definitely made him smile.

The woman who opened the door was not Celeste from last night. The Ice Maiden he had married three months ago stared out a face devoid of expression, dressed like a pioneer from the American West. Her hair was styled in a chignon, and he felt the icy barrier she erected between them before she even spoke.

"I have decided not to walk with you anymore, Solomon. Good day."

She closed the door quietly, and he heard the lock turn and the sound reverberated like the gong of a bell. Instinctively he knew even if he picked the lock, there was no way he was going to get past the brick wall she re-erected between them.

HONEYMOON AT ARCADIA

Arcadia was everything Mrs. Greene had said it would be. The view of the ocean from Celeste's bedroom window was spectacular in the setting sun. Its light lit the ocean surface to diamond brilliance. The waves soothed in a way nothing else could as they lapped against the beach in a steady soft rhythm. The palms trees swayed back and forth like native worshippers to gods.

She stayed in front of the window and allowed the beauty before her seep inside of her body and consoled the deep ache inside her. There was nothing quite like the beauty of God's handiwork to bring about tranquility. After a half hour, she walked away from the window and surveyed the room, her mind fixated on Morayo Hernandez.

Morayo was a very lovely young woman. Her skin shimmered like black satin and its contrast glorious to the white peasant blouse and flouncy multi-colored skirt she wore. A white head wrap with a large red flower design imprinted on it gave her an exotic appearance as she clashed with the opulent modern furnishing of Arcadia.

"Ek'asan Solomon," Morayo Hernandez greeted as she came forward to meet them. Her voice, accented in a lilting way, only added to her exotic persona. When she turned toward Celeste, she felt as if she'd found a friend in a single moment of time.

"This must be your iyàwó. Welcome to Arcadia."

In a half hour, she had been shown to her room. That had been an interesting exchange Morayo had gazed at the both of them when they told her they would be occupying different rooms.

"You're joking, right?"

Celeste didn't answer but waited while the woman called to the other house personnel to take their luggage to two different rooms.

"Would you like to have dinner soon, Solomon?" Morayo addressed her husband.

179

"Celeste?" Solomon had turned toward her. His eyes locked with hers, and she felt her heart start to thump. She willed the ice to coalesce and calm it.

"Ms. Hernandez," she started when the woman interrupted with a giant, ear piercing laugh. With such abandon, Celeste found herself relaxing. Solomon had glanced at her and they both smiled. "Morayo, can we have dinner in a half hour?"

"*Oda*! Good! In honor of your marriage, I made some traditional Yoruba dishes."

Now, as she went down the winding stairs, she anticipated eating foreign food.

Solomon was at the foot of the stairs and held her gaze as she came down. She wondered what she looked like to him, dressed in a blue gown from the early 16th century. The gown touted a lot of Spanish influence as a tribute to the history of Florida. The large ruff came up the back of her neck, and surrounded her entire head. A mantilla graced her shoulders.

It had been six days since they had spent any time together alone. Gone were the walks in the morning and the time in her den. She had stayed in her room and worked vigorously on learning videos, costumes, and correspondence. As a matter of fact, she kept her distance from him as much as possible. It was important for the void to be between them again. Vital for her to remember he married her for only a short time. Crucial to her survival to understand he married her for her lack of attraction.

As she came to the last step and started forward, the hand on her arms stopped her, and she turned and looked up.

Suddenly, he swooped down and kissed her, his lips hard and slightly bruising but she sensed he held himself back from her. She ached to respond to him, to pull her gloves off and wrap her hands around his neck and feel the delicious sensation of being held against his body. With an iron will, she forced herself to remain still although her insides quivered.

When he pulled away from her moments later, his breath came out harsh, and his eyes flashed down at her. Over bright, they were at the same time filled with another emotion she found difficult to define.

"Same old, cold, frigid Celeste, aren't you?" he spat.

Celeste remained silent and walked away from him.

Solomon blew out a breath of frustration as he watched her hips sway as she walked away.

Of course, Celeste remained unaffected by his kiss. He, on the other hand, only wanted more from her. One taste only made him hungrier. How could such a small kiss affect him? It wasn't the first time he wondered about that.

The last several weeks might as well not have happened. Their walk in the moonlight must have been a waking dream. The woman from that night had disappeared just as the ring had. Icy, the untouchable wife of Solomon Greene, had made her appearance.

His footsteps led him to the dining room where Celeste was already seated at the head.

"I am very happy to congratulate you on your wedding," Morayo said. Solomon saw she had changed. Somehow, the Yoruba woman had managed to look even more beautiful dressed in her native clothes.

"Morayo, I must tell you how lovely you look. You look like a queen," Celeste said as she stared with admiration at the woman. "May I inquire as to your —,"

"Well of course!" A wide smile creased her face as she came over to Celeste. "This," she pointed to the skirt part of the outfit, "is the *iro,* or wrapper. This is the *buba,* the top. And this," Morayo's hands fingered the shawl over her shoulder, "this is the *ipele.*"

Celeste's face brightened. *Leave it to a woman to get excited about clothes,* Solomon couldn't help but think. After all, if there was anything his wife was interested in, it would be clothes.

"I'd be happy to show you some more later. For now, enjoy your dinner."

Solomon glanced around. The room was nothing like the mansion in Michigan. The flavors of the tropics were heavy laden with bright colors and accents. It was made more pleasant by the smells. Tapas as an appetizer, with fried plantain, amala, or a type of pounded yam made into flour, and egusi soup—a soup made with seed from the egusi, a West African melon. A bowl of kola-nut sat on the table, as well. "For fertility," Morayo told them with a sparkle in her eye. He noticed Celeste's eyes dropped to her plate.

We need more than that, Morayo, but thanks anyway.

"Oh, Blaze would love this," Celeste said as she took another spoon of the egusi stew, "I have to call her and let her know."

It was a meager straw, but he grasped at it. He knew Morayo hovered in the background, taking note of the little conversation husband and wife were having with all the acuity of a television reporter.

"She would?"

"Oh yes. Blaze loves to cook. She always pushes herself to learn new cuisines."

"Who taught her how to cook?"

"My Great Aunt Beatrice."

"Self-taught?"

"Yes. But Great Aunt Beatrice had a knack for food. She used to say cooking and preparing food could not be taught by a formal institution but by learning to do it yourself. Leah took that to heart when she was younger. When she was about seven years old she somehow persuaded Mama to allow her in the kitchen. And Aunt Beatrice used to live with us for a while, and she showed her everything she knew." Her mouth smirked as she glanced up from her plate. "There was this one incident where Aunt Beatrice made Leah taste all kinds of seasonings, dried and fresh and then made her take a test on it. Every time she got one wrong, Leah had got whacked on the knuckles. Needless to say, she learned very quickly."

It was the most she had ever said the whole time they had been married and Solomon didn't want her to stop.

"So Leah's the cook in the family. I bet Jacob will be glad for that."

"Blaze took over the family meals when she was sixteen. It has gotten to the point where my mother and father are not allowed into 'her' kitchen." She put her fork down and leaned toward him as if he were a conspirator. "Once, she threw a dish towel at my father for coming into the kitchen where she was making a surprise cake for him for his birthday. I remember Father telling me she said, 'You may pay the bills in this house, but this is my kitchen so get out!'"

Solomon had to laugh. "Leah really is something."

"Oh, Blaze has always been that way. Her temper explodes like a nuclear bomb. My parents have thought for some time maybe she had some kind of mental disorder that made it difficult for her to control her anger. Alas, to their disappointment, that's just Leah."

Solomon laughed again and Celeste joined him. Then suddenly, the smile froze on her face, and her eyes went wide with shock.

"What's wrong?" he asked, wondering if she just realized she let her guard down.

He was correct. The grin dropped from her face, and she focused once more on her food. He sighed and dug back into his own plate. The food suddenly tasted like cardboard.

Dessert came, and it was a simple two layered yellow cake sheathed with white fondant and decorated with edibles candy pearls and flowers.

Morayo had said little, but Solomon could feel her curiosity as she served the cake. Sooner or later, she was going to question him about this marriage of his.

###

It happened sooner; that very evening in fact.

He was in the family room, the T. V. on and blaring but he had no idea what was on. Morayo came in.

"You and your *ìyàwó* act like no newlywed couple I know. What is going on between you Solomon?"

Morayo was a friend, and he smiled ruefully at her.

"Where do I begin?"

The Yoruba woman sat down on the sofa next to him, the red *gele* around her head bringing her face into prominence, her dark eyes intent as she waited for him to speak. Fifteen minutes later, she sat back and sighed.

"You have a problem, Solomon. I do not know of any woman who would marry a man after calling her ugly. *Oluwa o!* My gosh! I do not know what to say except this: Celeste is unique in a way that will be a blessing to you if you find out what burden she is holding on to. "

"What is she holding on to?"

"*Mi o mo!*"

"What?" His Yoruba was little more than non-existent.

"I don't know. It's up to you to find out." Morayo stood then and stared down at him. "Just as you have to let go of your past."

Solomon tensed. How did she know?

"I know, Solomon. I am not going to tell you how I found out, but I am glad you are not doing it anymore."

Solomon swallowed nervously. "I guess you're going to tell me to touch the hem of the Virgin's garment."

Morayo laughed, her head thrown back. "Oh Solomon! Was I ever a Washed Saint? The memory seems so vague now. *Oluwa o!* I am so glad the Lord Jesus is my savior, and it is His blood that makes me pure, not wrapping myself in fabric or putting the hem of a garment in my mouth."

He jerked his head up. "You're not a Washed Saint?" Morayo had been a devout follower of his mother and father. There were few that had been as zealous as her.

"No. I am a child of the King now. It is infinitely more satisfying than being a child of the Virgin."

"What happened? What made you change your mind?"

"I'll tell you about it some time." Her lips curved in a secretive way.

"Good night, Morayo."

"*Od'abo* to you as well, Solomon." She walked out the door and left Solomon with his thoughts.

AN OLD HYMN

It was a unique experience for her to wake up to the sound of the waves as they lapped against the beach, but infinitely pleasant. Celeste sighed with a sense of pleasure, and then she got up and began her day.

A half hour later, after she showered and put on her undergarments, she was putting on her hoops for her gown from 1865. The door opened, and Morayo entered the room, carrying a tea service with her.

"*Ek'aro* Celeste," Morayo greeted. She put the tea service on the vanity in her room. "I was going to surprise you with breakfast in bed but I see you are an early riser. It is just about 7:30 in the morning."

"I'm an early riser," Celeste said by way of explanation as she finished fastening the hoops around her waist and then walked over to the bed where she had laid out the petticoats and skirt, prepared to put them on. "*Ek'aro* means good morning, correct?"

The Yoruba nodded. "Are you wearing that?" Morayo asked, her dark eyes wide with surprise.

"Yes. I always wear costume clothes."

"Wow. So many clothes and layers. It is going to be a hot day today. Are you going out today?"

"I plan to traverse up and down the beach line, and then I will come in and be in for the rest of the day."

"You and Solomon are not going to sight see? Have you ever been to Tampa?"

"Oh, we'll sightsee some other time. But today, I want to relax in this lovely home. Would you give me a tour of the premises?"

"Well, I would think Solomon would that for you. After all, it is his family's house."

Celeste bit her lip to keep from responding. She didn't want Solomon anywhere near her. She couldn't forget the kiss he had given her the evening before. How much she enjoyed it. The familiar rage at God rose, and she tampered it down quickly.

"I'll ask him then," she finally said and turned to continue to get dressed.

"Do you need some help with all that?" Morayo's sleek eyebrow arched to the hem of her head wrap. She looked cool and comfortable in a blue and white skirt with a sleeveless matching tank and her feet shod with flat white sandals.

Celeste started protest and then stopped. She could use the help. "Yes please."

It took about fifteen minute to dress, but it was filled with a lot of laughter. Morayo was a chatty woman, but she made Celeste feel as if they were friends already. With the petticoats, underskirt and skirt in place finally, Celeste shook off Morayo's offer to help with the blouse and jacket and she finished dressing herself.

"Oh, let me do your hair Celeste," Morayo begged as she saw Celeste sit before the mirror and pick up the brush.

"Really, you don't have to."

It was different having someone with her, and she found herself nodding permission as Morayo came behind her and took the brush.

It took less time with Morayo doing her hair, and as she did it, the woman hummed a song. Celeste had never heard it before, but it had a melodious tune to it.

"What are you humming, Morayo?"

"Oh, a hymn I heard some time ago at the church."

"What hymn is it?"

"Oh, it is called Victory in Jesus."

A bemused Celeste asked her to sing the song, wondering why as she did. Maybe it was the way Morayo seemed free and happy. An inner glow shone from her dark eyes. Or it could be because she had entered her fantasy world and didn't say anything about.

Or it could be she just wanted to hear the song.

Morayo began to sing, her voice a deep contralto.

"I heard an old, old story.
How the savior came from glory.
How he made the lame to walk again.
And caused the blind to see.
I heard about his groaning
And his precious blood atoning.
And I repented of my sins and won the victory.
Oh, victory in Jesus!
My savior forever
He sought me and bought me
With his redeeming blood.
He loved me ere I knew him
And all my love is due him
He plunged me to victory
Beneath the cleansing flood.

Celeste felt her heart constrict inside as she listened to the words. She couldn't pinpoint exactly what it was that touched her so much but the words of the song made her soar.

"I like to say a little Bible verse in my mind when I sing that song," Morayo's voice interrupted her musings. "'For with God, nothing is impossible.' That is why I have victory in Jesus. Yahoo!"

"That's a nice song," Celeste replied. She assessed her reflection as Morayo finished her hair. She had styled it in an intricate braid on either side of her head and then a bun at the nape of her neck. It brought Celeste's face in sharp relief. "That looks so very good. Thank you."

Morayo put her head next to Celeste, looking at her from the mirror. "Isn't it something how God could make all of us different, and we are still the same? Look at me. I am dark chocolate and you are milk chocolate. And, shall I say, Solomon is white chocolate. Ha ha ha!"

Celeste laughed, throwing her head back in abandon. It felt good to release her laughter. Had she been so silent, locked in her icy cage?

"Aww, now that is better. Relax, girl. You are on your honeymoon! You should be more smiles, not polite expressions, or avoidance of each other's eyes. This man is your husband, and you should be enjoying him; and he, you."

"Don't blame me, blame God," Celeste said without thinking and then froze.

"What do you mean by that?" Morayo said.

"Nothing at all. I'm going to the beach. What time will breakfast be?"

Morayo told her, and Celeste was soon out the door and moments later she was on the beach, humming parts of the song.

CROWDED BED

Solomon sat on the patio and watched his wife as she walked along the beach early in the morning, brooding.

They had been at Arcadia for a week but in that time, he'd spent more time with Morayo than he had with his wife. He had taken her around the house that second day of their stay and she had enjoyed it, asking polite questions here and there. When they came upon the shrine of the Virgin, she had stood under it gazing at it with an inscrutable expression for the longest time. Then, she said, "There's something wrong with the statue, Solomon. It disturbs me."

"Let's leave then."

Besides that small exchange, she had barely spoken to him

That could hardly be said for the friendship that developed between Morayo and Celeste. They were as close as sisters. Every morning, he could hear them in her room down the hall, laughing at something or another. Morayo had gotten into a habit of helping her dress, sort of like a lady's maid, and she loved it.

"She has so many different and amazing dresses, Solomon. I cannot believe she made them all herself. *Oda*! It's really something!" Morayo told him one afternoon as they sat in the kitchen. Celeste had taken herself to her room, where she spent the afternoon. She came down at dinner, and Morayo fed them well, clucking her head at them both.

It was so far the sorriest honeymoon probably experienced by mankind.

He sat on the ledge of the balcony. Such high expectations he'd had for them. They were supposed to be sharing a bed when they came down here, not sitting around here doing nothing.

Agitatedly, Solomon rose from the balcony and leaned his arms against it. He studied the distant figure of his wife as she walked the beach line. What had gone wrong? The night they walked in gardens should have been the turning point in their relationship. For a moment, it had.

The next day, she literally and figuratively, slammed the door in his face. Why?

Was she still angry he had called her ugly and married because of that? If he could go back in time, he'd punch himself in the gut and rip out his tongue. The fact she was hurt by his words caused him agony. Why did it cause him to feel that way? Was it really because he wanted to sleep with her? These emotions roiled inside and threatened to rip him apart.

Before he married, his life had no order. There wasn't a Mrs. Greene, but one woman after the other. He'd had a good time. No misguided need to get involved because all he wanted to know was the quickest way to get them into bed. The most he'd known about them had been their first names, probably their last names, and most of their faces.

Now he had a wife and his life remained a cluttered mess. The ugly woman he had married to protect him from the beautiful women of his past now haunted his present. Those women he'd only been physically attracted to. With Celeste, the more she pushed him away, the closer he wanted to become. He couldn't get enough of the effort to dig deeper into her psyche. There were layers that he wanted to peel away. Burrow and find all her secrets. Go behind the costumes and see the real Celeste.

Solomon ran his hands through his hair as the ocean breeze caressed him again. He had thought the night in the garden would be all he had to do to get her.

He'd never expected it would be this hard to get close to a woman, much less his wife!

"Nice view, is it not?"

Solomon turned at Morayo's voice as she entered the master bedroom a cart in front her with his breakfast.

"Oh Morayo, you don't have to do that."

192

"Well, you and Mrs. Greene only eat together at dinner. You rarely spend time with each other. One would have hoped this honeymoon would have been an opportunity for you and her to become closer. Obviously that is not going to happen."

"How can I make it happen when Celeste doesn't want to have anything to do with me?" He walked back into the bedroom as Morayo placed the breakfast cart by the bed.

"You know, Solomon, your problem is you never have had to chase after a woman. The women you've had made it easy for you just to take what you want from them. But Celeste is different. She's not going to give in to you. And you thought she would because you're used to having women at your fingertips, literally. She is not impressed by your money, by your looks. She married you because you asked her, and you needed her, not the other way around."

"How could you possibly know?"

"I know you, Solomon. It is not hard to grasp."

"Well you're right. I had initially tried to get her; Gonzo told me he was going to take my wife from me."

Surprise mastered Morayo's features. "Gonzo? What does Gonzo have to do with this?"

"He's known Celeste for years. They were friends growing up when he went to visit his grandparents every summer. He was her knight," he spat in memory.

"You are not talking about Goodyard, are you?"

"Yes." Solomon felt his eyebrows draw together. Had she been talking about him to Morayo? Was she missing her knight in glittery, sparkly, shining armor?

"She has told me about him but I thought it was someone else. Gonzo and Goodyard is the same person?"

"That's his first name."

"What kind of name is that?"

"Like I know!" Solomon exclaimed, ticked off Celeste talked to Morayo about Gonzo but wouldn't give her husband the time of day.

"But what does Gonzo have to do with anything?"

"Celeste told him about our temporary marriage. She told him how we were going to divorce after a period of time and now, he's going after my wife."

Morayo sat down on a chair in his room. "He told you that?"

The memory played in his mind, and his hand rolled into a fist. "I came down the stairs and there he was, his arms wrapped around her waist. Touching her as if she belonged to him and she just gazing up into his face, smiling."

"Was she being inappropriate?"

"No! Celeste isn't that kind of woman. I've only known her for a short while, and I know she wouldn't do anything behind my back. I could see the way Gonzo devoured her with his eyes. I could have broken his hands and knocked his teeth down his throat. And she was clueless. Didn't have an inkling her knight wanted to do more than play their game." He blew out a breath. "And then Gonzo tells me he knows everything and he's going to take my wife from me."

"Are you serious?"

"Like I would make that up, Morayo." He stalked over to the cart and pulled off the top of the silver platter. Croissants, warm and soft met his gaze. He picked one up and bit into it. It could have tasted like paper and he wouldn't care.

"I have to be honest though Morayo. He would be a better husband for her. Not me. I have to admit that."

"*Kilo fa?*"

Solomon walked over to the bed and fell back on it, staring at the canopy above him. "Why? He knows her like no one else. Gonzo doesn't have the past I have."

He could hear Morayo move. She came next to his bed and stared down at him.

"I've been having these dreams."

"What kind of dreams?"

Solomon sighed and rubbed his eyes with his thumb and forefinger. "Dreams, or should I say nightmares, of women and candy."

"I thought you said dreams, not delusional male fantasy."

"That's just it, Morayo. They're not my fantasy. In all of them, I'm trapped by some kind of candy or sweet. I've been tied down by black licorice, held down by cotton candy weights, shot with jolly rancher bullets, drowned in a pit of rainbow sprinkles and blown to bits by chocolate malted milk ball bombs. In every single dream, the women are hot. Gorgeous. And they scare me to death."

Morayo didn't need to know about what disturbed him most about his dreams. In the beginning, the women made him eat an appendage of their body. Now, they were eating him and that, of everything, freaked him out the most.

"I think your dreams are telling you something," Morayo spoke slowly. Her dark eyes bore a hole into him.

"Why are you looking at me like that?"

"I was a santera, which is a female Santeria priest before my stint as a Washed Saint. As a priestess, I had to purify myself in various rituals and sacrifices. But they were simply outward things to be done that had no bearing on my inward state."

"Oh no! Not religion this early in the morning?"

"*Mi o selere rara,* Solomon," Morayo shook her hands in agitation. "I mean I'm serious. Just hear me out."

He sighed and sat up on the bed. When Morayo said that, she meant it. "I'm listening."

"You have to know every time you sleep with a woman, you are putting their spirit, their soul in you, so to speak. They are in your mind, your memory. You take a piece of everyone with you, and they are with you the next time you're with another woman and the next."

He'd heard this before but didn't really care. Something in his face must have betrayed that because Morayo said, "Solomon, do not ignore that. Imagine all these women are crowding the bed with you. You may be with one woman and then all of a sudden, a glimpse of past relationship pops in your head. Maybe the other woman was prettier, slimmer, bigger, doesn't matter. Then in some way, in the most intimate moment a man can have, suddenly there is a strange woman in his bed, and it is not his wife."

Now she confused him. "What?"

"Have you ever been with a woman and put another face on top of hers?"

"What does that—?"

"Why?"

"Why what?"

"Why would a man have to put another woman's face on top of the one he is with?"

Solomon jumped from the bed. "I don't know," he answered agitatedly, "How do you know all this anyway?" The conversation unsettled him.

She smiled. "I'll tell you sometime. But answer my question."

Solomon stared at her and finally gasped out. "Maybe because the other woman had something else I liked better than the one I'm with."

"And you have such a variety of ones to choose from."

"Look Morayo—"

"Now imagine if there was no one else. Just you and Celeste. You could not choose from your past sexual encounters because there would be no one to choose from. And the same for your wife. What woman, or man for that matter, wants to be compared to someone they cannot even see? Why do you think God said, 'Therefore a man shall leave his father and his mother and hold fast to his wife, and the two shall become one flesh'?"

"Are you done now?" Morayo had preached enough and what she said bothered him.

She smiled again. "After I say this: how can you be one flesh with Celeste when there is a crowded bed?"

A MATTER OF PROPRIETY

Three days later, Morayo had an idea why God had allowed her to see two people who were obviously meant for each other act like fools. Celeste with her hang-ups about her appearance and Solomon with his swagger with women. They may have thought God had little to do with their marriage, but Morayo knew without a shadow of a doubt He had everything to do with it.

Morayo walked over to the counter and pulled out the breakfast dishes and went about making breakfast for the both of them.

She liked Celeste. Behind her mask, a creative, caring woman waited for a man to turn her into the princess she wanted to be. Most women longed for Prince Charming in one way or another. Maybe not a drop dead gorgeous man with oodles of money like Solomon but a man that made her feel like Cinderella. Although Morayo's ancestry was Yoruba by way of Cuba, she'd seen nothing to change her mind on the idea.

As she prepared the tea to take up to Celeste, she thought about some of things Solomon revealed to her previously.

Gonzo was a fly in the ointment between them. And Celeste didn't know Gonzo looked to her to be his future wife. He probably thought he could win her based on what he knew about her and what he thought he understood about her. Poor Gonzo. Didn't he know a woman had the prerogative to choose? Celeste chose whom she wanted, and it wasn't him.

Morayo knew Solomon was falling in love with his wife. She laughed out loud, pulled the tea service and placed the various items on the cart. Fancy that. She wondered if he had any idea what that meant. The laughter died from her face as she thought about it. How sad for the man. To have been with so many women and never know a woman's love. The most he had received from them had been a physical joining. Peanuts compared to God's idea of the relationship between a man and a woman.

Blatantly obvious as well—Celeste was in love with Solomon, although she didn't know. No woman worked that hard at avoiding a man unless he disturbed her. Thus the reason why she went out her way to prove to herself and Solomon she wanted nothing to do with him.

But Morayo knew that another reason existed as to why Celeste avoided any kind of intimate ties. She felt the Spirit of God command her to tell her about His love. The kind that surpassed every boundary and every barrier that tried to block it.

The clock in the kitchen sounded out. It was seven o'clock, and Celeste liked her tea at 7:30am. She put the tea kettle on the massive stove in the kitchen and then took out the sausage, eggs and waffles she knew Solomon would want when the time came.

Tell her about my love, the Spirit of God whispered to her, and Morayo stopped, always thankful she could talk to God and hear His voice in moments like this. It made tears fall from her eyes as she thought about how far she had come from the pit of darkness to the light of God. In the quiet of the morning, with the sound of the waves at her back and the sunlight flooding through like rain she began to dance. There weren't any drums to call upon the *orishas* or a sacrifice for a cleansing ceremony. The Virgin's garments weren't going to clean her body from impurity. There was no need for her to be pure because she was made pure, not from her own efforts, but by the grace of God through the work of His Son. God was right there in the kitchen, and she could feel Him all over and she danced, and praised God and humbly told Him she would do as she was told.

She sang softly as she finished the tea service. "He loved me ere I knew Him and all my love is due Him. He plunged me to victory beneath the cleansing flood."

The water slapped against the beach, and the sun dipped into the horizon, casting thin streaks of purple-pink lines across the sky as night began to fall. The chilly wind from the ocean blew and with child-like alacrity found all the places on Celeste not covered by the large paisley shawl she wore over her dress. It tussled with her hair and played with the hem of her burgundy Regency gown, fluttering and exposing her bare legs as she dug her toes into the sand. She shivered, but she didn't move, dulled by the cold wind but quaking at the emotions rolling inside of her.

She was going to have to apologize to Solomon. Again. Tell him she in no way meant to act in any manner that would cause him to question her loyalty to him as his wife.

She shook her head and the ringlet curls bounced on either side. How could she have been so impudent as to allow herself to be entrapped by ignorance, especially of her own making? Morayo was a unique woman, five years her senior but with wisdom that seemed otherworldly as if she'd walked the earth many times before. Celeste had to thank her for assisting her in seeing her blunder.

The air grew chillier very quickly, and she got up and dusted off her dress, picked up her shoes lying beside her and started her trek back to the house. Goosebumps skittered over her skin through the long sleeves. She wasn't sure if was from the cold air or from the nervousness from the encounter she had to have with her husband.

Perhaps, it was both.

Morayo waited at the door, a towel in her hand as soon as Celeste closed the door behind her.

"*Otutu nibi,* Celeste! Very cold. Florida gets hot during the day but can feel like a Michigan winter at night, especially near the ocean."

"Thank you, Morayo," Celeste said. She took off her shawl and handed it unconsciously to the woman, her mind still focused on what she had to do.

"Do you know where Solomon is?"

"In his bedroom, alone. Where he has been for the past week or so," Morayo answered.

Celeste nodded and then started up the stairs.

At his door moments later, she stared at the grain of the wood and exhaled, then knocked.

"Come in," his voice called out.

As she opened the door, he turned and faced her. The sight of him made her mouth dry. How was it possible a man could wear a simple white T-shirt and black jeans and create a work of art? Green gold eyes appraised her, flashed in the light of the room. His usually spiky hair curled as if he'd come out the shower. It made him look boyish and rakish. The muscles on his arms bulged, rounded like the tops of smooth stones. She wanted to reach out and touch them, feel their strength.

What was wrong with her? Was she slavering over her husband?

She tried to call upon the ice reserve, but all she felt was a curious sensation of heat and vulnerability. Further, in the recess of her mind, a tiny thought whispered this man belonged to her, and she had a right to everything before her. In the past, seeing his handsomeness made her angry. But tonight, possessiveness took over. She hadn't felt this way about Jacob at all.

Her face flushed at that thought.

"Hello, wife," Solomon greeted. "What can I do for you?"

"I would like to speak with you, sir." She rubbed her hands together nervously, the satin brushing against itself loud to her ears.

"About what?"

"A matter of propriety."

Solomon's eyebrow arched. "A matter of propriety?"

"Yes. I, uh, I want to apologize to you sir."

He harrumphed. "I remember you apologizing to your knight's squire before. You even bowed down to the floor to show the depth of your apology and yet the next day, you reneged on our agreement. Why should this apology be any different? And what are you apologizing for?"

Guilt weighed down on her. "You are correct sir, in doubting my sincerity. But I need to apologize for allowing my friendship with Goijaart to cast any hint of scandal upon our marriage."

Solomon straightened from his relaxed position against the doors of the balcony. "Morayo's been talking to you, I see."

"She explained my association with Goijaart, no matter how innocent, could be incorrectly construed in an adulterous light. I would never do such a thing. I did not realize every time I met with Goijaart in your absence, I should have immediately terminated the visit. I allowed my affinity with him to obscure any sense of wifely sagacity. I deeply apologize."

Solomon stared at her, and she refused to move under his scrutiny. He walked over to her until he stood in front of her, and she was forced to glance up into his face.

"That's not good enough, Celeste. I don't want words from you."

She swallowed. "What do you want from me?"

He stepped closer, looming over her now and she back up until she felt the wall at her back. A long muscled arm came on either side of her head imprisoning her. Solomon's masculine scent filled the space between them, heady and male. Her heart started to thump inside her ribcage like a needle in a sewing machine. Where was her ice? Her control? It had melted somewhere from the beach to his room. Anticipation coursed through her, bubbly like ginger ale and heady as a narcotic. Would he kiss her now? She wanted him to. A lot.

"You." He bent down until all she could see was his green gold eyes.

Her heart threatened to jump from the confines of her chest.

"I can guess what you're thinking Celeste. That I'm going to force my 'connubial rights' on you as you so eloquently put it. Then you can say you've completed your wifely duty to me as if we're locked in some kind of time warp from 1492 or 1518 or 1 million b. c. for all I know." He brought his hand down and caressed her lips with his thumb. "I'm not going to make it that easy for you. Not at all. When I say I want you, I want your time, your company. This honeymoon has been cruddy so far. I want you to go sightseeing with me, eat breakfast with me, walk the beach, and act like a wife on a honeymoon."

Disappointment flooded through her. Of course, he would want her to be with him. Florida teemed with beautiful women as much as its waters swelled with sharks. He'd want his protection with him. She felt like a living prophylactic.

"Do you know why, Celeste?" He removed his thumb from her mouth.

"No," she whispered.

"I plan to use every moment, every minute we are together to seduce you, woman. And I'm looking forward to seeing you come to me of your own free will. Starting now."

Before she knew it, he bent his head and kissed her. Not the dominant presses of lips from before or the gentle seeking wonder from two weeks ago. This was a kiss of intent. It drugged her and made her knees weak. Their steady pressure caused her to want to respond, to kiss him back. But what was she supposed to do? Kiss him back, yes but how?

Stop thinking, Icy. Just feel, the small voice in her mind told her, and she decided to obey. She kissed him back, riding on the whirlwind of excitement in her.

He made a small noise and his arms started to go around her when an alarm bell went off in her head and God's constant reminder she wasn't meant to be happy reared its head. Swiftly she tore her mouth away and folded her arms.

"You liked that didn't you woman?" His voice throbbed with masculine knowledge of his effect on her.

Solomon smiled at her, his eyes full of warmth. Without breaking her gaze, he reached for the doorknob and opened it. "Good night, my lady," he said softly.

BELOVED

As he pulled on his socks and shoes, Solomon whistled heartily. The past week has been one of the best of his life. Seeing Celeste in the morning and kissing her good night in the evening made every day special. Morayo definitely approved of the change in their relationship, and she went about preparing delicious meals for them and then sending them off happily.

It amazed him that he had such a good time, and he hadn't slept with his wife. The most physical interaction they had were kisses at night. Even then he initiated them and not her.

Shoes tied, he leaned his elbows on his knees and let his mind wander.

The chase Celeste led him on exhilarated him. To discover her likes and dislikes had an addictive quality to it. It made him want to see what more he could do to make her maple syrup eyes turn to brown gold.

In the last week, they visited various parts of Florida. Unlimited funds made things easier. One day, he rented a car and they drove for miles all over Tampa, stopping at various places along the way that aroused their interest. They went into an antique shop where Solomon bought a brooch, necklace and earring set, and dainty white gloves the proprietor swore Marie Antoinette wore herself. Celeste had laughed at that and had glanced at Solomon, and his breath caught in his throat.

They visited Busch Gardens on another day. That had been a good day that lasted far into the night. They had walked from one end of the park to the other, astounded by the different animals they saw, learned about and petted. The roller coasters made Celeste scream and at one point she didn't want to go on any of them but he made her, laughing at her fear. They ended the night at a local restaurant on the way home and then they walked the beach before

205

going to their separate rooms. But not before he kissed her, a heated exchange that made his pulse quicken.

That had surprised him. He hadn't believed a kiss would ever have that kind of effect on him. It wasn't his first kiss at all but with Celeste, a kiss became a flicker of a candlelight that bloomed into a full fledge forest fire. It swept through his body and took him for a loop. How could he be so into this woman and he'd never seen her naked? Was it only because he hadn't had sex in a year? Was this just a physical response to abstinence?

The sunlight filtered through the balcony and blinded him for a second. The idea these feelings inside of him for his wife were only physical made him uneasy. He didn't want it to be just a material outpouring of body chemistry, hormones and testosterone. He wanted it to be something from his soul. In the last year and a half, at a time when he was saturated by women, he'd felt empty on the inside. There would be one beautiful woman after the other in his bed and nothing more. Just one more body.

Part of him had to admit while he wanted to make love to his wife, he was glad for the delay. What if she finally did capitulate and she invited him to her bed? Would it be any different from the countless other women he'd slept with? Would his first night with his wife be crowded by the memories of others? Or worse, the same old routine? A joining that did nothing for him?

"Solomon!"

He jerked from his thoughts and saw Morayo at the door.

"Sorry, Morayo. I was just thinking."

"Celeste wanted me to tell you she apologizes but she must decline going out with you today."

Hot searing anger coursed through his system. Was she trying to turn back into the Ice Maiden? After all the fun and connection they'd had this week, she was going to renege once again on their bond and try to get out of it. Well, didn't that woman have another thing coming!

"Oh yes she is," Solomon snarled as he jumped from the bed and stalked out the room.

Morayo called after him. "Solomon wait!"

"I got this, Morayo," he answered back. Each step took him closer to his wife's room.

"But Solomon — ,"

"Back off preacher," he called back.

Morayo's eyes widen in surprise, but then she turned and went back into his room. For a brief second, he thought he saw a grin on her face.

How could Celeste turn her back on them now? They were starting to get closer to each other, and she was just too scared to allow them to become more. Didn't she like their quiet meals in the morning as Morayo clucked around them like a mother hen? Hadn't their morning walks on the beach meant anything to her with just the ocean, the sun, and wind as companions? Wasn't it just the best thing to spend the day together? And now, she was going to turn into the Ice Maiden again. No, not while he was Solomon Greene he wouldn't let her

When he arrived at the door, he shouted, "Celeste, you open this door now."

Celeste's voice came back muffled. "I am sorry, sir, but I cannot. Please go away."

"Celeste! Woman you open this door right now!"

"I must insist you leave at once."

That did it! Without thought, he backed up, lifted his leg and kicked the door. "Gazow!" he screamed out as lightning sharp pain went through his foot and he hopped on one leg. Didn't the stupid label say the shoe had some kind of insulating support? He might as well have kicked the door with his bare foot! He made a mental note never to take action movies as literal ever again.

He heard a giggle from down the hall and looked up to see Morayo with his bed linen in her hand laughing at him. "Morayo!"

"Jason Stratham and Daniel Craig you are not, Solomon."

He spared her a glare and focused back on the door. He banged on it. "Celeste, open this door."

Silence.

The idea that she sat there in one of her dresses, regal as a queen and ignored him made him snap. He used his shoulder and laid into the door once, and then twice, ignoring the pain going through that side of his body. When he went to slam into it again, the door opened and before he could stop himself, he sailed through. The momentum of his body carried him almost half across the room and he landed in a sprawl on the carpet.

He groaned as the pain coursed through his body. He lifted himself up and turned to face her when he froze.

"Sir, I do not understand why you are being unusually obstinate. I made it quite clear I will not be able to accompany you this day."

Celeste had an old-fashioned mob cap on her head, the ruffled edge so long it fell on the forehead. The nightgown was straight from out of the Little House on the Prairie, long, and off white and just barely covered her toes. Her eyes were watery and red, and she sniffled. A second later, a deep bull-froggish cough landed into the large white handkerchief she had crunched in her hand. Her customary gloves were absent.

"Will you please vacate my chambers? I am suffering from a respiratory malady and would be most obliged if you could be so kind as to allow me to recuperate in the privacy of my room."

Solomon couldn't speak because the breath had left his body, whooshed out as if he'd been punched in the stomach. The pain that had taken hold of his body receded as new sensations flooded his system and flushed his body.

Gonzo's words came back to him: "I saw her again, and I could barely breathe!"

So this is what he meant, Solomon thought as he stared at this woman who in one instant became his beloved.

It was so sweet, this feeling. It gurgled inside him like a fountain in the middle of the desert. Fresh, it filled all the empty spaces of his soul with light.

Did the sun get brighter? The colors seemed to become more vibrant. His senses were enhanced, and he saw anew the clear, smooth nutmeg skin so soft to touch. The fragrant vanilla scent that clung to her tickled his nose. At a moment when she should have looked her worse, she became the most beautiful woman he'd ever seen.

How could he have ever thought she was ugly? His tongue should be scalded with hot bleach for saying such a heinous thing.

Gonzo should be given the Nobel Prize. His best friend had made the greatest discovery in all mankind. Celeste Martin, now Greene, was the best woman any man could ever have in all the solar system.

No wonder Gonzo had been willing to ruin their friendship for her. She was worth every sacrifice. Wasn't the phrase, 'all's fair in love and war'? Perhaps love and war were both sides of the same coin.

"Solomon? Is there something wrong?"

"No," he croaked out past the lump in his throat. He longed to tell her how he felt. The words fought for sound. Yet he had to wait. Everything had changed now. He wanted Celeste to love him back. If she loved him, she would never leave him, and they could stay married for the rest of their lives.

He inhaled and tried to calm down. After a moment, he could speak again. "I didn't know you were sick, Celeste. I'm sorry for jumping to conclusions. I thought you were trying to avoid me."

"The only thing I was trying to avoid was contaminating you with my contagion."

She didn't want him to get her cold. How sweet of her.

"I'm one of the few people on planet Earth who never get sick. Trust me on that one."

"Very well, sir."

"Get back into bed, Celeste."

"Sir, I am quite—" she started to say when she coughed again, more violently this time, and his concern mixed with his newfound love with acute sensitivity. She hurt, and he wanted to ease her pain in any way he could.

He walked over to her and picked up her slender form. Light as a feather.

"Solomon! Sir, this is most unseemly."

"Hush, woman," he commanded softly as he carried her to bed. He tried to keep her from noticing his heartbeat that thrashed inside his ribcage.

Celeste tried to protest again, but another fit of coughing wracked her body and he felt the strength of it tunnel through her slender frame. He ached for her.

"I'll ask Morayo to fix you some soup. You need to stay hydrated as well as eat some light foods. She will take care of you."

Like spun glass, he lowered her onto the bed. She didn't protest; a clue as to how bad she felt. He brushed his hand against her forehead alarmed at how hot she was.

"Solomon, how is Celeste?"

"She's got a fever. I think it's more than a cold."

"I'll try some Yoruba healing herbs first. See if they work. I'd rather try a holistic method first before drowning her in drugs."

Solomon tended to agree.

All day, Solomon kept by her side as his wife went in and out of sleep. During her wakeful moments, Morayo fed her soups packed with herbs from Yoruba used for various illnesses, made her drink water and toddy, and helped her back and forth to the bathroom.

He talked to her during her waking moments. When she slept, he sat by the bed, studied her, and drank in all her features so he could commit to memory the face of his beloved.

MORAYO

Someone tugged at the clothes on her body. Instantly, Celeste awoke and winced with pain. Her head pounded, and her nose stuffed as if embroidery cloth had been rammed into her nostrils. Heat rolled off her in waves and she shivered, her body sore. But she couldn't let anyone undress her.

"No," she murmured as she opened her eyes to see Morayo's kind concerned ones staring at her.

"I'm just going to help you change, Celeste. Nothing more."

"No. I'll take care of it."

"No, no. Celeste, you can barely stand up. Let me help you."

"I said no, Morayo. I can do it myself." Her voice sounded weak but her point was made when Morayo sighed.

"All right. At least let me help you to the bathroom, and I'll give you a change of clothes."

"No," Celeste said. "I'll do it."

Her legs trembled with the exercise, but she forced her body to move. Under no circumstances could anyone be privy to her secret.

It took forever. By the time she finished, her limbs shuddered with exhaustion. She didn't put her mob cap back on as it took too much energy.

"What you doing hiding all this hair, Celeste?" Morayo asked as she made her sit up on the bed. She then sat behind her and began to brush her hair and mix it with some kind of oil. She sniffed the air. Light, fragrant lavender. The scent floated in the air and wafted around. Muddled, Celeste realized it was some form of aromatherapy. It relaxed her as she inhaled.

A few moments later, her hair had been braided, and Morayo puffed the pillows behind her.

"Solomon's been worried about you."

"Indeed?" The thought made her feel a little bit better. She wondered what he'd said. Had he asked about her health? Brought some chicken soup? Called a doctor? She'd been self-reliant for so long it was nice to be pampered and fussed over.

"Yes. He only left just now because he wanted to get some more herbs we need for you to feel better. I hope you didn't mind, but we wanted to see if a holistic method worked instead of drowning you in drugs."

"I agree with your solution." Celeste rarely got sick anyway, and when she had, she nursed herself in a similar fashion.

"You may not notice, but you are starting to do better. You don't sound like a sex symbol for frogs now."

Celeste chuckled which turned into a hacking cough. "I'm still hot though."

"Well, the body is trying to burn out whatever is ailing you. But your temperature dropped about two degrees and will probably drop some more."

She nodded. "I miss the sound of the ocean right now."

"I had to close the windows."

As she started to straighten the room, Celeste watched her. Morayo had become a sister to her in a short amount of time. Unlike Blaze with her waspish attitude, the woman could speak her mind without abrasion. The song she hummed was the one that she liked.

"I like that song you sing. That hymn. Do you think I can go to your church with you the next time you go? Do they sing it there?"

Her face lit up, the white teeth bright against her dark skin. "Of course! Our congregation is diverse, but there are a number of us who are Yoruba and we've taken some of the songs and arranged them to the drums."

"Drums?"

"Before I became a Christian, I was a santera priestess. As a santera, the drums are used to call upon the *orishas*, our gods and goddesses embodied in the form of various saints. Since we have found Christ, we use our drums to celebrate the fact we do not have to call Jesus to come here. He is already here."

"Is it really so much different than what you believed before?" Celeste asked.

Morayo stopped her movements. The linens she clutched rested on her hips as her face grew thoughtful. "Yes it is," she said finally. "In Santeria, it's a mixture of *orishas* and a generic supreme creator. In the Washed Saints, the emphasis is on being pure by wrapping yourself in the Virgin's garments."

"That's rather odd." She had declined the invitation to visit the church with her mother-in-law.

Morayo sat on the bench near the balcony. "Yet, I believed in the Reverend Daughter and the Exalted Son. I even remember what she said that caused me to leave the belief of my family for generations. 'The purity of the Virgin will flow into and wipe you clean. Dear Virgin, nourish us with your heavenly form. Wrap us in your garments and let our impurity disintegrate and your purity enter in. Make us clean.'"

"You are a highly intelligent woman. At the risk of being judgmental, may I ask how could you fall for such a thing?"

Morayo stared off into the distance. "Perhaps that's why I fell for it hook, line, and sinker. The things she said were so outrageous maybe they had to be true.

"The Reverend Daughter didn't ask for adulation. She simply stated the Virgin came to her in a vision and revealed the truth about her status. As I look back, I believe God allowed me to have the doubts that would cause me to seek Him. In Santeria, there's an emphasis on purity, and following the way Ellegua gives you." She looked at Celeste "He is an *orisha* that guides the priest or priestess to their path. As a Washed Saint, the Virgin wanted to cleanse you from impurity but there were things you had to do. And I failed quite often.

215

"I began to feel dirty. I wanted the Virgin to purify me, but I had to do more. I could never do enough. Then one day, I was walking down the street in downtown Tampa, and I heard a man sing that song I told you about. 'I heard an old, old story. How the Savior came from glory.' There wasn't a need to perform an act or call upon a god or a goddess. God was already here! I stood there and listened, and the words pierced me like a needle. I wanted to know more, and the pastor there just happened to be Yoruba and he told me of Jesus and God's love. And His power and His majesty. God was so much bigger than the Supreme Creator. I didn't need to sacrifice animals or perform ceremonies to reach Him. He was already here, waiting for me. At that moment, I believed. And I left it all behind."

Celeste wanted to believe what Morayo said. That He really wanted her to be happy and bask in His love. But she was His leftovers, wasn't she?

She turned from the radiant glow from Morayo. "How can you be so sure?"

"Because He said so. The pastor, when he talked to me, showed me a verse in scripture. Jesus prayed for me thousands of years before my family was a thought."

"I don't understand."

Morayo got up and opened Celeste's closet. She pulled out a Bible. Going over to the bed, she perched on the edge and flipped it open.

She read out loud a lengthy passage. "I do not ask for these only, but also for those who will believe in me through their word, that they may all be one, just as you, Father, are in me, and I in you, that they also may be in us, so that the world may believe that you have sent me. The glory that you have given me I have given to them, that they may be one even as we are one, I in them and you in me, that they may become perfectly one, so that the world may know that you sent me and loved them even as you loved me. Father, I desire that they also, whom you have given me, may be with me where I am, to

216

see my glory that you have given me because you loved me before the foundation of the world. O righteous Father, even though the world does not know you, I know you, and these know that you have sent me. I made known to them your name, and I will continue to make it known, that the love with which you have loved me may be in them, and I in them."

As she listened, the words of Christ touched her. She knew she belonged to God. The thought soothed her. "And these words convinced you?"

"Yes. When the pastor showed this to me, in the margin of the scripture, he'd written his name. And then he asked me to put my name in there."

Celeste watched as Morayo's eyes moistened. "And when I read it that way, the most beautiful, wonderful thing happened to me. I became aware of His presence. I could feel it all around me. A tangible thing I couldn't see. Like the feel of the wind against your skin. God was there at that moment, and I felt His love and I knew then this is what I had been searching for. Jesus had died for me so I can be in communion with him."

Celeste could see the inner glow from her. She wanted the conviction Morayo had. But how could she? God didn't give her the mark that showed He considered her the leftovers.

"I'm going to tell you something Celeste. Something I've never told anyone else."

For a moment, Celeste wasn't sure she wanted to know. What secret could this beautiful woman possibly have? God had blessed her abundantly, and if it were some kind of deed from the past, then it would remain there. "Be confident it will go no further than this room," she assured her.

"I am not a whole woman. I am sterile because I have no uterus."

A jolt of surprise went through her. How could that be? Why did God do this to a woman who devoted her life to Him? "Oh Morayo, I'm so sorry. You would have been a great mother."

"During my *Asiento*, the time period of purification to become a full-fledged *santera*, Ellugea led me to become a priest of Yemaya, the 'Mother Goddess'. But I had never had a monthly. When I turned seventeen my mother took me to the doctor, and that's when I found out. So I saw being born childless as an act of hate from Yemaya.

"There are times sorrow overcomes me as I think I will never be a mother of a child of my own body. And men may see me as an easy take because I could never get pregnant. And then later, what man wants to be with a woman who can't give him children to pass on his line? Oh, I know there are some who would continue to love me, but I struggle with my inadequacy.

"So when I heard Jesus prayed for believers then and now, that He loved me so much to die, I started crying over and over again. It didn't matter that I wasn't born to have children." Morayo's voice broke up, and she started crying and then laughing with joy. "It didn't matter that I had impure thoughts. His blood would wash me clean. His love made me whole."

Quickly she turned the book and went to another passage. And she read out aloud. "'Three times I pleaded with the Lord about this, that it should leave me. But he said to me, "My grace is sufficient for you, for my power is made perfect in weakness." Therefore, I will boast all the more gladly of my weaknesses, so that the power of Christ may rest upon me. For the sake of Christ, then, I am content with weaknesses, insults, hardships, persecutions, and calamities. For when I am weak, then I am strong.'

"It made perfect sense to me then. In spite of my sterility, I am still His. That He will still be my God because he loves me. He makes me strong in my weakness. It clicked for me then, and I have never turned back. I've victory because I have it in Jesus."

Tears streamed down Celeste's face as the barrier she'd encase herself in and anger she'd always held toward God crumbled. If Morayo didn't see herself as leftovers and still worthy of God's love, then so could she. The jealousy she had toward her sister receded.

218

No, she wasn't Leah Martin, affianced to Jacob Othello Westwood. She was the wife of Solomon Greene, a man that accepted her and wanted her as his wife.

Thank you, dear Lord. You answered my prayer.

"Morayo, I thought I was God's leftovers. I thought He didn't love me. That He wanted me to be unhappy."

"I know, Celeste." The tone of her voice made her jerked back, and she studied the dark eyes that gazed into her own. She knew?

Morayo nodded as if she'd spoken out loud. "I haven't said a word."

Celeste wiped at her eyes. "But when?"

"Today."

Morayo told her how she had found out by accident and Celeste fingers knotted in the bed sheets. In spite her newly restored faith, panic seized her.

"Please, please, please don't tell Solomon."

"I won't say a word. I just wanted you to understand God loves you, Celeste. You can have the same victory I have. You only have to accept it. When Jesus died for our sins and rose again, He was victorious. That's why we have victory over every situation in our lives, no matter how hard, sad, or difficult they may be. After all, you did a reckless thing. You married a man you met a museum. He could have been anyone. Do you know how dangerous that could have been? How different your story could have turned out?"

Celeste bowed her head as a sense of awe pervaded her. She had been so angry at God for so long for thinking He didn't care. The magnitude of what could have happened dawned on her. She had spent so many years in comparison of her sister, alternated between love and jealousy.

"God sent Solomon to you and you to him. He made you for each other. Or actually, I think he made you for Solomon. Don't hold yourself back on him. Tell him the truth and let that bind you together."

Tell him the truth? The very phrase caused a wellspring of near hysteria to rise within her. "I can't. I can't tell him. I can't. I can't."

Morayo shushed her once more. "Okay. Ask God to give you the strength and the right time to tell him."

"I haven't prayed to God in ages."

"Thankfully, God's never too busy to take a call from a wayward child."

MAPLE SYRUP ACID

The web of lemon taffy stretched out under the glare of a hazy sun. An overcast cloudy sky created the backdrop for the four maple trees that upheld the web swayed lightly in a wind that caressed his bound body.

The threads of the web were hair strand fine with the elasticity of bubblegum and the tension of steel. Entangled in their gossamer hold, Solomon struggled. His teeth clenched as he pulled at the diaphanous binding. His feet kicked in the air, his pants clad legs jerked, his stomach muscles went rigid, and his chest heaved as he pulled and tugged with every ounce of strength he had.

He had to get out of there.

The more he fought, the more he became entangled in it. Lemon taffy strand after lemon taffy strand wrapped itself around him. Crisscrossed and bound him more and more against the web's hold until he was encased in a cocoon that left only his head free.

A movement caught his peripheral vision, and he saw them.

Two beautiful women crawled toward him, unencumbered by the taffy.

"Frank White," the darker of them whispered. Long wavy dark brown hair, dramatic black eyebrows painted on with a fine tipped brush lifted over amber eyes. Her skin was coffee mixed with cream and covered by a long-sleeved emerald nightshirt whose hem grazed the tops of her knees as she moved closer to him.

"Hans Bader," the other one spoke as she shook the platinum blond hair from her face. It contrasted starkly with the cobalt blue long nightgown she wore. Her milk and rose hued skin, long elegant arms and rounded shoulders adorned with the spaghetti thin straps were delicate.

Both women were exquisite in their splendor, their loveliness a testament to the glory of feminine beauty. The sight of them filled

Solomon with heat-robbing fear. It cascaded over his skin, raised goose bumps, and lifted the hair on his neck. The fear widened his eyes, made his mouth slack open and his heart slammed against his ribs like an animal locked in a cage.

"Go away! Get away from me!" he screamed out.

"No Frank," the emerald one smiled, as she came closer to him.

"We will never go away," the other added as she also drew nearer.

Simultaneously their faces began to harden into expressions of intense hunger, their breathing escalated as they crept closer.

This was worse than anything he'd ever experience. There was a sense of finality to it. He would never be able to escape them. There wasn't any amount of fight he could put up that would release him from this bondage. He was trapped and the thought of escape a joke. Solomon's head drooped in despair.

There was only one thing to do, one last desperate attempt.

Oh God, help me.

Something plopped on the lemon taffy threads. Without any real interest, he shifted his gaze to see what it was.

It appeared to be maple syrup, but there wasn't any syrup he knew of in the world that burned like acid. Another drop of maple syrup splattered on the web. The women had stopped in their tracks. The expressions of hunger morphed into fear.

It started to rain maple syrup. Each droplet disintegrated the taffy and left tiny wisps of smoke in the air. Both women flinched and jerked as each drop created holes in their bodies while it had no effect on him. Their faces were soon full of holes and rage contorted their beauty. The remnants of their lips snarled and curled up. Their teeth bared. The sultry eyes were narrowed and glowered at him. The threads had weakened enough to enable him to rip himself from their grip. He didn't waste another second as he jumped from web and landed on the ground. Syrup ran down his face in rivulets.

The small rainfall turned into a torrential downpour and syrup cascaded down in sheets of liquid with the effect of magma. The web and the women melted away under the onslaught.

As suddenly as it had come, the maple syrup rain stopped. The sun grew brighter and illuminated the four trees. With something akin to fascination mixed with a dab of horror, Solomon watched as the trees began to ooze out sap. It ran down the grooves of the bark and pooled at the bases. At each base, the puddles began to move as if they were alive and they all met at the center of the copse of the trees. The now massive puddle began to bubble and gurgle upward, growing into a tower that started to shape itself. Stretching, elongating, flattening out, or expanding, the sap formed itself into the shape of a woman.

At first, Solomon thought it was Mrs. Butterworth's come to life. But no, it wasn't a thing matronly about this syrup woman. She was exquisite, and she was all his.

Celeste.

She smiled at him, and his heart fluttered.

Love her. A voice whispered.

He swirled around, searched for the source of the voice.

Love her, the voice whispered again.

He turned back to the syrup Celeste and reached for her when woke up. His eyes to the darkness of his room. His heartbeat was steady and normal, his skin warm with heat.

The beautiful women were gone. Melted by maple syrup acid.

God had spoken to him in his dream. When he prayed, the maple syrup acid rain came and melted the lemon taffy web and the women on it. He was freed but how?

The answer came to him a moment later. Of course! His love for Celeste liberated him. And God had told him to love her. Well, that certainly wouldn't be a command hard to follow.

Rising from the bed, he opened the doors to the balcony and felt the early morning breeze caress him. The waves made a refreshing sound against the shore, and he inhaled the salty fragrance. The moon's light waned, but it still made a glorious picture in the sky and gave the ocean a pearly hue.

He walked over to his dresser and turned on the night light next to it. As he opened the drawer, he stopped as he saw a Bible reflected under the light.

Morayo.

A stick of paper protruded from it, and he opened the book to that place.

I Corinthians 13. Morayo had highlighted a passage, and he read it.

"Love is patient and kind; love does not envy or boast; it is not arrogant or rude. It does not insist on its own way; it is not irritable or resentful; it does not rejoice at wrongdoing, but rejoices with the truth. Love bears all things, believes all things, hopes all things, endures all things. Love never ends. As for prophecies, they will pass away; as for tongues, they will cease; as for knowledge, it will pass away. For we know in part and we prophesy in part, but when the perfect comes, the partial will pass away. When I was a child, I spoke like a child, I thought like a child, I reasoned like a child. When I became a man, I gave up childish ways."

The dream came back to him full force. Love her. What did that mean? He knew what he felt but what did he do with that? Until yesterday, he'd thought love was another word for sex!

What could he do to show he loved Celeste? And how the heck did Morayo know he needed to know this!

Shame came upon him. He'd ask God for an ugly wife and in return, God had given him the most beautiful one in the world. And he still had yet to make good on his part of the bargain.

He reread one of the highlighted passages: When I was a child, I spoke like a child, I thought like a child, I reasoned like a child. When I became a man, I gave up childish ways."

Solomon placed the book on the top of the dresser and rubbed his head, fixated on the verse.

Children can't make up their minds. They go from one fancy to another. He'd hopped from one bed to the other like a kid given free rein in a candy store. A man didn't jump from one bed to the other and sleep with every pair of legs. The last ten years of his life had been a complete waste. He'd acted like an oversexed but physically mature five year old in a store.

Yet, the candy wasn't a sugary confectionary but women. He'd pick and choose from the most colorful and the prettiest. Like gumballs in a jar.

If it hadn't been for the blueberry woman . . .

He could see her face now as she screamed at him, jabbed her finger at his chest, and hated him.

He hadn't even known her name. If she hadn't come and jolted him out of the routine of his bed hops, he'd probably still be there.

Celeste deserved a better man; a man who wouldn't have residue in his mind from other women.

Although he was free from their grip in his mind, he wasn't rid of their memory.

Solomon fell back on his bed, stared at the canopy.

Would he ever escape his past?

THIN VENEER

Patrick opened the door and moved back to allow the Reverend Daughter and Exalted Son into the house, the air between them so fraught with tension he could almost reach out and touch it.

They had dressed in white tonight for the new member's initiation into the Washed Saints. The white represented the purity from the Virgin's garments that would keep them from impurity. Each new member fasted for three days and dwelt on the impurity of their lives and confronted it. During this time, a journal was given to them to write down all their sins. After those three days, the member would go to the church, bathe and then stand in front of the Virgin's statue. Warmed water would be poured over them, symbolizing they were cleansed in the Virgin's purity and their impurities would be washed away.

Cordelia then said a prayer to the Virgin, and they would then be blessed by the Exalted Son and given the title of Washed Saint.

Usually, Cordelia came from the new member initiations in high spirits, her face aglow with satisfaction. Tonight, however, her face was drawn and tight, the corners of her mouth turned down. The Exalted Son didn't look any happier. His forehead creased, and his body held rigid as if he fought to control violent emotions.

By a thread, it would seem, Patrick thought.

"Batcher, prepare one of the spare bedrooms," Cordelia ordered.

Patrick went to answer in the affirmative when Theodore's hand reached out and grabbed her arm. From the wince on her face, it wasn't a light grip.

"That won't be necessary, old boy," Theodore objected.

"Oh yes, it will be necessary. You must be crazy to think I would want to stay in the same room with you."

"But you will," the Exalted Son bit out through his teeth.

Patrick backed away to leave them in privacy when he saw Cordelia snatch her arm out of Theodore's hand. It left a red welt on her skin.

"No, I will not. I saw you with Reanne tonight. You were both huddled in the corner of the church while I said a prayer to the Virgin. She could barely keep her hands to herself. And you just let her."

"I can't control others' actions Cordelia. Would you have preferred I interrupted your sacred initiation?"

"Yes! Instead you humiliated me in front of the Virgin."

Patrick coughed in an attempt to interrupt them even as he made sure to keep his face void of expression.

The diversion worked as they both jumped and stared at him as if he just appeared from the ground.

"Would you like the room prepared, Mrs. Greene?"

"No," Theodore answered as Cordelia opened her mouth to speak. "In fact, would you just bring up a night cap in a few moments?"

Theodore then took her arm and as she resisted, he tugged her up the stairs. Before Patrick knew it, he heard their bedroom door open and close.

He waited ten minutes in the kitchen before going up the stairs with the desired drink. As he came to the door, he could hear them screaming, and he stopped to listen.

"I did what you wanted!" Theodore shouted.

"I can't believe you expect me just to tolerate that woman in my presence. You're sleeping with her!"

"Reanne is a devotee. She's dedicated to us in a way that if you asked her to jump off the bridge, she'd do it! Her faith is so strong in the Virgin you can control her every action. Anything she does for me, she does because she wants to."

"How could you do this, Theo? All these years of being married? Of our church? How could you cheat on me?" Patrick could hear the tears in her voice.

There was a long silence, and Patrick almost knocked on the door when Theo spoke again. He tilted his ear.

"I didn't want to. But you were so occupied with the Virgin, Cordelia. She has taken up so much of your time you hardly have any for me. I realized it had been months since we'd had any time to ourselves, away from the church, away from the children. And when Reanne came into the picture, I couldn't resist."

"I wonder if you would be as understanding if I slept with one of our children!"

"This church has consumed you, Cordelia. To the point of everything else. We don't even talk about anything else but the church and what more we could do to grow it. Don't you see? Is this church worth our marriage?"

"Obviously, your sex drive is worth more to you than our marriage."

"Because this church is more important to you than our marriage, our son! He didn't even invite us to his wedding because we were so occupied with this church! Can't you see Cordelia? This church is eating us alive."

"No, it isn't! The Virgin demands our every sacrifice! Every part of our lives! Her purity must flow into our veins to replace the red blood of our impurity! I wrap myself in her garments and drawn from her purity!" Cordelia started to say, her voice high with entreaty and a quality of reverent awe.

"Shut up, Cordelia! Look at you! Here we are talking about my cheating and you go off into La La Land about the Virgin! This is what drove me to Reanne. She was concerned about me while my wife was praying to the Virgin!"

Patrick heard a scuffle, a grunt, the tinkling sound of something delicate breaking and then he heard Cordelia shout, "Get your hands off me!"

"No!" Theo said. "I want my wife back, not the Reverend Daughter. I want to be Theo darling again, not the Exalted Son."

More scuffling sounds, a short yell from Cordelia suddenly cut off, and then a long pause. Patrick once again went to knock on the door when he heard Theo say, "Do you remember that, sweet wife?"

"Don't you ever kiss me again, Theo. I don't even want you to touch me again. Let go of me."

Patrick thought it was prudent by then to knock on the door.

"What is it?" Theo shouted.

"You wanted a nightcap sir," Patrick answered.

"Oh," Theo responded, his voice sounded mollified and then the door opened just enough to let Theo slide through. He had taken off the suit jacket, and his shirt was wrinkled. The man's eyes were wide and dilated even as he scowled.

"Patrick old boy, get one of the spare bedrooms ready. I'll be sleeping in one of them from now on."

"Of course."

Theodore took the drink from the tray, downed it and then stalked off.

"Did you need anything, Mrs. Greene?" Patrick asked through the opening.

"Batcher, come in here and clean this up."

Usually, he would have taken umbrage to her tone but he wanted to see what had transpired between them.

The sitting area where the desk was in their bedroom was in shambles. The keyboard to the computer dangled on the side of the desk and papers were spewed all over the floor. Behind the desk the wall decorated by a custom-made wallpaper veneer of the Holy Virgin. On either side of it were pictures of the Reverend Daughter and the Exalted Son. Their faces were set in expressions of holiness but if their argument he'd overheard was anything to go by, their marriage was just as thin.

SECRET REVEALED

Celeste longed for her icy reserve of three, almost four months ago. She wished she could once again freeze her emotions and hide behind her mask, deaden all sensation and bask in the thought her unhappiness was God's plan for her life. In an odd way, she had been more comfortable then. She couldn't be hurt in that state. An insult wouldn't get past her frigid shielding, and she would never feel the sadness of her loneliness. In the past, when it tried to rise in her, she'd smash it down and, pummeled it with the strength of any wrestler.

Now, all that had changed in such a short time. The ice was gone and in its place a warm glow filled with excitement and anticipation promised to grow and fill all the empty spaces inside of her.

Morayo had forbidden her to leave the room on threat of taking all her costumes and hiding them, so Celeste was forced to lay there and think. She couldn't even get on her computer because it had been taken it away, as well. All the woman had left was a pair of knitting needles, a giant ball of wool yarn and the Bible. For two days, Celeste had been occupied with creating a sampler of all the stitches she'd learn, thinking about her husband, and reading the Bible.

Could she really tell Solomon the truth? Bare to him the secret that had been a part of her life for so long? The idea sent chills through her fingers, and she dropped her needles. She focused her gazed on the ocean outside.

Hope. She'd never allowed it to exist within her. It had grown when she thought she wanted to spend her life with Jacob and then shriveled when he fell in love with her sister. Once again hope took a stake to her heart. Was she brave enough to accept it once more?

She'd been reading the Bible over and over again. Passages leapt out at her. She was soothed by some, convicted by others, treasured by more. Obviously God loved her. She could not ignore that anymore and after a long prayer filled with tears, she'd released her anger at God. Could she trust God again? Trust that He would give her what she always wanted – a man to love her?

Once more, she picked up the Bible, and read Psalms 37: 4-5, "Delight yourself in the Lord, and he will give you the desires of your heart. Commit your way to the Lord; trust in him, and he will act." She dropped down further and read, "Refrain from anger, and forsake wrath! Fret not yourself; it tends only to evil."

"It tends only to evil," she whispered out loud.

Had her attitude been evil? There was no reason to think why it wouldn't be. She'd been jealous of her sister all these years. She'd closed herself away from meaningful friendships except Goijaart. She'd blamed God for her circumstances almost to the point where she'd almost hated Him.

Tears started to fall as she realized even in her disobedience, God had still protected her. She sniffled and more tears fell on to the page and she wiped her eyes and she flipped to another passage. It was from Proverbs 3: "Trust in the Lord with all your heart, and do not lean on your own understanding. In all your ways acknowledge him, and he will make straight your paths."

"Okay, dear Lord," she spoke into the room. "I will trust you. Trust you with everything."

And the warmth inside of her grew, and she sighed and wiped the tears from her eyes.

It was time to admit it.

She was in love with her husband. Heart throbbing, sexy, action hero physique, green gold eyed Solomon—a man that belonged to her. Kind, generous, and arrogant without being domineering. His kisses were so sweet and each time his lips met hers, she never wanted it to end.

And now, it didn't have to end. There wasn't a two year time boundary. Suddenly, forever was more than reasonable.

She laughed out loud and then ran to the door. She called out. "Morayo! Morayo! Come quick!"

Morayo came to the door moments later, her chest heaving.

"What's wrong, Celeste? Are you okay?"

Celeste giggled, and ran and hugged the woman who had in such a short time become a lifelong friend. "No, no, no, Morayo. I'm so sorry, everything is right not wrong. I need your help with something."

"What?"

"I'm going shopping."

Her forehead creased in confusion. "Shopping? For more material?"

Celeste threw back her head and laughed, so happy she felt as if she would burst from it.

"No. I need your help shopping."

"Since when do you go shopping? Don't you make all your own clothes?"

"Not anymore."

Hours later she arrived back at Arcadia with dozens of bags in her hand. In all her adult life, she'd never had such fun. Shopping with unlimited resources with Morayo made for the most enjoyable time she'd ever had.

She thought of the outfit she planned to wear. How Solomon would react to it? Would he recognize the significance of the change? Would he care?

As they brought in the last of the bags, she saw a movement to her right. Solomon stood in the hallway, arms folded watching her.

"Hello Solomon," Celeste greeted shyly. This new love seemed to get sweeter with each moment. She let Morayo take the bags upstairs as she drew herself closer to her husband.

"I see you've been busy today. Here I was worried about you being sick," he responded in a mocking tone full of humor.

"How could a person not get better with Morayo here to help them in their convalescence?"

Solomon remained silent as he walked over to her. His eyes snared hers, and she couldn't look away. Dressed casually in a pair of shorts rolled at the knees and sleeveless T-shirt he loomed over her as his masculine scent tinged by the ocean breeze touched her nostrils. He crowded her against the wall and rested his hands on her waist.

His eyes gazed down into hers, full of an emotion she couldn't quite name. An electric current flowed between them. This was a pulsing, magnetic connection.

"I missed you Celeste," Solomon whispered quietly. "I came home and you weren't here."

"I didn't mean for you to worry, sir," Celeste answered just as softly.

"It wasn't that I was worried, Celeste. I'm craving you."

It was the last thing she expected to hear, and excitement coursed through her veins.

"Oh," she replied lamely. She hoped he couldn't hear her heart beat like a drum.

"Oh?" Solomon mocked. "I'm hungry for you and the most you can say is, 'Oh'?"

If he said anything more, her body would match the temperature of the sun.

"I wanted to touch this flower soft skin with my fingers," He rubbed his fingers across her cheek. "So soft," he murmured as if he talked to himself. "I wanted to be close enough to you and wrap myself in your vanilla scented skin." He bent his head and anchored it against the column of her neck. "Ummm, you smell good, woman." Before she knew it, he nipped the base of her neck and a strangled sound of pleasure escaped her lips. "And I wanted to see what would happen if I did that," he continued, "And you did not disappoint. I wanted to drown in your maple syrup eyes and kiss these lips until I've had my fill."

As he bent his head, he said, "I hope you don't have anything planned right now."

Somehow, she made it up the stairs fifteen minutes later, her legs like water and Morayo in her room sitting at her vanity.

"Now that's what a woman on her honeymoon is supposed to look like," she laughed and then left Celeste to her thoughts.

They were all jumbled. Solomon had kissed her as if his very life depended on it, his lips expert but there was a hunger to them she responded to. She took in her reflection. Her lips were swollen and puffy. For the first time in her life, passion had gripped her body. She remembered her hands dug into his hair and tugged at the strands. She'd kissed him back with more fervor than knowledge. Her response had apparently been adequate because he'd groaned, and his ardor increased. His body became as rigid as steel although his mouth remained pliant.

She became lost in their frenzy until he suddenly ripped his lips from hers and pressed his forehead to her, his breathing harsh to her ears but such a delightful sound.

"Woman, not yet. Not yet," he gulped. His eyes were full of desire, and she couldn't believe she was the cause of it.

"Go upstairs, Celeste. Give me some time to calm down. Tell Morayo she can stop hiding and make us some food."

There must have been food at the table. Celeste was certain there was. It may have even tasted like heaven, but it could have been paper for all the notice she took of it. Solomon had held her gaze most of the time. His green gold eyes seared her with their heated intensity. Her insides knotted as the one thought kept coming to the forefront – how was this night going to end when she told him?

Dinner over, Morayo shook her head in mock shame as she cleared the dishes. "You both go outside on the beach. Cool off."

A large shawl wrapped around her and with Solomon's arm settled on her waist, they walked on the beach. The sun blazed fire across the sky for the final time before the night fell. The waves crashed against the sand, and the ocean breeze chilly but delicious. True to Morayo's words, a walk on the beach seemed to have a calming effect on their ardor. It hadn't dissipated but cooled some, from the temperature of the sun to the heat of lava.

She leaned her body against him. His forehead rested on her head. Eventually, she pulled off her shoes, and they waded in the water, laughing as they started to play. It hadn't even occurred to her to be concerned about her dress.

Solomon grabbed her from behind, his arms hard but she felt safe in their embrace. He turned her to face him, and the moon reflected in his eyes. She couldn't look away as he lifted her chin and pressed his lips to hers again. His lips were gentler this time but still as potent as ever. Her hands drifted to his hair to entangle her fingers in the inky silkiness. He groaned at her touch and pulled himself away from her mouth.

"I've never met a woman like you in my life, Celeste," he told her as he pressed his forehead to her own. "I thank God for you."

The words, spoken in a reverent tone were the most beautiful she'd ever heard. Poignant, they touched her soul and a tear fell from her eyes. He caught it with his thumb. As he held her gaze, he licked the tear away.

They stood there on the edge of the ocean . . . wrapped in their own world.

After twenty minutes, they headed back to the house. Morayo met them there and shooed them away to their separate rooms. As she got ready for bed, Celeste wondered where she would spend the night. Tonight she would tell Solomon her secret, and she was quite sure he'd still accept her.

She bowed her head and thanked God for the wonderful day.

A knock on her door jolted her from her supplication. Heart thumping, she went to the door and opened it.

Solomon stood at her doorway, dressed in a black silk robe and pajamas. She gulped. Was this it?

"Celeste, I need to speak to you."

She couldn't talk so she opened the door further and let him in and closed the door.

He stood in the middle of the room, and she noticed for the first time nervous tension surrounded him. Why would Solomon be nervous?

A loud sigh escaped his lips and then he turned to her.

"I want you, Celeste. I've never wanted a woman as much as I want you. But I need to tell you about my past. I care too much about you for you not to know, and if we are going to go any further in this marriage as man and wife, we can't have any secrets between us."

She smiled. "I agree." This had to be a sign from God. Once Solomon said what he had to say and she hers, they can put the past behind them once and for all. Tonight would be the first day of forever.

"I'll start from about five years ago and just go from there. I don't know how you're going to react to this but I won't lie. I'll tell you everything and it's up to you what you plan to do with it."

Celeste moved the chairs in her room to face each other and then she motioned for him to sit down.

He obeyed but still didn't say anything for a long while. She allowed him his silence. She would probably need the same consideration when her turn came.

Finally, he said it.

"Celeste, I used to be a porn star."

PAM

Five years ago . . .

"All women are desserts," Solomon said as he opened the refrigerator.

Ben Nomasters laughed. "Yeah, man. Tender, juicy, ripe pieces of—"

"I know, I know," Solomon grinned as he pulled out a can of orange juice and threw it to Ben who caught it deftly in his hands. He had the classic looks of a basketball player. He towered above Solomon by five inches and had brown bear skin. Nicknamed Doc Oct on account of his long arms and legs some had joked he could scratch his knee without bending. He sat on the leather couch in the living room in Solomon's penthouse.

As Ben opened the can, he asked, "Dude, who was that girl you were with last night?"

Solomon took a swig as he shut the door. "Dude, man I don't have a clue. We hooked up at Josiah's last night. She came onto me. I think her name was Pam. I can't remember."

The night had been a blur. As a matter of fact, the past year had been hazy. He took another drink. After all, when he'd left home after college, he had no need to work. He came into his inheritance when he turned twenty-five last year and with millions in the bank, he decided to leave the mansion and go off on his own.

The penthouse he rented was located in an affluent part of Bloomfield Hills in Michigan. Spacious and sparsely furnished, he had been excited to have a place that didn't ring with the sound of prayers to the Virgin, muted arguments from his parents, and he kept the place clean on his own without Patrick's help. He attempted to cook his own meals but nearly burned the place down. The next week he hired a cook to come and make meals that could be heated later.

It was pathetic, but that didn't matter. He had his own way of doing things.

He'd entered into some of the local X-Games, competed in the freestyle competitions, and won a couple of prizes. They occupied his time. Without those, he wouldn't even know what month it was. The whole idea of independence had seemed so hyped up in retrospect.

Night was when he came alive. At ten o'clock, he'd head out to a local bar or club and see what would happen. Most of the time, he came or went home with some female or other. Hot, gorgeous women with only one thing in mind, a quick lay.

"Well, Pam had it going on! Malita called me, so I stayed with her last night." Ben's voice brought him out his reverie.

Solomon frowned as he tried to think of where he'd heard the name before. "Malita? Malita Wood? Isn't that the girl you met like a month ago?"

Ben shrugged and tipped the can of juice back. "Yeah."

"Are you digging her?" His friend avoided monogamous relationships with almost fanatical ferocity.

"Dude." The one word said a lot.

Far as Solomon knew, his friend had almost as much action as he did. Ben had looks and money as his family came from a line of wealthy French black aristocrats that settled in Michigan about two hundred years ago in a small town near the Upper Peninsula.

"I just wondered man. Thought you were going soft on me."

Ben wouldn't meet his eyes and he lifted his hand and rubbed the top of it. Solomon's eyes narrowed as a sudden silence grew between them. Ben only rubbed his head when he was nervous about something. Then it hit him.

"Dude, you are serious," he exclaimed as his mouth fell open.

Ben scoffed but remained silent.

Solomon leapt over the small counter that separated the kitchen area from the living room. His eyebrows touched the top of his forehead in surprise. "Ben, dude. Really? You're only twenty-eight years old."

He watched as his friend got up and finished the rest of his juice. With effortless ease, he lifted his hand, aimed the can and watched as it sailed in a smooth arc and landed in the garbage can. "I didn't say we were getting married, man."

"But you've been kickin' it with her for a month, right?"

"Yeah. So?"

"When did Ben Nomasters become a one gal guy?"

"Dude, you trippin'. I'm just kickin' it with her for a while, that's all. Pretty soon, another dessert will go on the table, and I'll have to sample some of that."

Solomon and he laughed as they fist-bump.

Two days later, the doorbell rang and he opened the door to see Pam.

"Uh, Pam," he greeted in an awkward voice, shocked at the sight of her.

"Hello Solomon," she responded back. Her dark eyes watched him intently even as her lips curved upward. He let his gaze rove over her. She came prepared to spend the night. Her black hair shone with luster as it contrasted with her grape-hued eyes. Against her powdered sugar skin, they blazed with a sultry fire. She wore a black form fitting dress made all the more seductive because it emphasized her shape while it covered her completely.

"If you're finished," she said, and he lifted his eyes back to her face, "may I come in?"

He stepped back to allow her in, his eyes fixed on her. His breathing escalated, and he felt the familiar sense of desire heat the blood in his veins. Pam whatever-her-last-name-was had the body of a temptress and the swag of confidence. Every step she took was calculated to draw a man's gaze to some part of her anatomy. He could remember at Josiah's two days ago the way the black light from the dance floor had illuminated her in a way that she seemed like a neon-lit fairy.

The door closed behind him and locked in the strawberry scent she wore in the small hallway. It intoxicated him all over again.

But when hadn't a woman's body affected him? Since the time he turned fifteen and lost his virginity with Stacy Pell, he'd never said no to a woman who offered. The older he got, he became more selective about the women he slept with. After all, why exert so much energy for an ugly woman? He knew how to give a good time – being sexy was a small price to pay for one night with him.

"I had such a good time the last time, I wondered if I can get an encore?"

All the blood in his body rushed through him. It heated every vein, every artery, every single nerve cell. Solomon's lips stretched into a grin as he put his hands on her waist and started to caress her.

"Well, I could never say no to a sexy lady."

Pam Oliver had started to become a weekly fixture in his life. His days were filled with practice at the skateboard park or going to Ben's practice sessions with his team. His nights were a steady stream of night clubs, bars, and random hook-ups although more often than not, he ended up with Pam at his or her place.

One night, they were lounging in his living room; she dressed in some silky thing that hung off her shoulders and he in pajamas when she suddenly said, "Hey, let's record it."

Confused he turned toward her. "Record what?"

"Us," she said as she rubbed her hand over his thigh. Her purple eyes were filled with invitation. As far as women went, Pam had to be one of the hottest he'd ever slept with in his life. Furthermore, she didn't want a real relationship with him. The only thing they gave each other was physical gratification and that they did well together.

"Really? That's something you want to do?" The idea completely blew his mind. He'd always considered lovemaking a private act.

"Why not? I think it would be hot." Her voice had taken a sultry quality as her hand lifted to his face. His heart started to beat faster in response. She leaned closer to him, her breath in his face warm and sweet. The scent of the perfume she wore coupled with the fragrance of hair all worked together to send every other thought to oblivion.

"Sure, whatever you want," he responded.

After that night, she wanted to record every time they were together. Initially, he had been hesitant about it, but after some time, he'd learn to tune it out.

Ben had come by a few times and on one of these occasions he told him about it.

"I knew that Pam chick was a freak!" Ben exclaimed.

They were in the second bedroom he'd converted into a game room, and they played video games.

"Why would a woman want to do that? I would think a guy would be more into that," Solomon said as he and Ben fought aliens on the screen.

"I'd never get into that kind of thing myself. When I'm with a girl, I don't want to think how this would look on camera."

"I just tune it out."

They were quiet for some time except for grunts and curses as they played the game. Their fingers flew over the controls. After they died the fifth time during a difficult sequence, they stopped.

"Where are you going tonight?" Solomon asked as they went into the kitchen and he tossed him a can of Pepsi.

"Malita and I are going to the opera house in Detroit."

Solomon whirled around, his eyes wide. "The opera house? Dude, are you serious?"

"Well, Malita wants to go, so why not?"

Solomon walked over to where Ben sat on the couch and sat down on the adjoining loveseat. "Ben, the one and only time I remember you went to the opera house was with your mom about three years ago. You said you hated opera."

Ben shrugged, but he rubbed his hands over his head and avoided his eyes.

"How long you been with Malita?"

"Three months."

"That's the longest you've ever been with a girl, Ben." Solomon said, amazed at the thought Ben Nomasters, semi-pro basketball player, heir to the Nomasters fortune, and all around playboy would be held captivated by one woman.

And from what he could remember about Malita — he only met her once — she wasn't extremely attractive. She had a nice body, but her face lacked anything that made her stand out.

"Where did you meet her again?"

"At Fred's club," Ben answered and then dipped his head as he rubbed it. "She was passing out," he cleared his throat and then continued, "gospel tracks."

"What! Security let her in there?"

"Well, it was ladies' night that day. And they didn't look like tracks. They look like those cards people leave on your windshield at in the parking lot."

"I thought you didn't like that type. Religious and all that."

Ben got up and looked out the window, but Solomon doubted he'd even notice.

"I thought I didn't either," Ben said, as he folded his arms. "At first, I couldn't believe this girl was in the club passing out gospel tracks. I knew she had to be crazy. Then she started talking about

Jesus and I thought, 'Yeah, right. If I turned it on the right way, she'd drop her—'" He stopped and then cleared his throat again. "Well whatever."

Solomon knew what Ben started to say. Why the restraint?

"So I made it my business to prove she was only talk. How many church girls do you know walking around with three or four kids?"

He inclined his head in agreement.

"Malita is different, man. I know she's digging me. I've seen that look before. Last month I thought for sure she'd give it up. The only thing she'd let me do is kiss her, and that's it."

Solomon's eyebrow drew together. "I thought you said you were at her place a few times."

Ben rubbed his head. "I lied. That woman won't even let me near her house. I have to meet her at the church or the library or some public place like that."

"I don't get it," Solomon said as he leaned back, "why go through all the trouble? There's plenty more women out there."

"I've thought of that. I even told her I wouldn't see her anymore. Dude, you know what she did?" Ben half turned to him, the sunlight behind him silhouetted his figure. "She opened the door to my car, shoved me in, and waved goodbye. When she walked away, she never looked back. She didn't care. So for three weeks, I went back to doing what I had been doing. I tried to hook up with a couple of different girls, but I ended up going home by myself. So last week, I met up with this Asian chick, but when I took her back to my place, I just ended up talking to her about Malita. The girl said if I wanted to see where it would lead, then take a chance.

"I couldn't get Malita out my mind. Everywhere I went, I saw her. So I went to the same club where I met her, and there she was, sitting at the table, passing out tracks. I don't know if I ran to her or jumped over the tables but before I knew it, I sat down next to her and I told her I'd have her any way she'd give me."

Ben laughed and rubbed his face. "You know what she said? She said, 'I knew you'd come back. God already told me you would.'"

Solomon groaned. "You have got to kidding me."

"I'm not. So we've been dating since then exclusively. The crazy woman won't let me even kiss her. Said I'd have to earn the right again. So if she wants to go to opera house, I will dress like a penguin and go with her."

"All this just to get laid? Screw that. If a girl won't give it up, I'll just move on to the next one."

"Anyway, that's what's going on." Ben glanced at his watch. "And if I don't get out of here, I'm going to be late and she'll make me wait longer."

As Ben raced out, Solomon noticed his face had settled into an excited expression.

He didn't get it. Malita wasn't hot, and she barely tipped the scale on pretty. Yet Ben ran out of there like he'd won the lottery. What would be the point in waiting to have sex with a girl? There were way too many of them more than willing to give it up. He shook his head. He felt sorry for him. Variety was the spice of life he believed. Why would a man get married and sleep with the same woman over and over again? That was like eating the same sandwich every day for years!

A monogamous relationship had a certain appeal, but it would have to be short lived. There was the off chance the woman he met would lose her attractiveness and then it would be time to move on. Even with Pam coming over every week, he'd still saw other women. Solomon got up and cleared the cans from the living room. Ben had to be out his mind.

The next week Pam showed up at his place, but she wasn't alone.

248

An Indian woman stood next to her. Solomon couldn't take his eyes off her. She had bright angel cake skin almost as pale as Pam's, wavy cocoa brown hair, long tapered eyebrows over large chocolate cake eyes and dressed in a sari that bared most of her midriff and a wide scarf over one shoulder.

"Who is this?" he'd asked even as a wild, impossible thought crossed in his mind. Pam would never do that, would she?

"My name is May. It would take too much effort to give you my real name," May answered her voice heavy with its accent. His eyes dropped down to her lips. Even her mouth moved sexily.

"I told her about you," Pam said as both women came further into the apartment. They deliberately brushed their bodies against him and the scent of strawberries mixed with musk lifted to his nostrils. He inhaled them deeply. He closed the door.

"What did she tell you?" He asked as he went over to the refrigerator and pulled out a bottle of wine.

"How good you are in bed," she answered as her mouth curved in a provocative gesture.

The bottle slipped from his hand, but he caught it in time with his other hand. May laughed the sound throaty and deep as she threw her head back. The exposed column of her neck tantalized him. He could imagine the kisses he'd place there.

"When I told her," Pam's voice interrupted his fantasy, "she wanted to sample the goods for herself," A wide smile curved her lips. "I thought maybe she could join us."

His hand lost their ability to hold anything. The bottle of wine barely made it to the surface of the counter. 'Pam, if this is some kind of joke," he croaked out as his blood heated to a boiling point.

In response, May shrugged and the scarf fell from her. She stood, exotic and sensual.

"Well," he said as he sauntered toward them, "I could never say no to a sexy lady, much less two of them."

MALITA

A loud bang woke him. The sound slammed against the inside of his head like a hammer. He held his forehead as he slowly got up and stumbled out the bedroom to the door.

"Hey man, you just getting up?" Ben said as he came into the room.

"Dude, do you have to talk to so loud?" Solomon moaned as the door closed.

"I'm not. You just have a hangover."

The hammers inside his head banged incessantly, and Solomon blindly made his way to the counter. He put his head to the cold surface, his eyes closed. Maybe if he just stayed there the pain would seep into the granite and then the counter could have a headache.

"Man," Ben exclaimed from somewhere on his side, "you're wasted."

"I'm not wasted," Solomon responded and winced again. Apparently there was an alcohol fairy in his head who replaced the hammer with a one ton mallet.

"What did you do last night?"

What didn't I do? Solomon thought as he slowly lifted his head and went to lay on the loveseat. Ben sat on the couch opposite him.

"Pam brought over some friends and we partied."

Partied? The word couldn't begin to describe the orgy that took place in his apartment last night. It had turned into the wildest night of his life. He only had impressions of women and alcohol. A couple of guys had been there he didn't know but only one of them had participated. The other had a video camera, and he guessed he recorded the proceedings but the whole thing was vague.

"Yeah, your place is a mess," Ben said as he surveyed the disorder.

"What time is it?" His tongue tasted like cloth.

251

"It's one in the afternoon man. I came to invite you to come with me and Malita to her parent's house for a barbeque but I guess not."

"When are they having it?"

"Tomorrow at three."

He'd only seen this woman once his friend couldn't get enough of. They had been dating for almost seven months now, and he still hadn't slept with her. How lame was that? Such a waste of time. However, the girl intrigued him. What could possibly be so different about her that made Ben act like an idiot?

The next day brought clouds and a temperature drop but as Solomon pulled up to Malita's parents' house he saw the weather change did nothing to deter people from the barbeque. As he stepped out the car, Ben came out the house to meet him.

"Hey man. Glad you could make it."

Solomon looked around. "Wow, my bedroom is bigger than this house."

He nodded. "Mine too but that doesn't matter. Come on, everyone's in the back."

People congregated in different groups while a few younger kids played basketball at a small court. There were two grills going, and the smell of grilled hot dogs, pork, chicken and burgers filled the air. His stomach growled loud enough for Ben to hear, and they laughed.

"C'mon man, say hi to Malita."

A short woman, she barely came to his shoulder and Ben towered over her like Goliath to David. She did have a nice figure, but her face did nothing for him. She looked bland. Medium brown skin met with hazel colored eyes, a wide nose, and full lips.

"Hi Malita," Solomon greeted as she shook her hand.

"Hello Solomon. Ben's told me so much about you," she replied as she studied him.

"Same here. I remember seeing you a few months ago, so it's nice to catch up again."

"It is. Here's my mom." She inclined her head to a woman behind him, and Solomon turned to see an older woman that showed where she definitely got her looks from. Much more, she had a giant fleshy mole near her eye! Woof!

"Hi Mrs. Wood," he greeted as he took her hand as well.

"Hello Solomon. It's so good to have you join us. Please feel free to eat whatever you want. If you need anything just let me know."

Mrs. Wood's friendly manner made up for her lack of beauty. *It would have to*, he thought.

Solomon enjoyed himself. Mr. Wood turned out to be a short, midnight dark man with dark eyes and a face that reminded him of a pit bull. A wide forehead with broad, bushy eyebrows peppered with gray and a wide nose that flared often. His voice boomed like a preacher although he was a deacon at the church they attended. The man knew how to barbeque, and Solomon found himself going for thirds. A few people came over to him and invited him to play some board games, or watch T. V. He ended up playing a rousing game of ping pong with a couple of older kids.

He watched Ben as covertly as possible as he engaged with other people. For the most part, he stuck by Malita, his long arms around her shoulders as people came and went. The woman didn't dress provocatively, and her conversation was friendly and polite. Several times, he caught himself enjoying a joke or an observation she'd made. She seemed nice.

But her face! If only she had smoother, clearer skin. Earlier, he saw a smattering of tiny moles near her ear. The sight almost stopped him in is track. He would have offered to have them removed for her for his peace of mind but knew he'd probably get his teeth knocked down his throat. Ben would see them when he slept with her. Wouldn't that turn him off?

An hour or so later, people started to leave. Ben went to help Mr. Wood clear up the grills, and Malita came and sat by him.

"I hope you had a good time, Solomon," she said. The sun had set. It left faint purple streaks against the canopy of the sky. Insects buzzed and flew around them in dense swarms.

"I had a great time. Thanks for the invitation." That much was true. The Woods, for all their lack of beauty, were very nice people. But then, they had to be.

"You're welcome. So, Solomon, what do you do with your time?" She settled back into her chair.

"What do you mean?"

"Where do you work?"

"I don't. I live off my inheritance."

"Must be nice to have so much free time," she said. "I wish I had that kind of free time. I'd probably be down at the detention center most days. "

"Well, I do participate in the X-Games whenever they have them. I'm a skater."

"Oh wow! I wish I had known. Some of the teens at the detention center my father volunteers at skateboard. Maybe one day when you have time, you can come and show them a few moves."

Detention center? Not likely. "Let me think about it," he said instead.

"Sure." She took a sip from the lemonade she brought with her. "Ben's going to ask me to marry him soon," she said unexpectedly.

Solomon's eyes widen. Oh no. "He is? How do you know?"

"I know. Probably in the next month." She took another sip.

"He never said anything about it to me and I would know."

"I know. When he does tell you, make sure to tell him to make the proposal special. I want something to remember for the rest of my life."

If this wasn't the oddest conversation. "Why would Ben want to marry you?" The question came out before he could stop himself, and he slapped his hand against his face. Now she was going to call Ben, and he'd be driving home with one less appendage.

"What? Because I'm not drop dead gorgeous?"

Solomon jerked in surprise. How did she know? He'd been careful not to show any hint of his thoughts.

Malita smiled at his discomfiture. "I saw the way you were looking at me. You can't believe this short mama had your boy running crazy. But she does and do you know why? It's because I am beautiful. Not by man's standard butGod's. Only His love makes me worth looking at."

What could he say in response to that? He opted to remain silent, and she continued. "I fell in love with Ben the first time I saw him at that club where I passed out tracks. I knew I wanted this man for my husband. But I saw he was a playboy and despite the fact I fell for him then, I had to ask God for permission. When he left because he couldn't sleep with me, I cried. I thought I would never get over it. I even thought, maybe if I did it just once. The Spirit helped me restrain myself. I think restraint is good in a person, don't you?"

Her expression made him wonder if she implied more than she said. He didn't say anything.

"And then, three weeks later, I came back to the same club. The next thing I knew, Ben stared down at me with those eyes of his and I knew he was here to stay."

"Why are you telling me this?"

"Why not? You and he are friends, aren't you? I know he's going to ask me very soon. So," she said briskly, "do you have a special someone in your life?"

"Oh no," Solomon laughed, "not at all. I plan on being a bachelor forever."

"Really? You don't think you'll ever get married?"

"Not likely. I could never limit myself to one woman."

"Why is that?"

He glanced up at her, expecting to see censure in her eyes. She simply looked curious. And of course, Malita had a way about her that made a person want to talk.

"Now, don't get offended but I see women like desserts. Variety is the key. I can't imagine just one. I'd died of boredom."

If they do get married, I probably just got myself kicked off the guest list.

"Oh I see. Well, be careful. You can't survive on that. Too many sweets get you sick."

"That's just something our mothers say," Solomon quipped.

"Is it?" she replied. The tone in her voice caught his attention. Her eyes had him in their grip. She seemed to be telling him something that was just out of his reach of comprehension.

"Hey honeycomb," Ben said as he came over to their table. "What ya'll talking about?"

Honeycomb? His friend had traveled into that strange world of relationships where odd cutesy names were considered endearments.

Malita broke contact and Solomon released a breath. "Nothing much, Ben. Just shooting the breeze."

A few moments later, Solomon left. As he went back to his penthouse, he couldn't stop thinking about her. She'd left an imprint on his thoughts. Malita was the antithesis of all the women he knew. Pam would have laughed till she got sick at the thought of a monogamous relationship, much less marriage. The orgy from the night before last proved that. How could Ben just want to be with one woman for the rest of his life? It didn't make any sense.

He hadn't seen Pam in over a week. With a vague sense of alarm, he hoped nothing happened to her. Of course, she could be just busy.

256

After all, a person couldn't stay in bed—figuratively speaking—all the time, could they?

At the skateboard park, he started to gain a small following. Some of the kids, older and younger, watched as he practiced, and he gave them some pointers for techniques. Others he helped to perfect their style. Every time he went there, a sense of accomplishment lifted his heart. What a great feeling it was to pass on the love of skateboarding to someone else. To see their faces when they executed a trick or see them as they watched his style and tried to copy it.

By himself, he practiced a new trick. He couldn't get the mechanics quite like he wanted, but he kept at it. If he used the trick to create a freestyle maneuver, he wanted it to be stationary for the most part. A freestyle move just required his board and a flat surface. If he wanted to go more street style, then he would want to use some kind of implement like a ramp or a rail. He toyed with both ideas back and forth.

A few hours later, he executed a grind, a trick where he slid along the rail using the trucks instead of the wheels. Once he landed back on the ground, he rolled till he got the ramp and then performed an airwalk where he took both his feet off the board, flipped it, and then landed back on it again. The series of tricks became his move, and as he started to go back to his car, he tentatively called it "Greene Storm" but he'd have to call it something else later.

As he opened the door to his penthouse a half hour later, he stopped. Pam sat on his living room couch, drinking a glass of wine.

"Hi Pam," he started as he closed the door. "How did you get in?" He put his skateboard in the small hall closet next to the front door.

She shrugged the movement of her shoulders fluid. "I had a key made."

"What! Pam, you can't do that."

She smirked at him, the purple eyes filled with amusement. "But I did already. Don't worry. I just got here about ten minutes before you."

"Why did you go through all that trouble? If you really wanted a key, I would have given you one."

"So you say," she whispered mysteriously as she took a sip of wine. Her throat moved as she swallowed the liquid, and he felt his mouth go dry. How often had he'd caressed the same slim neck and place hungry kisses on it? It had been a while.

"Before your hormones get all randy, I do have a proposition for you. In order words, I came here to talk business."

"Business? What kind of business do we have together?"

"Sheet business," she answered as she set the glass down on the table in the middle of the living room.

"Well in that case," Solomon replied as the desire welled inside him, and he jumped over the couch. Just the thought of being with Pam had him excited.

Pam threw her head back and laughed. "Not that kind of sheet business. Not right now anyway. I want you to work for me."

"Work for you?"

"I own an erotic production company. I produce pornographic films and I'd like to contract you for a series of films I'd like to have you star in."

The blood rushed through his head as shock ran through his body. He couldn't have been more shocked than if she told him she came from the planet Mars. Pam Oliver a porn producer?

"Why are you so shocked?" she asked him.

"I just am," he replied after a few moments of silence while he came to grips with the idea.

"Oh, please don't tell me you're a prude." Her voice filled with scorn.

"We've been kicking it for two months Pam so cut it."

"Good. You had me concerned for a moment. I've been auditioning you for a while," she started and then began to give him all the details of their encounters. The way she talked about it, she could have been discussing the stock market. As he listened to her, a sense of incredulity came over him. Could this really be happening? Was this some kind of joke?

As she continued to talk, he went over their short term acquaintance. He saw everything through with a new perspective. She had approached him. She introduced the recording, the multiple partners, and everything else. And thirteen days ago, she'd planned the party.

"So all those people from last week?"

"They are part of my crew," she answered him.

That's right. The guy with the camera. It all made sense now.

"Were you doing a movie then?"

"Yes but you won't be credited in it. After all, that would be against the rules."

Suddenly, he got up and went to the refrigerator. He pulled out a can of orange juice and took a deep gulp.

"So what do you say, Solomon? Why not work for me? It's the best job in the world."

The answer seemed so easy to say. But at that moment, a wave of uncertainty crashed over him. Did he really want to do this? What about his mom and his dad? Although his parents had strangely left him out the spotlight when it came to their church, he didn't want to risk them being associated with the porn industry.

"I don't want to use my real name in the films Pam," he gushed out.

"Not a problem. But we have to on the contract."

He couldn't believe his stroke of luck. Solomon Greene had just been given access to have unbounded sex with as many women as he could handle. Gorgeous, scintillating women with bodies made for his hands. They would be, in a sense, at his beck and call. The enormity of it rocked him to the core. And at that moment, he felt so sorry for Ben. He'd certainly missed out. He'd been given the ultimate dessert platter.

"Fine." He set the empty juice can on the counter. "Let's get this over with."

"Oh no," Pam interjected as she got up and walked over to him, her movements sensuous as they always were. "We can always sign that later."

As his arms went around her and he bent his head, he murmured, "I never could say no to a sexy lady."

The next week as he watched the game, Ben came over and told him he wanted to ask Malita to marry him.

"You want to marry her." It wasn't a question.

Ben rubbed his bald head, but he didn't avoid his eyes as he had before. "I can't imagine my life without her. I feel as if I'm connected to the most wonderful, the most beautiful woman in the world. I don't want to let her out my sight, for an instant. She's perfect."

Beautiful? Perfect? Hardly, Solomon thought.

"That's a giant step Ben. You sure you want to do this. After all, she's kinda too religious in my opinion. And I thought you didn't like those kind of girls."

"These several months, we've talked about it. She's never forced her faith on me at all. As a matter of fact, she did everything she could not to browbeat me over the head with it. I was the one who wanted to know more about God. I got baptized last week. I'm a Christian now. The best decision I'd ever made. I can't tell you how good I feel."

Solomon spat out the juice he'd sipped. "Baptized? Like thrown into a pool of water?"

Ben rubbed his head. "Yeah."

The news floored him. Ben Nomasters a Christian? What was the world coming to? Now he'd be stuck with one woman with some outdated notion he was to sleep with one chick for the rest of his life because Jesus said so. And when he got tired of her, then he'd divorce her like everyone did and then he'd be back to his old self.

Now that he thought about it, Ben did change. He became a bit calmer, and a sense of serenity encompassed him. He didn't even know the last time he'd hit the night scene. When they gamed together, he'd didn't curse anymore. As a matter of fact, about two weeks ago, they both saw a sexy short girl walk by them, and Ben didn't even respond to her.

"Wow," he said after a few moments of silence between them.

"You know, Sol. It's kinda weird. I went at Malita to prove she wasn't a real Christian, and she ended up converting me. I love her so much just for that and now, if she becomes my wife, I'll be the happiest man in the world."

"Love is another word for sex, Ben. You sure this getting married thing isn't because you're just hot for her?"

"I'm sure man. I've never felt this way about any woman before. Never."

Remembering what Malita told him, he said, "Well, if you're going to propose to her, you have to make it good. I mean, really romantic."

"I have to talk to her dad first and see if he'll let me marry Malita. I don't know if she'll marry me without her father's consent."

Her father should just be ecstatic he had a man willing to marry his daughter. Ben was one of the heirs to the Nomasters fortune. Mr. Wood could hardly expect there would be anyone else better. "Ben, this is the 21st century, not the 18th century."

"Some things are timeless man," Ben replied. "I've been praying about it for a while now even before I got baptized that he would be open to me marrying her."

"What about your parents?"

"They liked her when they met her. My mom got excited when I told her I wanted to get married. She never thought I would."

Neither did I, Solomon thought.

"I'm heading over there to talk to him now. I know Malita and her mom are at the detention center working with some of the girls there. This will be the only time I can talk to him." Ben rubbed his head. "I'm so nervous."

"Good luck I guess," Solomon said as he walked him to the door.

"I need more than luck, Sol. I need divine intervention."

The restaurant sparkled with luxury as Pam and he sat down across from Ben and Malita.

She hadn't wanted to come but capitulated when he said it would be her job to distract Malita while Ben went to get everything set.

"This is my date, Pam Oliver," he said by way of introduction after their orders were taken.

"It's great to meet you, Pam," Malita said warmly, a big smile on her face as they shook hands over the table. "Wow, you have a very firm handshake. I like that. I hate when people shake hands, and they act like you have the plague."

Pam laughed. "I do too. I remember one guy said I almost broke his hand because I shook it so hard."

"Rather than act like you've been quarantined by the CDC."

Pam's demeanor relaxed. Solomon wondered how Malita would act if she found out that Pam produced erotica.

He didn't have long to wait.

"So Pam," Malita asked after they ordered appetizers. "What do you do for a living?"

Here it comes, Solomon thought.

"I produce erotic films and television shows," Pam answered.

Now Malita would start in on talking about God, and Jesus and rain hell and brimstone on Pam.

"What an intriguing line of work," Malita responded. "I've always admired people who can market quite well."

Pam had jerked in response. Obviously she hadn't expected that. "What do you mean?"

"Well think about it. If you can market erotica, which in the scheme of things, doesn't need to be marketed, think what else you can do with those skills."

"There is that," Pam said slowly as she stared at Malita, her face a study of confusion.

"Do you enjoy your work?" Malita asked.

"I do like bringing the film together and working behind the scenes. A lot of work goes into that. Plus, as you said, although I produce the films, I do a lot of marketing for it as well."

"Maybe we can talk later. Do you have a card?"

Solomon watched as Pam pulled out her business card and handed it over, the confused look still on her face. "Great. Thank you. I was talking to Ben . . ." and the conversation went on another line.

Hardly had he expected Saint Malita to be so casual about it. When he found out Pam was in porn, it had taken him for a wild ride. Ben's hope-to-be-future-wife was an amazing woman.

The dinner went well, even though Solomon could tell that Ben became more nervous by the minute. He knew because Ben rubbed his head so often that it began to reflect light. The girls talked like best friends. It shocked him to find out both liked to collect rare books. Strange, he'd slept with Pam on so many occasions but he didn't know a thing about her.

Ben murmured to them and then gave Solomon the look. It was time. As unobtrusively as possible, he touched Pam's shoulder to let her know to continue the conversation and then he left the table to go back to his car. Ben had asked him to bring a silver antique box to place the ring in.

As he entered the restaurant again, he saw a small gathering of people at the kitchen doorway. Mr. and Mrs. Wood stood next to Mr. and Mrs. Nomasters. The mothers held hands, their faces lit with excitement.

Ben studied him as he came back to the table and slipped the box to him. He then made his exit.

"Sorry Malita," he interrupted, "but I just got a call. Pam and I have to run."

"Oh!" she said. Her mouth curled down, "and we were having such a great time. Well Pam, I had such a great time getting to know you. It's nice to have a new friend. I'll be calling you soon, okay?"

Pam hugged her and scooted out the booth. Solomon grabbed her hand, and they left the table.

"Let me run to the restroom first," she said out loud although he knew that as a ploy. She wanted to see what would happen as much as he did. In a strange way, he was excited for his friend. What would Malita say? The woman had the choice to say no but then she wouldn't have told him what she did.

They scurried like mice to the back of the restaurant where presumably the restrooms were and then waited by the parents to watch the scene unfold.

Ben had scooted closer and wrapped his arms around Malita's shoulders. He started speaking. They were too far away to hear what he said, but she nodded her head in response. After a few more seconds, he reached into his pocket and placed the box Solomon gave him on the table. Malita glanced down at it in confusion and then picked it up. Ben obviously told her to open it because she bent her head to do that. As she did, he quickly went down one knee. Her gasp was audible. When she glanced up again, her hand flew to her mouth and Solomon saw Ben ask the ageless question.

Sniffles caught his attention. All the women were crying. Despite his aversion to the whole marriage thing, he had to admit, what Ben did was very romantic and touching.

He just couldn't see himself doing that.

Malita shouted yes and then threw herself at him. Her arms wrapped around Ben's neck. He lifted her against his body as the other patrons laughed and clapped, cheering. Then he bent his head and whispered something to her before he kissed her.

They were at it for some minutes. Solomon's eyebrows arched as he realized it must have been the first time Ben kissed her in months.

Mr. Wood grumbled deeply in his throat, and Solomon turned to see the man's face wore a scowl. Mr. Nomasters merely shook his head.

They were still at it thirty seconds later when Solomon intervened. Mr. Wood's face had darkened.

"All right, all right," Solomon yelled out and the two broke apart. Ben glanced at them as if seeing them for the first time.

"Aww man, I forgot ya'll were here," Ben said as everyone came forward. The wait staff brought champagne glasses and what looked like a bottle of wine. Yet, when Solomon took a sip as he toasted the now engaged couple, he found it was sparking grape juice.

Later that night, Pam and he sat on his couch in the living room and stared blindly at the T. V. For the first time since they met, they weren't in the mood. So the T. V. blared in front of them and before long, Pam curled up into his arms and they went to sleep.

THE DESSERT LIBRARY

Three years ago . . .

The next two years could only be described as a giant flesh party. True to her word, Pam contracted him to act in her films. He didn't know until later but she had gained notoriety in the industry as a quality filmmaker. She also headed an empire of erotica including magazines, TV shows, films, and books. Strangely enough, she preferred to stay out the spotlight.

During that time, Solomon thought he lived every man's dream. Beautiful sexy women were part of his dessert tray. They came at him left and right in some ways. Not just the actresses he worked with but well-known up and coming celebrities, politicians' daughters, high-powered female executives, and others. He'd never been able to resist any of them. Why should he?

Being a male porn actor didn't necessarily pay well but he figured most men weren't in it entirely for the money. He certainly wasn't.

After he started with her company, Pam ceased her physical relationship with him. She'd done her part, she told him. Now it was time to do his.

Most of the women he met were nice but he'd never sought to know more than their names. They were only delicious desserts, readily consumed and just as easily forgotten.

He had time to be the best man at Ben's wedding. As he watched them marry a whole year later, he once again felt sorry for Ben but he refrained from telling him. Let the man find out himself. They looked happy enough, and Ben seemed enamored by her. Solomon wondered if the poor man would be bored to death before the year was out.

Yet two years had passed since their nuptials and Ben still seemed to be in wedded bliss. He had apparently become a deacon in training at the church they now attended and did a lot of volunteer work at the detention center with her family. He'd given up his semi-pro basketball career.

The Nomasters donated large sums of money to the center and they were able to do outreach programs. It all seemed very worthy but it may have been compensation for something else. He didn't know.

One day, Solomon woke up alone in his penthouse. Winter had come and he felt a chill. He wrapped himself in the blanket as he headed to the thermostat but he realized it wasn't coming from there. It took some time for him to recognize the source of the coldness came from inside him. A bone-numbing sensation encapsulated his heart. He rubbed at his chest, the strange sensation tangible. Even odder, he walked over to the bathroom mirror and stared at his reflection. A good looking man stared back at him but the man had no more substance than a painting. He touched his face, the hair pricked at his fingers. He had a body, but there wasn't a soul.

Frustrated with himself at his thoughts, he went into his bedroom and flung himself on his bed. However, the chill didn't leave him all that day. And at night, when he hit the club scene, he still felt it.

It had to be in his mind. He tried to drown it out with several drinks and all he got was a hangover and an empty bed. Someone had driven him home apparently when he woke up the next morning with no recollection how he'd gotten there.

As the weeks went by, the feeling intensified. It had transformed from a chill to hollowness inside. Morbid thoughts flowed in and out his mind. He wasn't a person simply parts that moved and processed information.

He went to Pam for more work and she consented. More work came along and even then the hollowness stayed with him.

One day, as he stood in his apartment, staring at the blank TV, he had a sudden urge to go see Ben. He jumped in his car and sped there, his hands clenched the wheel. He had to go talk to Ben. For some reason, it was imperative to see him.

Half hour later, he stopped in front of the house and got out the car. The house seemed like a beacon to him. Even from the exterior the warmth inside pervaded him. His heart constricted in response.

Ben came to the door a huge smile on his face. "Hey Sol! Come on in! We haven't seen you in a while."

As he stepped into the interior, Malita came out, smiling. "Hello Solomon! It's so good to see you. Strange, I knew you'd be coming soon. Come on in."

"Actually, I need to talk to Ben for a few moments Malita. Do you mind?"

"Not at all. As long as you promise to have dinner with us."

That warmed him on the inside, and the coldness receded. "Thanks. I'd be glad to."

"What's wrong man?" Ben asked as they sat down in the game room moments later.

What was he supposed to tell Ben? He face grew hot. It was silly to come over here.

He plunged on anyway. He'd gotten this far. "It's kinda hard to tell you this. I had this gnawing need to come see you, and now I feel stupid."

"Dude just tell me."

Agitated, Solomon jumped up. "I've been having this feeling lately. It's been going on for three months now." He stopped and blew out a breath. "I feel cold inside. I can't get rid of it."

"You feel dead inside," Ben uttered in a low tone.

Solomon whirled around, surprised. "You know?"

"Yeah. I know."

"Well, then what is it?"

"If you had asked me two and a half years ago, I would have told you I'd come down with some kind of virus or flu. Now I know what it is, and I know I will never experience it again."

"What is it?"

"It's loneliness, Sol. Simple, pure loneliness."

Loneliness? Solomon scoffed at the idea. No way.

"Dude I'm not lonely. I'm surrounded by gorgeous chicks all the time. Remember?"

"Yeah, I remember," Ben said as he leaned back and folded his arms. "How's that going for you?"

"It's going good, never better."

"Is it? You know, before I would have thought you were living the dream. Gorgeous women, unlimited sex, and getting paid to do it as an added bonus. And yet, here you are, feeling lonely."

"I'm not lonely." If Ben said that again, he'd clobber him. And why should he be upset about it?

"I think more than that too, Sol," Ben continued as if he hadn't spoken. "I think the effects of your lifestyle are starting to get to you."

"What do you mean?"

"All those women and you're not close to any of them. They're only there for a few hours, a few days and then gone. Like bubbles. I felt the same way until I met Malita, and she led me to the Lord. He has filled all the empty spaces in my heart. And then, He gave me this incredible woman just because He can. I don't know why she married me. She certainly could have done better."

"What does that have to do with this loneliness?" He didn't want to listen to what Ben said but his hearing remained intact. Besides, something Ben said held his attention. The talk about emptiness. It couldn't be loneliness.

"None of them mean anything to you. You've never gotten close to them at all. Simply hit it, quit it, and move on to the next one. They're not even women to you anymore. Just a different dessert you consume. But they don't satisfy you, those women. All you focus on, and so have I in the past, was the outside. But there's so much more to them than what you get from them sexually."

Ben reached over and pulled out a Bible from somewhere behind him. Solomon rolled his eyes. "Aw man, don't get all preachy on me."

"Hear me out man," Ben responded and he flipped open a page and read out loud. "'But King Solomon loved many strange women.'"

He put a finger to bookmark the page as he looked up at Solomon. "Sol, just like you, the king had money, power, influence, and wisdom. He had it all. God had given him everything. But the king, for all his knowledge, lacked one thing. Restraint when it came to women. In the context of this scripture, when it says 'strange,' he's talking about ethnicity. He had 1000 women and they all took him away from God. He ended up worshipping idols and turning his back God, the one that had given him everything.

"These women in your life, Solomon, are strange. Not in ethnicity but in the lack of connection you have with them. They are leading you further and further away from God. As a porn actor, and doing as many movies as you do, you have no idea what restraint is. Nor the freedom that comes with boundaries. Think about it, Sol. You sleep with them, but you don't connect with them. Sex, for you, has become a job, not a physical outpouring of the love you have for your wife."

Ben had hit the nail on the head. Lately, he had been calling his sexual activity work. It had become a job instead of a pleasurable act.

He heard the pages of the Bible turn and then, "And Adam said, 'This is now bone of my bone and flesh of my flesh.' I didn't get that before but I do now. Remember when I told you I couldn't imagine my life without Malita?"

"Yeah. So?"

"This verse tells me what I couldn't express. Since we've been married, my feelings for her have deepened. I'm part of a unit with her. She's the most beautiful woman in the world to me. I'd die for that woman."

"At the risk of a head injury, aren't you kind of stretching it a bit? I mean, c'mon!"

Ben stared at him, his eyes narrowed in anger and Solomon back away. "Hey man, I'm sorry. I shouldn't say that."

"I know. Thanks be to God, I'm a Christian now or else you'd be on the floor."

"And I would deserve it," Solomon answered by way of apology. Ben was almost seven feet tall and bigger than him.

"And to answer your question, sure there may be other women who appear to be prettier than my wife, but I wouldn't know. I've only got eyes for her."

Ben rubbed his chin, apparently in some deep thought. "You know, God describes his relationship to the Church as a marriage where He calls the Church His bride. I think that's significant."

"Now you're going to give me theology?"

"Hear me out. When God told the prophet Hosea to marry a prostitute, a lot of people focused on Gomer and Hosea's relationship and how it relates to God's attitude toward us. However, I think it's also important to note God told Hosea to marry her. In other words, commit only to her. The greater responsibility fell on Hosea not necessarily on Gomer. This is just my opinion mind you and I could be wrong. Even in the New Testament, God gave the greater responsibility to men: husbands love your wives. Look at you Solomon. You can't commit to anyone. All you can do is have sex with them."

Solomon stared at Ben. He had to have it wrong. He wasn't lonely. Every week, he had some woman in his bed or he was on set with another. That didn't matter. The feeling inside of him had to be from the fact he was becoming disillusioned from his job. Maybe it was time to do something different in the industry. He had started to gain his own sphere of recognition after all.

with him, handsomely paid of course. And so for a whole month, he'd slept with a different woman.

It should have been the pinnacle of his success. Hugh Heffner should have given him an award for his prowess.

Yet, for all that, the coldness inside of him remained. Finally one night, as he stood in the bathroom draped in darkness, he stared at his reflection. He gazed into his own eyes and saw the truth.

Solomon Greene had been saturated by pleasure and in exchange, lost his soul.

THE BLUEBERRY WOMAN

"Three things happened to me," Solomon continued as Celeste listened, "that changed my life and led me out the industry."

Celeste could hardly bear to hear more. She wanted to tell him to stop. To desist with his narrative that ripped every ounce of hope from her chest. It became necessary to clench her hands in her lap to keep from running to him, falling on her knees and beg him to say no more. To end the nightmare he started with his words. With each word, the chains tightened on her heart. Each second that passed, the cold shield she'd wrap herself with for years formed once more.

Yet, she knew he had to continue. So she remained silent and listened once more.

"Frank had got it into his head the last film should be called the Virgin Fruit. We would audition college girls who were still virgins and if selected, we would pay for their college education. By this time, I didn't care who it was. As long as she was hot and sexy, that's all that mattered.

"Frank set up everything and candidates came in droves. Medical students, lawyers, journalists, cooks, I don't know. I left it to Frank to select who it would be. And he had to do an extensive background check. I didn't want some chick lying to me about her virginity. After all, she was going to get an education for one night of sex. Was that too much to ask?"

Celeste's lip almost curled in disgust. How could he be this way?

"After weeks, the girl had been selected. I was looking forward to it. It had been a while since I'd been active."

Solomon's face tightened as he focused his gaze on something only he could see. "I can remember that day so clearly. It had rained and the ground was still wet. I'd step into a puddle of water on my way into the studio. Frank had come to meet me and we started talking. And then he introduced me to the Virgin Fruit. And when I saw her, I froze. It was my high school chaplain's daughter. Her name is April Houghton. I can't tell you who was more surprised. We stared at each other for a long while. She looked so embarrassed and I—I—could feel this bile rise in my throat. Disgust at myself for what I had become and for what I was about to do."

He turned; his green gold eyes were wide with entreaty. "I had bought her virginity for a few thousand dollars. She'd sold it to me for the cost of a four year degree. And I could feel this dirty, nasty film come over me. All of a sudden, I could hear Ben's voice in my head. I promise you I heard him as if he were standing next to me. And it said, 'For the lips of a strange woman drop as a honeycomb, and her mouth is smoother than oil: But her end is bitter as wormwood, sharp as a two-edged sword. Her feet go down to death; her steps take hold on hell.'"

Solomon's eyes had widened to the size of saucers. "I knew then I couldn't do this. I told Frank to cut a check for her in the amount she needed. He thought I'd lost my mind but he did it anyway. I never saw April again after that day."

His hands pulled at his face, and Celeste thought how much she'd wanted him to touch her barely an hour ago.

"I walked out there, got in the car and drove to Ben's house. I think I left the car running I was so anxious to get to Ben and Malita. They'd had the baby by this time, a little girl named Carla. She was only a month or so. I can't remember now. I banged on the door and Ben ripped the door opened and cautioned me to be quiet. 'The baby's asleep,' he whispered to me.

"I grabbed him by the shoulders and I asked him, 'Were you just reading your Bible just a few minutes ago?'"

He looked at me like I'd lost my mind, but he said he had. I asked him to read me what it was. I think he wanted to drive me to the shrink but he did as I asked. He'd read the very words I heard in my head. My legs shivered like a little boy caught without his pants on. I fell on the floor. I told him what happened. It shook him up too and we talked about it. He told me a lot of things, some of which I remember and others which I can't. He talked about God too. He prayed for me. There are times I can remember what he said but most times, I can't."

Her heart had galloped in response to what he told her. Could God really talk to someone like that? It seemed incredible, but Solomon wasn't a man to make up something like that.

"I wish I could remember what he said. I really do. The next day, Ben, Malita, and Carla were dead."

Celeste gasped and her heart constricted. Of all he had told her, their story had touched her. A bright spot in the cesspool of sexual promiscuity that made up her husband's past. How could two wonderful people be gone?

"What happened?"

His eyes had gathered water, and a small tear ran down the side of his face. "A truck driver fell asleep at the wheel. He rolled over into the freeway and landed on their car. They were crushed."

She winced and closed her eyes. What a horrible thing.

"I went to the funeral and saw three closed caskets. The Woods and the Nomasters were wrecks. There were so many people there. At the end of the service, I got up and bumped into Pam. Her face was covered in tears. 'Malita saw more in me than anyone ever had in my life,' she told me. 'She became my friend when she should have stayed fifty miles away from me. Her parents invited me to dinner more than once and she wanted me to be there when Carla was born. She'd name me the godmother. All I had ever been was a porn star, and she turned me into a godmother of her child. The day she died, I had shut down my enterprises. I was going to ask if I could be a full time nanny for Carla. I wanted to go to church with her and learn more about God. My life had started to change. Now she's gone.'

"I hadn't even known Pam and Malita had kept up with each other. Yet, it should not have been a surprise.

"When I went home that day, I cried like a girl. Ben was gone, and now I had no one to turn to."

Solomon took a deep breath and then another. His pain touched her almost as tangibly as wind. Long moments went by and Celeste let the silence linger. A few tears fell down his face but he wiped them away. She could only imagine what he was going through.

"The final straw was the blueberry woman."

She knew her face reflected her confusion when she saw him lift a corner of his mouth. "I call her that because I don't know her name. I can remember her face though. It had freckles on it and a long thin nose. Dark blue eyes stared at me with hatred in them. And later on, they filled with tears. I can even see the clothes she wore that day. A pink sweater and a pair of jeans. And she jabbed me in the chest over and over again."

His voice trailed off and Celeste waited for him to continue. This blueberry woman didn't seem like any of the other women in his past. Not from the way he told the story. Why did she hate him? Why had she poked her finger into his chest?

His voice interrupted her thoughts. "It was a few weeks after the funeral. I hadn't been out in all that time. I stayed around the house, miserable. Finally, I decided to go to Denver. I had no particular reason to go there. I'd done a couple of films there but I think I liked the mountains. So I flew down there and stayed at a hotel for a while. I walked down the street and went into a small coffee shop.

"The door opened and this woman came in pushing this guy in a wheelchair. When the guy looked around, he saw my face and the oddest expression came over his face. He obviously recognized me. It wasn't the first time I'd been recognized by anyone. Most times, people came up to me and wanted my autograph or something. But the look on this guy's face was different. He simply seemed shocked to see me there.

"The woman also stopped and stared at me. She stared at me a long time. I tried to ignore her. I turned away from them but I could feel her eyes still on me. It made me uncomfortable. I remember thinking maybe they were stalkers or something. Boy was I wrong."

Solomon paused again. The temperature in the room had dropped, and Celeste went over and closed the balcony doors. The cessation of sound was abrupt and the silence heavy in the air. She returned to her seat and clasped her hands together. She waited.

"I ordered blueberry pie with my coffee. As I went to take a bite of it, I felt someone suddenly standing over me and I looked up to see the blueberry woman.

'Aren't you the guy that made all those sex tapes called the Dessert Library?' she asked.

'Yes,' I said.

'I see,' she said in this weird little voice almost as if she were ticked off.

'Was there something you wanted to know?' I asked. 'I'd like to finish my pie.'

'I've waited a long time to tell you this,' the woman said as she sat down across from me. 'You see, I know every inch of your face by now. I've seen you so many times I even know you have a tiny mole on your shoulder. I know everything about you physically because I've had to watch you for almost two years. First when you were with Pam O Productions and then when you started your own company.'"

Celeste interrupted. "She told you all this at the coffee shop?"

He nodded. "There this woman sat, talking in this really quiet voice but I was sure she was holding back her temper. I could tell from the way her eyes remained wide and the way the muscles in her cheek twitched. So I said, 'Well, it's nice to have fans.'

"She gave the strangest laugh then. It sounded like a combination between a snort and a scream. 'A fan?' she said. 'I'm not one of your fans. I'm one of your victims!'

'Whoa lady. I don't have any idea what you're talking about. I've never seen you before in my life.'

'That's it, isn't it? You've never seen me, but I've seen you more times than I care to remember. I hated you before I saw you today. But right now, sitting here in front of you, you make me want to puke.'

'Look, Miss you need to leave. I'm trying to eat my pie in peace.'

"She took my pie from me and set it next to her. I could have caused a scene but I noticed the way her hands were shaking. Her lips shook. 'What's your problem, lady? How are you one of my victims?'

"She stared at me, this blank look on her face. Then she said, 'The man in the wheelchair is my husband of four years. About two years ago, he came across the movies you made with Pam O Productions; and they just lit up his world. I would come into our bedroom and he would have them on the TV. I thought it was just a phase. He always got interested in one thing or another. I didn't like the stuff in my house but I never did anything about it. I thought that he would get over it.

'Only he didn't get over it. He started to watch the movies all the time. I'd come home, and he'd be doing that while he watched you with some actress. It got to the point where he couldn't even make love to me without having the movie play in the background. And then he wanted me to act like those women on the screen. And it got worse. I won't go into those details but let's just say it took much trouble to make love to me instead of going solo with you and some girl in the background.'

'Ma'am, I really have to ask you to go,' I said. I didn't want to hear anymore.

"'Oh, you're going to listen to everything I have to say,' she told me, as her lip curled. She leaned forward, and almost put her face on top of my nose. I could see the little hairs on her upper lip, that's how close she was. And she sneered at me. 'I don't care you're sitting there trying to eat a blueberry pie. I don't care if you think I'm being too personal for you. I don't care how you feel about anything. I'm going to say my piece and be through with it, so you just sit there and listen.'

"She leaned back then. 'Now, six months ago, our marriage was all but over. He preferred you and those stupid films to me, a real woman. You see, he replaced you with him. And I didn't fit into the fantasy. I didn't look like the black woman in Brown Sugar Girl or the red head in Heartthrob Candy Cane. He stopped having sex with me. Then one day, he got into a car accident, and it paralyzed him from the neck down. Can you imagine how I felt? This man wouldn't sleep with me when he could and now he can't?'

"I remembered the way she laughed, Celeste. It was almost like she was crying. My throat clogged up as she told me her story. But I still didn't understand how that made her one of my victims. I guess she saw the question on my face. She said, 'He was so involved in trying to be like you that he pushed me to the side. And now, his injury is so bad no amount of modern medicine can help him. He's worried I'll leave him now. And he has every right to be. I say I am a victim because of people like you in porn who turn women into objects and men into masturbators. Apparently there are hundreds of women with husbands, boyfriends, and sons that cannot perform with real women. Do you have any idea what it's like to have your husband prefer a computer image or a movie flick than his own wife? To see him try to make you into his fantasy because of some porn actress who's paid to look as if she enjoys men degrading her? Don't you get it? It's people like you that help bring up the next generation of masturbators. And your *Dessert Library* collection made it worse. Not only have you helped to propagate this perception of women but now, you've made them into confectionaries! Sugar and sweets!

'I hate you for what you turned my husband into. Now he feels sorry and keeps wondering if I'll leave him. Well, he better wonder, because I don't have an answer to that! Eat your pie, you scum.' She threw it at me and it splattered everywhere. By this time, she started to cry and yell and screech at me. Then she took her finger and jabbed it into my chest. 'I hope you rot.'"

Solomon stopped talking. His head hung, and Celeste continued to sit. The ice she thought she'd seen the last of had encased her again, stronger than ever. The love she felt throbbed inside her, but she forced her icy defenses to contain it. Yet, her curiosity had been stimulated, and she asked, "Solomon, do you agree with the blueberry woman?"

He glanced up at her, the green gold eyes sad. "Yes. At first I didn't but later on, I realized something. I've never had to go solo. I've always had a woman in the wings to assuage my appetite. And yes, I could say I never put a gun to anyone's head to go buy the flicks. But I helped to make them available. I added to the problem. At the end of the day, even in some small way, I have to take responsibility for that couple and possibly more than that. I am as much to blame as her husband.

"So that's when I left the industry for good. I closed down Greene Flesh and left it all behind. I've been celibate for a year now but I still could feel the lure of women. Every time I saw one, my senses went into overload. I knew all I had to do was turn on the charm, and I'd have some luscious sweetness in my bed. It became almost too much for me to resist. So I made a deal with God and the rest you know."

Just like that, it ended as suddenly as it began. For a moment, she couldn't move as she took in everything he said. She would never be able to compete with the women in his past with their perfect bodies and personalities. They had been beautiful, sexy, and promiscuous. A kiss meant nothing to them, nor did intimacy. He would expect her to act like them. She thought that he had started to desire her because he'd felt some kind of emotion for her. But that was erroneous on her part. He was celibate and she available. For a while there, she almost believed he wanted her, quirks and all. His kisses had expanded her knowledge of desire but for him, they must have been run of the mill, tolerated until he got what he really wanted.

"How many women have you been with, sir?"

Solomon, who had been watching her, said, "Does it matter?"

She didn't respond and waited for him answer. He cleared his throat. "Three hundred."

The very number ripped the breath from her body. A small army had gone down in history for their valiant efforts against a massive enemy. That many people had been killed in a single bombing. A research company would need that many test trials to determine the validity of a product's results.

"Now that you know, wife, does it matter?"

No, it didn't matter. Nothing mattered anymore. She thought about the shopping trip she'd made earlier that day. How excited she'd been about tonight. How close she thought she connected to God as He answered her prayer.

I trusted you God. I stepped out on a limb and put my trust in you. It would appear I can no longer depend or count on you to make me happy. I cannot fight against omnipotence. You win.

She cleared her throat. "Thank you, Mr. Greene, for being frank about your past."

Solomon sat up. "Mr. Greene?"

She raised her hand as she cut off his words. "You have told me much, Mr. Greene. I appreciate your candor. I have a better understanding of why you married me. However, I am sure you understand why we cannot consummate this marriage."

He gulped. "Why not?"

"You are a whore, sir. In retirement, but nonetheless, a whore."

"A whore," he exclaimed, his mouth slacked open.

"I assure you, Mr. Greene that is the correct terminology. Though you seem to be remorseful of your past, it is however, part of your makeup and therefore I must take into account you will repeat your actions. You may even be diseased in some manner."

"I can't believe what I'm hearing," he said as he got up. "Celeste, I told you all of this because I wanted to be honest with you. I know you feel this connection between us. I couldn't make love to you otherwise. And for the record, I've gotten tested every year and don't have an STD."

Did he think that made a difference? "Should you receive some kind of reward for being safely promiscuous? Should I just succumb to you because of some strange modern euphemism about practicing safe sex? Should I be honored I have married a man with a worn phallus?"

"A worn what!"

Her anger grew colder and she stood as she allowed it to take rein. "Let me make you aware of something, Mr. Greene. I married you because I was in love with my sister's fiancé. It agonized me daily to see them together and to know I would never have her husband. He was everything I longed for. Now I have discovered my husband is little more than a prostitute. You are nothing compared to him. Do you think I would let you touch me? I am glad for your honesty, but I will not stay here another day. Tomorrow I return to my father's house and after the duration of two years, we will dissolve this marriage as originally discussed, and I will be rid of the stain of you as my spouse."

He came forward and grabbed her arms. His eyes were filled with entreaty and his face tight as he said, "No Celeste, don't go. I don't want you to leave me. I can't change my past. It is what it is. But I promise you are the only woman I want to be with. "

"For right now. And then afterward, you will grow bored and seek new, greener pastures."

"No!" he shook her, as his eyes bore into her own, filled with desperation. "No! Don't do this to us. Not now. Don't go back. Please Celeste, don't leave me."

"I must Mr. Greene. Nothing you say will keep me with you. Take your hands off me."

She struggled against him but his strength succeeded her own. His robe fell on the floor in the tussle and the light fell on his body, bringing its perfection into sharp relief. The iron hard pectorals against her face as he dragged her against him were warm. Her hand had brushed the solid, well-defined abs and the heat of his skin seemed to burn her. The long column of his neck rested on top of her head and the masculine scent of him enveloped her. For a brief moment, she wanted to bask in this, to forget all he had told her. He was *her* husband after all. Shouldn't that mean something?

Your husband but not your man, a voice whispered.

Three hundred other women had been held against this same body. They'd been caressed by the same hands that now held her. Their mouths plummeted by the same lips that brushed the line of her hair and had sent desire through her veins. Those women all had a piece of him and she'd never have all of him to herself.

"Please don't leave me. I'll sleep in another room. I won't touch you but don't leave me woman. You mean too much to me," his voice had a husky tone to it and for a moment she almost capitulated. The love inside her sought for recognition but she squelched it.

"Release me, Mr. Greene," she told him.

He jerked as if burned and leaned back. As she allowed him to study her, she committed his face to memory but would never see him again. His arms fell from her and his face turned to stone. Then he picked up his robe and walked out the room.

She took several deep breaths and then closed the door.

REMEMBER ME

Celeste left Arcadia the very next day. Solomon watched her from the top of the stairs as Morayo had the driver take her suitcases. The Yoruba's eyes were filled with sadness and Celeste stood by, dressed as an American pioneer. At that moment, he started to see the pattern of her costume. She'd worn a similar outfit when they first married, the day after their walk in the twilight, and now. The outfit represented difficulty. Why did he just now understand it?

As the chauffeur drove his world down the pathway, he knew he'd never be the same.

Morayo had tried to talk to him afterward but he didn't want to hear any preaching. And she must have grasped it because she remained silent after a few attempts. His anger wasn't directed at God. After all, he was given the wife he wanted and more. The most beautiful woman in the world. Every other woman seemed like worms compared to his Celeste.

Later on that night, he sat on the beach and remembered their stay in every detail. He could see the light in her eyes as she smiled, feel the softness of her lips under his turn him into mush, and hear her gentle voice as she made some observation. He missed her like air.

But she didn't want a whore for a husband. And as he always suspected, he would never be able to escape his past. Perhaps if he had kept his end of the deal he made with God, she wouldn't have left him. He should have gone to Father Ian and got back to his church duties. God had held up His end of deal, but he did not; so maybe that's why Celeste left him.

He went back home a few days later. As he got out the car, he stared at the mansion and thought of it as a cemetery. He would die here, alone and unloved but held captive by the one woman in the entire world that he'd given his heart.

When his parents asked about Celeste, for the first time ever, they were cognizant he didn't want to discuss the reason behind her leaving. And such an action didn't seem too far away from them either. He'd notice his parents were sleeping apart. They hadn't argued but the coldness between them made every family gathering a battlefield.

September led into October and then November. Each day that passed was an endeavor to go on with his life now that his heart had vanished and left a crater in its place. The skateboard park had closed as the weather grew colder. Most days he worked out in the gym and muddled around the house. He thought about getting a job but declined. He didn't need the money and he may deprive someone else an income desperately needed.

His board saved his sanity. He was in the gym room, balancing on his board when he had the idea to develop a YouTube channel to show freestyle tricks and techniques. Celeste had taken her love for hand crafts and did the same. Why not he?

It turned out to be the best idea he had. He started his YouTube channel and soon had a following. Other skateboarders from around the world connected with him; soon he had a network. He also garnered attention as being one of the best. In a way, he thanked Celeste for this, too.

At the beginning of November, as he worked out in the gym room, his father came in.

"Sol, can I talk to you for a minute?"

"Yeah sure," he invited as he placed the weights back on the stand and wiped his forehead.

"It's been some time since Celeste went away. Your mother isn't here right now, and I want to know the truth. Why did she leave?"

Solomon debated on what to tell him. He and his father hadn't been very close but he loved him as much as any son would.

"Did she find out about the porn?"

The words doused him like a bucket of water and Solomon froze in surprise. How did he —

"Yeah, I know," Mr. Greene sighed as he made his way over to the bench at the back of the room.

"But how, Dad? I never did a movie under my name at all."

The large meaty hands were clasped together as his father continued to look at him for a few seconds. And then, the truth all of a sudden slammed into him.

"You watched one of my movies?"

"Imagine my surprise, son," Mr. Greene started to say and then he rubbed his hands over his face. The tips of his ears were red. "I'd saw this DVD in the adult store called Jolly Rancher Cowgirl. I had no idea what it was about, but it intrigued me. I hadn't looked at porn in some time and your mother was — well, let's just say she had other things that occupied her time. I bought it and took it home. When I started the movie, I saw you as the titular character. Your name was David Brander I believe. At first, I was too shocked to do anything but stare as you. Then I stopped the video. The truth stabbed me. My son is a porn star."

A rush of emotions went through Solomon, varying from incredulity to embarrassment.

I've hit a whole new level of weird.

"I'm sorry Dad that you had to find out like that. I think," he responded, lamely.

"I didn't watch it, Sol. I turned it off before I saw anything significant."

"I guess that's okay."

An awkward silence built between them. Finally, Mr. Greene said, "Is that why she left, son?"

Solomon sighed. "Yes."

"You want to tell me about it?"

Solomon told him, from the first day he met her until the day she left. As it unfolded his father sat quietly. At some points, his eyebrows had risen especially when he related he married her because he had at one time considered her unattractive.

"I can't believe you told her that Solomon," Mr. Greene stated after he had finished.

"I can't either, Dad. I wish I could go back in time and rip my tongue out I wish I could do so many things differently."

Solomon walked a little ways from his father, his head bowed as he thought out loud. "You know something, Dad? Being in porn was supposed to be the life. Having sex with some of the hottest women on the planet. But after a while, no matter what I did, it took more out of me than I got from it. I remember the first time I started correlating sex with work."

He turned and glanced back at his father. "I've had these crazy dreams for a year now.

"In the dreams I see this beautiful woman and she hurts me even though I can't feel any pain. At first, in my dreams, I used to eat a part of their flesh that looked like candy. And then, they began to eat me. In the last one I had, I was held trapped by a web of lemon taffy. The women were coming at me and I couldn't escape. Then I called out to God for help and they were melted away by maple syrup acid rain. And then the rain formed into Celeste.

"After all this time, I understand the dreams. The women consumed me. Their memories eat at me all the time. There's not a day that goes by where some girl from the past rears her head and say, 'Remember me?' in my mind. I'd do anything to take away the last ten years of my life but I can't. The woman I love, the only woman I ever felt this way for doesn't want me. You know what she called me? A whore. I'd never felt ashamed of my past until she said that."

"If you love her son, why not go after her?"

"It's Gonzo's turn." The image made him want to slam his fist into the wall. Was Gonzo even now at his wife's house, on bended knee? Had he already stolen the kiss that Solomon had stopped earlier?

His father's face scrunched. "Gonzo? What does he have to do with anything?"

When he told his father about their rivalry, he stood up and walked over to him. "Solomon, never let another man get a foot hold between you and the woman you love. You fight for her with everything that you have."

"Dad, Gonzo knew her before I did. They are good friends just like he and I were. He knows her and understands her in a way I never will. He's the best man for her. I'm not. I tried to be but it wasn't enough."

Mr. Greene placed his hands on his shoulders. "Look, Solomon. I like Celeste. I want her in this house, and you do what you have to do to get her back."

"But how? Dad, she told me that she never wanted to see me again. And even if by some miracle, I did get her back, would it be any different."

"What do you mean?"

"I've been with three hundred women, Dad."

His father's eyes widened into saucers. "Three hundred?"

"Yeah. Will it be any different with her than with anyone else? The thing about porn is you perform so often it turns into work. And I've seen hundreds of women's bodies. Will there be anything about Celeste that's going to change the way I feel about having sex with her? She's going to have the same equipment all the others had. I want it to be special and I don't think, as much as I love her, that it's going to be anything more than one more job."

Mr. Greene stared deep into his eyes. "I can be honest and say I've never thought of it like that. But I will say this. Do not give up Celeste without a fight. I like her. I want to get to know her better. And I want to see some grandkids running around this monstrosity of a house. And paramount to even that, I want you to be happy and I believe she's the only one that can do that for you."

"And what about you and Mom?"

"What about us? I don't want you to have the kind of relationship we have. And I want you to be a better man than I am. Go after her, Solomon. She's your wife and she deserves your every effort."

###

"Icy, do you want me to make you some crumpets?"

Celeste lifted her head from the quilt she was stitching. Blaze's face, lovely as usual, looked at her with inquiry. The morning late November light filtered through the windows in the living room.

"Yes, please, if you wouldn't mind."

"No. I made a breakfast casserole since J-hun's coming over for breakfast."

J-hun. Celeste allowed herself a tiny smile. A year ago, the endearment would have cut her into two. Now, it meant nothing to her except a name her sister called Jacob. Despite everything that had happened, she would never again feel the longing for him. As a matter of fact, she looked at him with new eyes. When he came to visit a few days ago, she noticed he wasn't as muscular as he used to be. He'd developed a slight paunch, probably from all the food Leah cooked for him. No one, in the right frame of mind, could resist Leah's cooking, much less her fiancé. His eyes, that periwinkle blue she once thought were serene had a cold touch to them. Solomon's eyes always blazed with warmth. Even in anger they were never cold. The gold flecks like flames. She knew he worked out often in his gym and his physique was hard and roped with muscles.

She sighed. After three months without his constant presence, his memory should have receded like an old quilt pattern. Yet, there it remained, vibrant as ever. Like now, she found herself remembering the clasp of his arms around her as they walked on the

294

beach at Arcadia and played in the ocean. The way his face wrinkled in confusion at an unfamiliar word she used. The press of his lips on hers as he kissed her senseless.

That's quite enough. You are very well aware you are not the only one who has received his kisses.

The cold anger swelled again. Why had God let her fall in love with this man? What could she, one woman, do for a man who had his pick of the most beautiful in the world? He would never be satisfied. She was so glad she didn't reveal her secret to him. A man used to perfection would not have settled for less.

"Icy!"

Leah's voice broke through her thoughts and she glanced up. "Blaze?"

"I asked if you wanted anything else with the crumpets."

"Just tea."

"Look, Icy," Blaze said as she came forward and sat on the chair across from her. "You can't keep doing this to yourself."

"Do what to myself, Blaze?"

"Go back to him. You don't have to tell me why you left him, but obviously it wasn't a good choice to make. I know you love him still."

Celeste's head jerked up. "What?"

"You love him. That's why you've sat here day in and out, moping around. Go back."

She set the quilt on the ottoman next to her. "I can't quite believe I'm hearing this from a woman who poured lemonade on her brother-in-law the first day she met him."

Leah pulled her curls. "You're right. You should be surprised. While you were gone, I had time to calm down and think about things. Solomon married you, and he has treated you well. You live in a mansion like you always dreamed. He didn't try to change you but embraced who you are. When he should have kicked me out his house for the way I acted, he didn't. So maybe, he's not so bad."

"You do not know his past like I do."

"True. But the past is the past. You can't hogtie a person because of their mistakes they can't change. I know I don't want God to hold my past against me. That's why Christ died for us, so our past sins won't continue to separate us from God. It's the future we have to look forward."

Celeste stared with some amazement at her sister. Where was the volatile and fiery sister? Apparently an alien had taken residence in her body.

"You are being extremely level headed, Blaze."

"Well, when you stopped talking to me for a month after the reception, I knew I had to evaluate my actions. I realized I couldn't continue to have diarrhea of the mouth anymore."

Celeste's eyes rolled. "Must you be so vulgar and crass, Blaze?"

Leah smiled. "Baby steps, Icy."

A Bible lay on the table in front of them, and she reached over and picked it up. As she flipped the pages, Celeste's remembered Morayo doing the same thing. There seemed to be continuity to the faith both her sister and her new found friend had. Whenever there was trouble, they went to the scriptures. Leah found her spot and began to read.

"'Then Peter came up and said to him, "Lord, how often will my brother sin against me, and I forgive him? As many as seven times?" Jesus said to him, "I do not say to you seven times, but seventy-seven times. Therefore, the kingdom of heaven may be compared to a king who wished to settle accounts with his servants. When he began to settle, one was brought to him who owed him ten thousand talents. And since he could not pay, his master ordered him to be sold, with his wife and children and all that he had, and payment to be made. So the servant fell on his knees, imploring him, 'Have patience with me, and I will pay you everything.' And out of pity for him, the master of that servant released him and forgave him the debt. But when that same servant went out, he found one of his fellow servants who owed him a hundred denarii, and seizing him, he began to choke him, saying, 'Pay what you owe.' So his fellow servant fell down and pleaded with him, 'Have patience with me, and I will pay you.' He refused and went and put him in prison until he should pay the debt. When his fellow servants saw what had taken place, they were greatly distressed, and they went and reported to their master all that had taken place. Then his master summoned him and said to him, 'You wicked servant! I forgave you all that debt because you pleaded with me. And should not you have had mercy on your fellow servant, as I had mercy on you?' And in anger his master delivered him to the jailers, until he should pay all his debt. So also my heavenly Father will do to every one of you, if you do not forgive your brother from your heart.'"

Leah glanced up. Celeste asked, "And you read all that to me for what reason?"

"Whatever Solomon did, you have to forgive him."

Forgive him? How could she forgive him when three hundred women stood between them?

"Why?"

"Because God has forgiven you. How many years have you spent spitting at God for making you — "

"That's quite enough, Blaze," she retorted as her face burned with shame.

"No, it isn't. Whatever Solomon did, it can't be worse than what we as people have done to God. And if God can forgive us for all our sins, no matter what they are, then we are obligated to forgive each other. Are you still angry at me for what I did at your wedding reception?"

"No," she answered slowly.

"Why?"

"It doesn't make sense to hold on to anger for that long."

"Then why would you give me a break and not your husband?"

"You're my sister."

"And you love me don't you?"

"Of course I do," Celeste answered. She had a sneaky suspicion she knew where this was going. And she didn't like it.

"Whatever Solomon did, is it so bad God cannot forgive him?"

"But—"

"But nothing, Icy. You love that man and it's time for you to stop hiding and let him know. Whatever he did, it shouldn't be enough to break you apart."

Hours later, she sat in her room and went over what Leah had said. In her lap lay the Bible and she marked the passage Leah read earlier.

She did love Solomon. After all this time, that hadn't changed. In fact, the absence made the feeling more poignant than ever. She missed him so much.

Would it have mattered if the women had numbered in the hundreds or the single digits? In the scheme of things, no. If he had told her just one woman, she would have acted the same. But she turned her back on God, not once but twice. Yet, she knew if she came to Him again, He would take her back into the fold. God loved her and He forgave her.

Morayo had shown her a passage in Psalms, and she flipped to it and read it aloud. "For as high as the heavens are above the earth, so great is his steadfast love toward those who fear him; as far as the east is from the west, so far does he remove our transgressions from us. As a father shows compassion to his children, so the Lord shows compassion to those who fear him."

If God had thrown her sins away, then she needed to do the same. She loved Solomon and it didn't matter if the number had been a thousand, she would not hold his past against him.

A feeling cascaded over her. It flowed through every part of her body and melted the icy defense she built up again. Peace at last.

A hard thump interrupted her and she called out. "Come in."

The door opened and her father poked his head around the corner. "May I come in?"

She nodded and closed her Bible up. "Yes, Daddy."

Mr. Martin came in and settled on her bed. His heavy bulk weighed the bed down. "I want to talk to you."

She waited.

"It's time for you to know."

An icon daffodil appeared on her computer and she sighed. She didn't feel like trading barbs with Daffodil right now.

"That can wait Dad, go ahead."

"No, answer it. They'll just see me sitting her next to you," her father grinned.

She answered the call and Daffodil's face filled the screen. "What do you want Daffodil?"

The arrogant smirk that had arrested the other's girl face fell as her focus shifted to her father who had risen from the bed and stood in the way of the camera.

"Who is that?" her voice was barely a whisper.

"This is my father," Celeste answered as she wondered why Daffodil looked as if she'd seen a ghost.

For a moment, the woman stared at Mr. Martin. Then she finally spoke, "Well, well, well. How is our father?"

Celeste froze. "What did you say?"

Mr. Martin said, "What are you talking about, young lady?"

"Both of you heard me well. How are you, Dad?"

Time seemed to have stopped as Celeste took in what Daffodil implied. She could barely speak.

"What makes you think I am your father?"

"My mother described you well, Dad. I'm sure you remember her. Heather Simmons?

Celeste stared up at her father. His eyes had widened to the size of golf balls, and his whole body went rigid. It couldn't be true.

"Remember now?"

A KNIGHT'S KISS

The doorbell rang and with something akin to relief, Celeste offered to answer it, thus leaving the dining room table with its strained atmosphere. As she gripped her 1902 evening gown with its long train, she scurried out the room as fast as her slipper feet would carry her.

When she saw Goijaart's face, relief flooded through her. "My lord, I am most pleased to see you this day."

He came in as she stepped back and placed a bouquet of lilies in her hands. "For my queen," he replied, his dark eyes bright.

"Thank you, my lord, you are most kind. Please come in. Did you drive down?"

She placed the bouquet on the small foyer table and made a mental note to put them in water later. She took his coat as he answered and hung it in the hallway closet. Strange, she'd gotten used to Mr. Batcher handling when visitors came in. She missed his face and his efficiency. How easy one became accustomed to luxury!

"Did Blaze make dinner?"

"Yes," she answered quickly, determined to avoid the awkwardness that would surely come if he joined the dinner table. Everyone's tempers were contained by hair-fine restraints. Anything could set if off and then war would erupt. "But dinner's almost done so let's go into the den."

She ushered him in and then sat across from him. "What brings you here, sir?"

"You," he answered as he got up and sat next to her on the small loveseat.

"Indeed?"

"I sensed you needed me, and I came."

How so like her knight to understand she did need him. The last few days at home had been hard.

"Well, your extrasensory perception is quite accurate. I do need you. A lot has happened in a short amount of time."

His brow furrowed. "Such as?"

She got up and walked toward the other side of the room. "Do you know of my rival on my YouTube channel?"

"That woman with the flower name. Dahlia? Daisy?"

"Daffodil Simmons," she corrected him.

"Yes, I know of her. And forgive me, my lady, but your channel, as informative as it may be, does not make my list of interest."

A gulp of laughter escaped. "Really? You mean to tell me learning how to brioche knit does not capture your fancy? How could you say such a heinous thing?"

"Easily, my lady. With these lips."

As they laughed, the tension flowed out of her. Only her knight knew exactly what to say. Goijaart had to be the best friend a woman could ever have.

"But what about this woman?"

The smile fell from her face. "Well, sir." She stopped and then started again, even after several days, still not quite able to believe it. "Well sir, it appears she is my sister."

Her knight's mouth dropped. "Would you say that again?"

"She is my younger sister on my father's side."

"Your father!" he exclaimed as he shot up to his feet. She shushed him, hoping her parents hadn't heard. Swiftly she went over to the door and pushed it closed.

"Sir, maintain a respectful volume. I do not want my parents to know I've told you."

"But my lady, when—" Goijaart stopped abruptly as he went over to her. "Did you say *younger* sister?"

She nodded. Perhaps that had been the worse of the knowledge of her father's other child, the fact she'd been conceived after her. Which meant twenty-five years ago, when she was two, her father had played loose with another woman behind her mother's back. If Daffodil had been older, the news would not have had as much impact. Everyone in the family would have attributed this to the past before he married his wife. Sadly, that wasn't the case.

Mrs. Martin, a sunny person by nature had retreated behind a wall of silence. Blaze, for once in her life, kept her opinion. As shocked as they both were, they knew this issue was between their parents, not the family.

To add more fodder to the situation, Daffodil had developed a hatred for their father as he had abandoned her mother after the affair. Now after all this time, Celeste finally understood the resentment Daffodil had had toward her, even though it wasn't her fault.

Suddenly, Solomon having slept with three hundred women before their marriage didn't have the same ring of wrong it once had.

"I'd hate to be your father right now, my lady."

"I would not disagree with you, sir."

"How are you holding up under all of this?"

"An easy question to ask, isn't sir? What can I say? I found out my father had an extra-marital affair with my rival's mother and she is my sister. How does one hold up? But to be honest, Blaze and I have distanced ourselves from the situation. We recognize this is a situation our parents have to work through. I still love my lord father with all of my heart. Yet, one finds it difficult to keep one's high regard of one's parent when their fallibility has been exposed."

"That I know well, my lady." Goijaart's voice had taken on a dark quality, and she knew he thought of his mother and uncle.

"But let us speak of other things. Although dinner is done, Blaze made peanut butter cream pie decadently displayed with pieces of miniature peanut butter cups and drizzled with caramel and chocolate syrup."

"My lady," he said as he wrapped his arms around her waist, "you had me at 'Blaze made'."

They laughed again, and her head rested on his chest. Through the past upheaval of the last few months with Solomon and these days with her father, it felt good to have her knight with her to relieve her spirits.

"It is so good to have you with me, sir."

"I am aware your husband is not with you," he stated quietly as his warm breath teased the hair along her scalp.

"Your deductive powers are acute as ever, sir," she answered, unable to keep the sarcasm from her voice.

He pulled away from her and gazed down into her face. "Why? Will you tell me?"

She hesitated, and he reached into his pocket. He led her back to the couch, and they both sat, the handkerchief between them.

"I left him," she stated bluntly.

"What did he do to you?"

She jumped at the vehemence in his voice and the scowl on his face. She'd never seen this side of her knight before.

"He did nothing, sir. It is what he told me."

"What did he tell you?" The scowl had disappeared but his eyebrows were drawn together.

It was all right to tell Goijaart. He would never betray her trust. She could always depend on him. A great friend.

"Are you aware of his occupation for the past three years or so?"

"No. We drifted apart although we stayed in contact off and on. What does that have to do with anything?"

She got up once more and walked to the other side of the room. "My lord, my husband performed in and produced pornographic cinema."

It was almost comical the way his eyebrows lifted into his hair line. His mouth dropped wide open and his eyes bulged. "My lady? Surely you jest."

"Would I make up such a story?"

"Solomon was a porn star?"

She waited for the hurt that she originally felt when he first told her. It didn't come. Not since she'd forgiven him. The act had grown less and less significant. It happened in the past, let it thus remain.

"I never knew. He never told me."

"So it would seem."

"Is that why you left?"

"Yes," she said. "I couldn't stand the sight of his face at the time. I didn't want those hands or those lips upon my person. I called him a whore, and I left him in Arcadia. I've not seen him in three months."

She heard him get up and come toward her. Mindlessly, she allowed him to put her in his arms again, hold her against his body. Safe, sweet, steady, Goijaart. She sighed in contentment.

"Would you prefer another's hand on you?"

Her head raised and she looked into his face. A warm light came from his eyes and his face softened by a smile.

"Whose hands?"

"Mine, my lady."

She gave a small laugh. "But you are already holding me, sir."

"Not like I'd want to," he stated and she felt his hands grow tight around her.

"I don't understand," she responded as a feeling of alarm went through her. Goijaart acted rather peculiar to her.

"I want to hold you like I've desired to do for so long," he murmured and his arms grew even tighter around her waist. Warning bells went off in her head. What was he doing?

His face came closer; his black eyes glittered as they peered into her face. "You are so beautiful my lady."

"Sir, you jest," she responded as she tried to put some distance between them. And the way he gazed at her. He had the expression of a hungry man and she was the cure to his appetite! But that wasn't right. Goijaart was her friend, nothing more. So why was he acting like this?

"No, I am not. You are very beautiful to me. I've wanted you for a long time. I knew all I had to do was wait for Solomon to mess things up and then you would be mine." His head bent and anchored itself in her neck. Truly alarmed now, she tried to push him back but she might as well have moved the Great Wall of China. He didn't budge. She could feel him inhale deeply. "Umm, you smell so good, my princess, my queen. Like vanilla and roses. I can drown in your scent and never get tired."

A flicker of a memory popped in her mind. Solomon had said something similar to her once. The words from his mouth had increased the desire in her. Goijaart's words made her wish she hadn't taken a shower this morning.

How could this be happening? How could she not have seen her knight cared for her more than she did for him? She pushed against him once more. The comfortable embrace from earlier suddenly felt like a cage.

"Goijaart, please let me go. I believe Blaze is ready to serve dessert."

His grip tightened and she had the awful thought she unwittingly made things worse.

Her hunch was correct with his next words. "Nothing could be sweeter than a taste from your lips. I would wager they drip with sweet—"

His arms tightened their hold and flushed her against his body. Alarm transformed into fear.

"Delicious—" his hand reached up and tumbled itself into her hair, and forced her head up. She began to resist in earnest but her efforts made no impact. In the midst of the rising turmoil and this change in Goijaart's behavior, part of her mind took time to recognize if her husband had said this to her, she'd melt in his arms. Yet, with Goijaart saying these things, it only filled her with dread.

"Honey." His lips closed over hers, and his body hardened as if a jolt went through him. He groaned into her mouth and she struggled, the taste repugnant. His fingers had gripped her hair in his hands, and she could barely move away. He kissed her with violent ferocity. How could she have not seen this?

She heard the door open and then a loud gasp. A whoosh of air went by her and then suddenly Goijaart's grip weakened as a giant fist slammed into his face, barely missing her own. With relief, she gulped in air and then lifted her head as she saw Solomon standing over Goijaart sprawled on the floor.

"I told you before to keep your hands off my wife, Gonzo," Solomon shouted as he lifted her knight by his shirt and punched him again in the face. He sailed further back and fell against the wall.

He lunged at him again when Celeste realized she had to stop him. If he continued, he'd do his friend serious harm.

"Solomon, desist!" She ran forward, but her feet tripped in the folds of her long trailing skirt. She fell forward and landed on Goijaart. Her elbow slammed into his head. The impact hit her funny bone, and her knight slumped forward.

Had she knocked him unconscious?

"Get off him!" Solomon screeched as he reached forward and gripped her arms, nearly flinging her in the air as he pulled her up.

"Solomon, you must desist. I believe I've rendered Goijaart unconscious." For Pete's sake her elbow screamed in agony. Why people called it a 'funny' bone was a mystery as there wasn't a thing humorous about the pain going through her arm.

Solomon yelled, "You play the Ice Maiden with me and leave me because I've slept with three hundred women and yet you let Gonzo kiss you! If I hadn't stopped him, you'd both be rolling on the floor. Woman, are you out your mind?"

"THREE HUNDRED!"

Celeste jerked her head up. The whole family was in the doorway, faces slack with surprise. Unfortunately, so were Jacob and three of Leah's bridesmaids. She groaned to herself. She'd forgotten they were coming over after dinner.

"Solomon, please let's take this elsewhere private," she implored him in a low tone.

Even now as he trembled in rage, he looked magnificent. The black hair gleamed like satin, spiked as usual. His face had slimmed down but the gauntness added to his handsomeness. She drank him in even as her heart throbbed to the heat that blazed from his eyes.

"No! I came back to beg you to come back to me. Give me a chance to prove I love you with everything inside me. That I will take you any way you give yourself to me. I wanted to start over again."

He loved her? The shock of the word sent a hot bolt down her back.

"And I find you lip locked with my former best friend? We're married! Remember that matter of propriety we talked about? Well, you've definitely stepped over the bounds this time. If you want him so bad, then take him. I won't bother you anymore. You and your black knight can go riding into the danged sunset on your stupid valiant steed with roses and fairies flying around you. I don't care. I don't ever want to see you again!"

He stalked away and the crowd at the door parted like the Red Sea to let him pass. The sound of the front door opening and then slamming shut reverberated through the house. Several pairs of eyes slowly turned back to her as a great silence engulfed them. She heard her mother whisper to her father, "You know, as upset as I am with you, I do believe I'd rather the illegitimate child than the three hundred women." Her mother reached down and gripped her husband's hand. "You're not out the woods yet, but we'll get through this."

A loud snore came on the edge of that statement. Goijaart had fallen asleep.

"This is better than a soap opera," one of Leah's bridesmaids said as they walked away. "Now where's that cream pie you made?"

Jacob was the last to leave. As she met his gaze, he nodded once and then closed the door.

Solomon *loved* her? She drifted to the floor and her skirts settled around her. Tears fell down her face and she lifted her hands to the heavens, and shouted with the loudest voice she had, "Thank you, Jesus!"

Finally, after all this time, her final prayer had been answered.

SAVED

Thanksgiving and Christmas had been miserable holidays. His parents hadn't talked to each other, the food Mrs. Houston put on the table had the culinary delight of sandpaper, and he missed his wife. He lied when he said he didn't want to see her again but pride kept him from going back. It had been three months since he'd caught her with Gonzo. The memory made him snarl again. And Celeste was the type of woman to take a man at his word, so she wouldn't come to him and make him eat his words.

He couldn't go back after he told her what he had. Instead, he worked on his videos and worked out and kept himself busy.

He started to read the Bible, too. He never had before, but when Ben had told him about King Solomon, he wanted to read everything he could about the man. The more he read about the man, the more intrigued he became. He was shocked that in the Song of Solomon it talked about sexual relations. There were several prevailing theories about the book, but two prominent ones were at the forefront. The first stated the book spoke allegorically about the relationship of the Church and Christ as bride and groom. The other theory maintained Solomon talked about his relationship with his bride.

After he read it several times from three different translations, he came to the conclusion the latter applied. He found it highly unlikely a man who had a thousand women at his beck and call would be thinking about theology with verses that spoke of what Solomon wanted to do to his Shulamite wife, not for her. It was also significant that the Song of Solomon spoke of only one woman, not many.

He went to Proverbs next and mentally ate up the verses the King had written. He even found the verse Ben had read the day before he died. As he continued to read, he noticed how often the king had personified wisdom as a woman. More than once, he'd read the verses: "Blessed is the one who finds wisdom, and the one who

311

gets understanding, for the gain from her is better than gain from silver and her profit better than gold. She is more precious than jewels, and nothing you desire can compare with her."

On New Year's Day, in the gym room, he read those verses again. Then his mind traveled back to the day before Ben died. Almost without realizing it, he flipped the Bible back to the beginning and reread what Adam said and heard Ben's voice in his head: "This is now bone of my bone and flesh of my flesh."

That described how he felt about Celeste as if she were a part of his body. Being away from her was killing him.

He flipped the pages again until he came to another verse in Proverbs: "He who finds a wife finds a good thing and obtains favor from the Lord."

That definitely was true. Celeste was the best thing that ever happened to him. Yet the passage that stuck out to him the most had been a simple one. "Let your fountain be blessed, and rejoice in the wife of your youth . . . Let her breasts fill you at all times with delight; be intoxicated always in her love. Why should you be intoxicated, my son, with a forbidden woman . . . He dies for lack of discipline, and because of his great folly he is led astray."

It took a moment to realize that fountain meant a man's sexual prowess. Strange the King would say to bless it. But he remembered the blueberry woman and her husband. Her husband had at one time been able to enjoy being with his wife until the Dessert Library came along.

Solomon hung his head. He got it now. All those women. All those strange women. God had released him from them but now he had to learn how to love and commit only to Celeste. He worried if Celeste did agree to be his wife in every sense of the word would making love to her be any different. But if he allowed himself to be intoxicated only with her and no one else, then lovemaking would truly be special for both of them.

"Solomon?"

He jerked his head up. He'd recognize that voice anywhere. "Pam?"

Pam Oliver sauntered in and he watched her. She had changed since he'd last seen her. Gone was the continual expression of seduction. She walked sedately without switching her hips. She wore a sweater and a long black skirt that came to her feet.

"Surprised to see me like this?"

"Yeah." Even more than that, as he watched her walked closer, he didn't feel a hint desire for her. And though she remained as lovely as ever, she had nothing on Celeste.

"I gave my life to Christ two months after Malita died and my life has never been the same. I took all my flesh clothes, as I used to call them, and burned them. I went on a shopping spree for modest clothes but I needed help in other areas. The women at church helped me out a lot. I thank God for them all the time."

"What have you been doing?"

"How much time do you have?" he quipped.

She sat next to him and crossed her legs. "Spill."

"I can't believe you're married," she said as he finished a condensed version of Celeste and his relationship. "But I am happy for you."

As he studied her, he could tell she had a new serenity about her. Ben had been the same. He wanted that. Wanted that so much.

"I want what you have," he said all of a sudden.

She turned to him, her purple eyes filled with tears. "I've had several people say that to me and every time they do, I am humbled God took me, a used up, aging porn star and turned her into one of his disciples. And I'm not the first one He's done that for. He did it thousands of years ago and He's still doing it today. Of course you can have what I have. It's meant to be shared. I know you believe in God Solomon but it's not enough. You have to submit your life to him, fully and wholeheartedly. When Jesus died for you, he died for all the sins you would ever commit because He loved you even before

313

you were born. Our sin separates us from God. Without the blood of Jesus, we can't ever see God but with Jesus' blood covering our sins; we can ultimately live with him in heaven.

"I thought being a porn star would always be written on my forehead for everyone to see. But Jesus' blood has washed the stain of all my sins away. My past is no more as far as Christ is concerned because I've accepted him as my savior."

Solomon's heart resonated with the words. He wanted to be rid of his past. He wanted the effects of it to no longer be a hindrance between him and his wife.

"Do you believe Solomon?"

"I do," and he felt his heart constrict. He really did believe. A tear fell from his eyes as the bonds across his heart were loosened. Only the Almighty could take a woman like Celeste and make her desirable for a man who'd been saturated by many strange women.

Pam then led him through a simple prayer where he acknowledged he was a sinner and he needed and wanted Christ in his life. For a moment, in a fanciful way, he expected angels to drift from the ceiling and surround him but nothing of that sort happened. He didn't feel anything at all but he was fine with that. From this day forward, he would devote his life to the Lord and to his wife, if she would let him.

They stood up and Solomon asked, "Why did you come by? I didn't know you knew where I lived."

"You've been in my prayers for some time. I remembered you once said your parents were part of the Washed Saints and I looked up their address. That's how I found you."

"I'm glad you did."

"I hope things go well with you and your wife."

Hope filled his heart. With God on his side, there was a good possibility they would. "They will."

She smiled at him and he drew her into his arms and held her tight. "Thank you Pam."

He leaned forward and kissed her lightly on the mouth. It meant nothing to either of them but an expression of friendship. A goodbye kiss to the past and a bright glimmer for the future.

"Get your hands off my husband!"

PERFECT WOMAN

Please God, don't let him be disgusted when he sees me, Celeste prayed as she knocked. The snow on the ground crunched under her boots as she waited for the door to open. A brisk, cold wind flittered with the hood of her feather down coat.

A moment later, it swung open and she looked with relief to see Mr. Batcher's brown face.

"Hello Miss Celeste," he'd greeted, the light in his eyes filled with warmth. "I have missed your presence in this house."

"Thank you, Mr. Batcher. I hope to be back to stay."

As he stepped back and allowed her to enter, he replied, "I hope so too."

She allowed him to take her coat and then waited to pensively to see if he would notice the change in her.

"Miss Celeste! You're wearing jeans!" Mr. Batcher's voice reflected his surprise and she turned to see his eyes wide and his face a mask of incredulity.

"Yes. I've decided for the New Year I shall leave my fantasy world behind."

Modern clothes still took time to get used to. She'd worn old-fashioned petticoats, corsets, bum rolls, layers of skirts, underdresses, and overcoats for so long the weight of them had become a second skin. They had been her comfort for such a long time, a shield to protect her from the modern world and a defense for her emotions to remain behind an icy demeanor. Her hands were also bare and the ring Solomon gave her rested comfortably on her left hand.

However, the time had to come to let fantasies of yesterday go and embrace the reality of the present.

A reality that included being a complete unit with the husband God have given her.

After he'd left her home, she'd waited for him to return and get her. That's how it always happened in the romantic fairy tales she'd encased her whole perception on. But as time went by, she knew what she had to do. She'd rejected Solomon for so long. If he was to accept her, she had to make the first move.

Three days ago, she'd sat in her room, surrounded by the dozens of costumes she'd worn over the years. Each one had been crafted by her hand. But now, it was time to put her play things away. If she was to be the wife of Solomon Greene, she could not be the dress-up princess of her fantasy.

She cried for an hour as she packed away her costumes. They would come out once in a while as she still went to the fairs, balls, and other exhibits. And of course for her YouTube channel. But she would no longer hide in them. Her gloves, she kept. Although she decided to no longer work as a model, she still wanted to protect her hands.

"Where is Solomon, Mr. Batcher?" she asked as she came out her thoughts.

An expression of unease crossed his face although he concealed it quickly. "He is in the gym room, Miss Celeste. Do you want me to let him know you are here?"

"No, I would like to surprise him."

"Of that, I'm sure he would be," Mr. Batcher murmured in a low tone, a strained smile on his face.

She placed her booted foot on the steps and started up. Her heart pounded as each step brought her closer and closer to him. Her love, her life!

Her hand brushed the banister, and she glanced at it to see the scratch on it. It must have been made the day he performed his dangerous trick on the banister. The day she had reconnected with Goijaart.

She paused in her ascent as her heart constricted. It still confounded her that she had no idea of Goijaart's feelings toward her. In her mind, he was only her childhood friend, her knight. The one who lived in her fantasy world with her. She would always be grateful for their friendship that had sustained her for so long. And yet, she had to let go of him as she did her costumes. The letter she wrote him had been one of finality. In it, she made it clear that, though she was grateful for his friendship, she could never return his affection for her. It had been two months since she'd sent it and she hadn't heard from him. Celeste had an idea she wouldn't for a long time. Her knight was a man of deep emotions, and the severance of their friendship would be difficult for him to endure.

She would not torture him with her presence in his life for the foreseeable future.

The stairs beckoned to her, and she proceeded once more. The sunlight from the window blinded her for a moment and then her vision cleared. As she glanced out the window, a frozen snowflake glinted. It resembled a flower, and her mind went to her rival.

The situation with Daffodil had not resolved itself. And even now, after two months of this knowledge, her father and mother were still at odds with each other. Daffodil had not spoken to her since she'd revealed her familial relationship to her, but Celeste had adjusted her mind to the fact she had a younger sister besides Leah. It would be a long road as the family recovered from her father's infidelity. Maybe one day, the three would become fast friends.

Blaze. Her mouth curved upward as she thought of her sister. How good it felt not to have the tug-of-war between love and jealousy for her sister. For the first time ever, she was truly happy for her. She no longer wanted Jacob. God had given her the most wonderful man on Earth. She only hoped Leah and Jacob would be as happy and content as she planned for herself and Solomon.

A door opened somewhere above, and she stopped. Was it Solomon?

As footsteps came closer, her breath caught. She wasn't ready. Not yet!

"Celeste?" Her father-in-law's voice lifted her head, and she released the breath lodged in her throat. He stood a few steps ahead of her. He had a suitcase in one hand and a long coat in the other.

"Hello Mr. Greene," she greeted as she started forward again.

"My girl, I'm happy to see you." He set the suitcase on the stair and hugged her to his wide frame. When he released her, his eyebrows lifted, the steel gray filled with inquiry. "Are you here to stay?"

"Yes, if you don't mind."

A giant smile relaxed his face and he hugged her again. "My dear, nothing would make me happier than to know I leave this house in the care of a sane woman."

Her brow furrowed. "You're leaving, sir?"

"Yes. It's for the best after all. But I will be back once when my grandchild is born."

She dipped her head and her face flushed in embarrassment. Leave it to in-laws to want grandchildren. Unconsciously she placed her hand on her stomach. If by some miracle Solomon still wanted her when she told him about her secret, soon her belly would protrude with the fruits of their love.

"If I can get ahold of you, Mr. Greene?"

"Nothing would keep me away when that happens, my dear. I have to go now. My plane leaves soon." He patted her on her shoulder, picked up the suitcase, and continued down the stairs.

"Celeste?" he called from behind her.

She turned around and saw her father-in-law at the landing.

"Yes?"

"I've always enjoyed your costumes and admired your skill with handcrafts. But I must say, Celeste. Modernity becomes you."

The compliment warmed her from the inside out. "Thank you. You are most kind."

He waved and continued his descent.

As she neared the top of the stairs, a movement caught her peripheral vision. Mrs. Greene stood at the head of the stairs with her arms folded. Her eyes were bloodshot as if she had been crying and the tip of her nose red like Rudolph's.

"Hello, Celeste. I am thankful to the Virgin she has allowed you to come back to us."

Oh Lord, help me to reach her. Let her find the truth in your love just as I have done. "I am glad to see you as well, Mrs. Greene."

"Did you see my husband?"

"Yes."

"And did he appear to be leaving?"

Celeste felt unease travel along her spine. "He did have a suitcase with him."

Mrs. Greene's face scrunched like wrinkled paper, and a sob escaped her lips before she whirled and scurried away.

When she got to the top of the stairs, she turned and made her way to the gym room.

How would he react when he saw her? How would she react when she saw him?

The light from gym room door lit the small expanse of the hall. She took a deep breath and stepped into its light and froze.

Solomon had his mouth pressed against another woman.

The sight of it nearly made her weep. This couldn't be happening.

No! No, Solomon, not this!

For a moment, she wanted to revert to her old self, ice the emotions that whirled inside her. Retreat to the comfort of numbness. An instant later she rejected the idea as the scorching, boiling anger welled up and erupted like a volcano. There was no way she would allow another woman to have access to what belonged to her.

"Get your hands off my husband!"

###

At the sound of Celeste's voice, Solomon jerked back from the sweet, innocent kiss he shared with Pam as a wellspring of joy gurgled inside him. Celeste had come back! Thank God!

Yet nothing could have prepared him for the sight of her as he faced her and then froze in shock.

Long, slender, perfectly proportioned legs were encased in black jeans fit her like a second skin. They emphasized her shape as he studied the oh-so-tempting curves of wide hips she had hidden under layers of skirts. A narrow waist was accentuated by a bright orange, ribbed sweater that flowed over her torso. The crown jewel of her magnificent change was her hair. She often wore it up or braided, but now the long mass had been styled in large soft curls that cascaded in a glorious waterfall of brown hair.

Her beauty surpassed any other women he'd ever known.

"Celeste, you look — wow! I can't get over—. You are so —" he stuttered.

Her eyes were focused on Pam and he saw she stalked over to the woman. "Who are you? What are you doing with my husband? No, ignore that. I am aware of what you are doing, but I am here to serve you notice the only bed my husband will be in from now till eternity is mine."

Solomon's mouth went dry. What did she just say?

"Mrs. Greene, you've got the wrong idea," Pam responded, flustered as she held up her arms.

He watched as Celeste nearly stabbed her finger into Pam's face. "I've got the wrong idea? Let me make something clear to you. You have about three seconds to rid yourself from my presence before I break every bone in your body!"

This was a side of his wife he'd never seen before and it thrilled him in a purely masculine way. His woman had a possessive streak in her. But he couldn't let her hurt Pam, not when there wasn't a thing for her to worry about.

"Celeste I—"

She whirled around. Her face snarled. "I'll deal with you in a moment."

Her anger made her all the more alluring. If he didn't touch her he'd go crazy.

He pulled her into his arms and bent his head to kiss her. He missed her scent, the intoxicating vanilla scent he wanted to drown in. Smooth nutmeg skin begged his fingers to caress it. The maple syrup eyes had from the very beginning enraptured him.

"Solomon, I—" she attempted to speak.

"Quiet woman," he commanded and lifted her chin to fit his mouth to hers again.

Long moments later after he drank his fill from her, he lifted his head and saw himself reflected in her eyes.

"Oh, Solomon," she breathed, "I love you. I love you with everything in me. Why were you kissing that woman?"

Pam? He'd forgotten all about her. He turned to look for her but saw she'd gone, and the door was closed.

"Pam Oliver. The woman I told you about."

"The one who—"

"Yes," he finished for her, "but she's not in the industry anymore."

"Then why was she here?"

He kissed the tip of her nose. "To lead me to Christ. She'd been praying for me, and her prayers were answered."

"But why did you kiss her?"

"I'm sorry, my sweet. However it appeared, the kiss we shared meant absolutely nothing but friendship. In the porn industry, kisses are mere illusions of intimacy. I want you to know something woman. When I kiss you, what I feel for you isn't an illusion. But you were right to be upset. I should not have allowed that. Please forgive me."

Her eyes gazed up into his for a long moment. Then she sighed and said. "All right. I also need to explain myself. Solomon, I was not kissing Goijaart when you came. He'd grabbed me, and I couldn't push away from him. I had no idea until that moment he'd had feelings for me. Feelings I could never return. I have, for the time being, severed my relationship with him."

Relief flooded through him. Although he knew how deeply Gonzo cared about Celeste, there was no way he could share in their life right now. He'd pray one day his friend would find his own wife to have and to hold.

She pushed against him, and he let her go even as he felt bereft of her presence. Yet, she had put space between them in her customary manner for a reason.

"There is one more thing I need to tell you in order for our marriage to begin anew and fresh. I want to be your wife in every way. To make love to you, have your children, and grow old with you. But there is something about me that may affect your desire for me and I cannot continue this relationship with you in the dark."

"Nothing could do that, Celeste," he assured her but she shook her head.

"Wait until you hear and then make your judgment."

He wanted to go to her and hold her, but he sensed she needed the space in order to tell him what she thought was important.

"Solomon, I have a condition called unilateral amastia. It basically means I have only one breast."

He went stone still. Of everything he expected to hear her say, that wasn't one of them. It threw him for a loop and then a second later, everything made sense. The reason why she married him because he'd wanted an unattractive wife, the clothes she wore hid her shape, her resistance to his kisses, and the deep rooted belief God had marked her for unhappiness.

AFTERWORD

I hope you enjoyed Solomon and Celeste's story. I believe every woman has a right to be the only one to occupy her husband's heart. However, this is not always the case. Too often, with premarital affairs, a man has his pick of any woman in his memory. What wife wants to be replaced by a memory? Men too, are victims of their minds as with each sexual encounter, a bond is made with that woman, etched forever in his mind. Perhaps that is what makes the women of the past . . . strange.

Made in the USA
Lexington, KY
01 March 2014